RESISTING FATE

MELANIE SHAWN

CONTENTS

1

"WHO HERE HAS SEEN *SCHITT'S CREEK*?" SUE ANN Perkins wearing her signature long floral skirt and cardigan asked from the podium on the stage of the community center.

Audrey Wells had never known her own grandparents, but she'd always thought of Sue Ann as the quintessential grandmother. She ran a café in Hope Falls, which Audrey, her mother, and sisters frequented when they had vacationed here every year from the time she was four until she was ten.

Six summers she'd spent in the quaint small town. The best six summers of her life. Which is why she'd moved here after graduating college and convinced her sister Vivien to relocate from Los Angeles and open up a coffee shop with her, which had been a dream of hers since she was a kid.

Growing up her favorite TV show was *The Gilmore Girls*. Her father left when she was two and her sisters were three, four, and five, leaving her mom to raise the girls as a single parent. Audrey liked the show because the main character was a single mom named Lorelai, who was cool and fun and beautiful, just like her own mom. The Wells sisters had been raised in Los Angeles, but Audrey used to dream of living in Stars Hollow, the fictional town the series was based in and owning her own business just like Lorelai.

Hope Falls was Audrey's real-life Stars Hollow. A tight knit community filled with colorful, quirky characters. She even found her very own Luke who was Lorelai's main love interest on the show. Unfortunately for Audrey, Josh was less of a love interest and more of a best friend. There were other minor differences as well. Instead of running a diner like Luke did on the show, Josh owned Pine Auto Shop. And unlike Lorelai who owned a B&B called the Dragonfly Inn, Audrey owned a coffee shop called Brewed Awakenings. But like the television characters, they did have good banter and there was *a lot* of sexual tension, well…on her side at least.

Every time Audrey saw Josh, her heart sped up, a tingly sensation would spread from the top of her head to the tips of her toes, and she had a difficult time breathing. She basically had an allergic reaction to his sexiness. And she wasn't alone in her reaction to him. She'd seen plenty of women have the same physical response to being near him. Viv liked to say that he was the Tom Hardy of Hope Falls. Not just because he looked like the actor, although there were definitely similarities, but because he had an air of mystery about him that drew people to him. He had a quiet authority and commanding presence that was like catnip to the opposite sex. He was a motorcycle riding, tattooed, bad boy with a heart of gold, a smile that sizzled and spread through you like butter in a hot frying pan, and eyes so deep and so brown that Audrey found herself getting lost in them and never wanting to be found.

So yeah…on her part there was *definitely* sexual tension.

"Come on, show of hands." Sue Ann lifted her arm in the air. "*Schitt's Creek*. Who's seen it?"

Audrey had thought Sue Ann's question was posed more rhetorically and hadn't realized that this was a participation exercise, but she quickly lifted her hand to indicate that yes, she had seen the show. As she looked around the room, she saw that about half of the crowd of a hundred people or so had their hands up.

It was a good turnout tonight for the Small Business Association's monthly meetup. That was probably because it was the first meeting of the year. She'd noticed, in the eight years she'd lived in Hope Falls and been part of the SBA that as the year went on, the number of attendees for the monthly meetups dwindled significantly.

Audrey always attended. Every meeting. Her sister Viv, who she owned Brewed Awakenings with, never had. Which was why she'd been so surprised that she'd shown up tonight. Beside her, Viv's arm was also held high. The sisters had binged watched the show several times together.

Another surprise guest this evening was Josh aka her Luke. He rarely came to these things but was in attendance tonight with his grandmother who everyone called Nonna. Nonna was a spitfire, to put it mildly, who had developed an unlikely friendship with Viv. Despite the sixty-year age gap, the two women got their nails done together, they regularly binge watched reality television shows together, and even frequented JT's Roadhouse, the local bar together. They'd even gotten matching tattoos. Audrey wondered if Nonna was what Viv had always wanted in a grandmother, just like Sue Ann was to Audrey.

Behind her Audrey heard rumblings of someone asking what Sue Ann had said followed by a gasp and a stage-whispered, "Well, I never!"

She knew exactly who the gasper/stage whisperer was without even looking. Mrs. Winifred Minton owned a small antique shop on Main Street. She had a sign in her window that read: NO Smoking. NO Profanity. NO Children.

Although Audrey loved antiques, she'd never visited the shop because both the sign and the woman intimidated her.

Renata Blackstone, a community leader and elder in the Washoe tribe who co-chaired the SBA with Sue Ann stood from her chair and walked up to the mic. Renata was the opposite of Sue Ann in every way.

Sue Ann was soft, friendly and approachable. She stood at five-foot-two, on a good day, always wore a version of the same long floral skirt, matching shirt and cardigan combo, had reading glasses hanging from her neck, and wore her hair in the same short style. Her rounded cheeks were always rosy and she had a smile on deck for anyone who needed one. She spent her days at the café she owned where like the Olive Garden, when you were there, you were family.

Renata was tall and reed thin. Her waist length jet black hair had threads of gray running through it and she always wore it in the same braid that hung down her back. She was the definition of grace, and class, and held herself and those around her to a higher standard. She was a formal woman who commanded respect and was not given to emotional displays.

And like Winifred Minton, she intimidated Audrey.

"Relax, Winnie." Renata addressed Mrs. Minton's gasp as she stepped up to the mic. "Sue Ann didn't curse. Schitt, S-C-H-I-T-T is the last name of the family that the show is about."

Audrey didn't dare look behind her to see what Mrs.

Minton's reaction to Renata singling her out in the meeting was. But, not surprisingly, her sister did. And whatever Viv saw caused her to her clasp her hand over her mouth as she stifled a laugh.

"Don't," Audrey admonished beneath her breath.

Viv turned to face forward again and whispered, "Her face looked like she was sucking on a thousand lemons. I've never seen anyone so puckered before."

"Shh," Audrey hushed her sister which caused Mr. Brooks who owned Two Scoops ice cream shop with his wife Marlene to turn around from the row in front of them, his expression was one of amusement at her sister's remark, not irritation.

Audrey should have known that shushing someone would do the opposite of what her goal was and draw more attention to them. Viv had no problem with drawing attention to herself or being the center of attention. She thrived on it. Audrey did not. In contrast to Viv, Audrey actively worked to blend into the background and not stand out.

"Okay," Sue Ann continued as Renata gracefully glided across the stage and returned to her seat. "For everyone who hasn't seen the show, you're missing out. But the reason I'm bringing it up is because on the show they had an episode that featured the town hosting a singles week to boost the town's economy. As you all know, our tourist seasons are booming, but revenue drops off *significantly* in off-season months, one of which is February. So, this year Hope Falls is going to host its inaugural Valentine's Week specifically targeted to singles. We already have couples that come and stay for romantic getaways, let's give singles something to do as well."

There was a murmur in the crowd and Audrey was already thinking of Valentine-themed drink specials that she and Viv could offer at Brewed Awakenings. Audrey and Viv had owned the coffee shop for almost eight years now. They ran the day-to-day business, but their other sisters Ava and Grace were part owners. They'd been silent investors up until last summer when Ava moved to Hope Falls permanently. Then, right before Thanksgiving Grace, the oldest Wells sister, relocated from LA.

Now that both her older sisters were in town, they'd been more hands on. It was nice to have her sisters so close by, especially since for the past few years Viv had been taking off on a lot of trips lasting anywhere from two to four days.

Her sister had gone to Vegas, San Francisco, Phoenix, Seattle, Dallas, and about a dozen other cities always leaving at a moment's notice without any warning. Viv had been secretive about her trips, which was very unlike her. Viv was an open book, and what most people would describe as an over-sharer. But when it came to her trips, she was very tight-lipped.

Because Viv had been absent so much, Audrey had hired two part-time employees, both of whom were amazing. Manny was a retired sumo wrestler who was the barista equivalent of a master sommelier. He loved finding new blends of coffee beans to combine and create rich, unique, and flavorful concoctions.

And then there was Carly. Carly had over eight piercings on her face alone, including her lip, eyebrows, nose, and dimples. Her hair was always a colorful expression of whatever mood she was in. One day it might be pink, the next jet black, the next gray. She'd shaved it off completely once and had rocked a mohawk for a few months. She was a hard worker and brought a vibrancy to the coffee shop.

"This event is going to start on the seventh of February

and go right through the week, culminating with the Valentine's Day Festival down at the Riverside Recreation Area. I can see from your faces that everyone is excited about this plan. I can't take credit for it. This is the brainchild of Miss Vivien Wells and Nonna Bianchi. They will both be spearheading this project so all questions and or concerns should be directed toward them."

Audrey whipped her head, turning to look at her sister who was staring up at Sue Ann with a grin on her face. Viv had not said anything about this. Apparently, trips weren't the only things she was keeping close to her vest.

JOSH BIANCHI TURNED his head when Sue Ann announced Nonna's name.

"Nonna?" He spoke in a hushed tone. "Why would you—"

His grandmother kept her head facing forward but she cut her eyes toward him and gave him The Look: capital T, capital L. It was the look that he'd been getting since he was three years old. Maybe even before then, but the first memory he had of The Look was when he'd scooted Nonna's kitchen chair over to the counter to try and get a cookie from the ceramic frog shaped cookie jar she kept beside the bread box. Nonna walked into the kitchen and literally caught him with his hand in the cookie jar. She hadn't said a word. She didn't need to. One look and even at the tender age of three, he'd removed his hand, stepped down from the chair and pushed it back into place.

Thirty-three years later The Look had not lost any of its potency. Josh returned his attention to Sue Ann Perkins.

Sue Ann moved on to other topics while his mind was like a needle skipping on a record. It was stuck on trying to puzzle out why in the hell Nonna had volunteered for a project of this magnitude. She was ninety-two years old, lived on her own and still came in every day to work.

When was she going to slow down?

For the past five years or so, he'd been trying to convince her of two things. One, to stop coming into the auto shop he owned and operated every day and just enjoy her life. And two, to move into Golden Years Senior Living. She adamantly refused both. Her response to cutting back her hours at the shop was always, "*When you stop, you die.*" And when he brought up the senior citizens home, she said, "*People move out of there in a body bag, you want me in a body bag?*"

Nonna knew exactly what to say to shut him up. But that didn't mean he stopped worrying about her. She lived in a two-bedroom cottage alone. It was only a block from the auto shop, but he still lived in constant fear that something would happen and he wouldn't know about it. He'd even bought her a lifeline alert, but he found it in the trash less than a week after he'd gifted it to her.

To say that Nonna was stubborn, was like saying that Mt. Everest was a little hill. No one and nothing stopped that woman from doing exactly what she wanted to do. So as much as he'd like to think Viv was the driving force on this project of theirs, he knew better. He wouldn't be surprised if Nonna was the one who'd convinced Viv to do it.

He still didn't quite understand the duo's friendship, but there was no denying it existed. From what he had observed the two had bonded over their mutual love of hair, Taylor Swift, getting their nails done, reality television shows and the fact that neither of them had a filter. They both said exactly what they were thinking when they were thinking it, consequences be damned. Nonna always said that Viv reminded her of herself as a young woman, which was both terrifying and somewhat amusing.

He did appreciate that Viv cared about his grandmother and spent time with her. He wasn't exactly thrilled that the duo frequented JT's for drinks on Friday and Saturday nights, or that they'd gone to a male review show in Lake Tahoe, or that the two of them had gotten matching heart tattoos during Spring Break last year. But hey, if that's what floated his ninety-two-year-old grandmother's boat, who was he to judge?

Viv wasn't the only Wells sister that had taken a special interest in Nonna. No one was as sweet and generous to his grandmother as Audrey Wells. She was a lot quieter and behind the scenes about her affection where Viv was in your face and flashy, but that spoke more to who they were as people than anything else.

Audrey always remembered when Nonna's doctors' appointments were and she made sure to have drinks and treats ready for them before they made the ninety-mile one-way trip to see her heart specialist in San Francisco. When Nonna had hip surgery six years ago, Audrey had brought her puzzles, magazines, and other things to keep her occupied while she was recovering. She'd even put together a dinner train, so Nonna would have homemade meals since she couldn't cook.

Audrey had even learned how to make samsades and sfogliatella which are Greek and Italian pastries that Nonna's parents used to make for her. She did that just so Nonna would feel taken care of like when she was a child.

Josh's great-grandfather was of Italian descent and his great-grandmother was Greek. Nonna had inherited all the passion and fire from both her parents' lineage. Even at ninety-two the woman was a force to be reckoned with.

She had grown up in Italy but spent her summers in

Greece. She and Josh's grandfather had been married when she was barely twenty, and they'd emigrated to the States when Nonna was in her early thirties. When she moved here, she was pregnant with Josh's father and neither she nor Josh's grandfather, who sadly passed away before Josh was born, knew how to speak English. Josh had always been so impressed that they'd moved to a country where they didn't know anyone and learned a completely new language in their thirties. He couldn't imagine doing the same thing in his.

As the meeting came to a close Sue Ann opened the floor for questions and Mr. Reed, who owned the local bookstore Read Between the Lines in downtown Hope Falls, lifted his hand. "For this singles week thing, I'd like to do a reading event at the bookstore. Maybe get an author who has written a book on dating to come for a signing."

"That sounds great!" Sue Ann smiled before calling on Mr. Brooks who owned Two Scoops ice cream parlor.

He asked, "Is there going to be a group promotion for downtown vendors?"

"I think we should do some sort of discount system that increases with each place you visit. Maybe some sort of punch card or something," Jim Grady who owned the bowling alley suggested.

Sue Ann held up her hands. "Like I said, you'll have to speak to Nonna and Viv about all of that. This is their baby."

Everyone seemed excited about Nonna and Viv's "baby" but Josh was still in shock that his grandmother hadn't mentioned a word to him about it. She told him what she planned on cooking for dinner next Tuesday and what color she was going to change her nails to before she went and got them done. If she was going to change laundry detergents. And how many times she got up in the night to use the restroom. But this she hadn't said a word about. It made zero sense.

He looked over at Audrey, and as if she sensed him looking, she turned in her seat and looked right at him. When their eyes met, hers widened as if to say, *can you believe this?*

He knew exactly what her expression meant. They didn't need words to communicate. The corners of his mouth tilted up in a private smile as he shook his head.

Over the past eight years he and Audrey had grown… close. It was strange but their relationship was simultaneously not close enough and too close. He loved Audrey. She was the most important person in his life besides Nonna. And he would do anything for her, including keeping the feelings he had for her to himself.

When she turned her attention back to Sue Ann at the podium, he looked around the room and still had a hard time accepting that this was his life.

Unlike most people that grew up in Hope Falls, he hadn't wanted to settle down and live his life here. He'd promised himself as a kid that the day he turned eighteen he'd be out of there. And he was. He'd joined the Army and spent seven years serving his country. He was an EOD (Explosive Ordinance Disposal) specialist. Ultimately, his time in the service was cut short by an undetectable IED that detonated and ended his career. After a few months stay in the hospital he was medically discharged.

Without having another plan, he'd returned to his hometown a broken man. He ended up taking over the reins of his family business Pine Auto Shop after his father passed away just a few weeks after he came back. The timing of his dad's death was shitty, not that there was ever a good time for someone to die.

Josh shifted in his seat trying to relieve some of the pain in his lower back.

Beside him, Nonna reached into her purse, pulled out a butterscotch candy, unwrapped it, not caring that the crinkling noise was loud, and popped it in her mouth. She offered one to him, just like she used to do every Sunday when she'd drag him to church as a kid and he was getting antsy, but he declined.

In church he used to get antsy because he was bored. His restlessness now had nothing to do with boredom. Whenever he sat or stood in one place for a prolonged amount of time, his back rebelled. His pain ranged from good days being about a four and bad days being a full on ten on the pain scale. Since the explosion that changed his life forever, there hadn't been one day where he was pain free. And the physical pain was only part of it. After returning to the States, he'd fallen into a pretty deep depression that was exacerbated by night terrors and debilitating anxiety.

Not that he had the right to complain. He was alive. He was breathing. He was one of the lucky ones. Or at least that's what he kept telling himself.

2

AUDREY TAPPED HER FOOT AS THE MEETING WAS WRAPPING up. She'd been doing everything she could to stay focused on what Sue Ann was saying but her mind kept pulling her in the direction of how much work this singles week thing was probably going to be for her.

Viv was incredible. Amazing. When Audrey had asked her sister to move to Hope Falls, she hadn't batted an eye before agreeing. And Viv had been dedicated to making their business successful. She showed up, not necessarily on time, but she always showed up. While she was at the coffee shop, she worked hard and then as soon as the clock struck midnight, or five when they closed, she partied hard. That was where her passion lied, it was in her extra-curricular activities.

Things just didn't keep Viv's interest very long. She would be obsessed with something one week and then the next week on to the next shiny new thing. Big picture ideas were where she shined. Follow through-grunt work was not her strong suit.

And as much as Audrey loved Josh's grandmother,

Nonna wasn't exactly someone who was going to be picking up Viv's slack. She barely knew how to use her smart phone for calling people. She never used it to go online, and as far as Audrey knew she didn't own a computer. Oh, and she was ninety-two.

Audrey was torn between thinking it was sweet that Viv had teamed up with Nonna and wanting to wring her sister's neck for taking this on. Especially right now. It couldn't be a busier time for the Wells sisters since one of their sisters, Ava, was getting married on Valentine's Day. It was the seventh of January, which meant that there were only four weeks until the inaugural singles week was scheduled to commence on February 7th. And five weeks until Valentine's Day which was the culmination of the week-long event and their sister's wedding.

What was Viv thinking?

"Okay." Sue Ann hit the gavel that she used to call the meetings to order on the podium. "In the infamous words of Porky Pig, tha tha tha that's all folks! See you next month on the twenty-first."

Sue Ann barely got the parting comments out of her mouth before Audrey turned to her sister. "Why would you take on something of this magnitude when we have Ava's wedding on Valentine's Day."

Viv looked wholly unimpressed by Audrey's concern. "We barely did anything for the first one and that was when Ava lived in Chicago and the wedding was here. She actually lives in Hope Falls now. I doubt that's going to mean more work for us."

Their sister Ava had been engaged to Ian, her childhood sweetheart of twenty years, and had planned on marrying him the summer before in Hope Falls. But on the morning of her wedding, Ian slid a Dear Jane letter under her door explaining that he'd been having an affair that spanned over a decade and he was leaving her for the other woman.

It had all worked out in the end. Ava was now set to walk down the aisle with the man of her dreams. Their late mother would have called it fate. Cora Wells was a firm believer in true love, fate, destiny, serendipity. She was a true romantic.

Nothing wavered their mom's faith in love and all things associated with the word. It was actually quite remarkable considering their father, who their mother maintained was the "love of her life" until her dying breath, had abandoned her with four daughters ages five, four, three, and two.

Audrey had no memory of her father, Mason Wells. She'd seen pictures. She'd heard countless stories, but she didn't have any memories of her own since she was barely out of diapers when he took off. From the stories her mom would tell about him, he'd been a magnet that people were drawn to. Sort of like Viv. Their mom always said that Viv took after their father. She was outgoing, fun, fearless.

The exact opposite of Audrey.

The Wells sisters might be considered Irish twins since they were all born within a year of each other, but the foursome could not be more different in both personality and appearance. The only physical characteristic they shared was the hourglass figure that they'd inherited from their mother, which they were all grateful for. Other than that, they looked nothing alike, and they all had very unique personality traits.

The oldest, Grace, had been like a second mother to the rest of them. She had taken custody of all three of the sisters when their mother passed away when Grace was eighteen, Ava was seventeen, Viv was sixteen, and Audrey was fifteen. And she had taken care of the household for the years their mother was sick leading up to her death. Grace was textbook Type A. She needed to have control at all times or her world was not right.

Up until a couple of months ago Grace had been a high-powered entertainment law attorney in Los Angeles where her nickname had been The Ice Queen, or 'Elsa' from *Frozen*. The nickname worked on two levels because not only was Grace considered cold and detached by her colleagues, she also resembled the Disney princess with her light blonde hair and icy blue eyes.

But that's not who Grace was deep down. She was loyal and selfless and would do anything for the people she loved. She now lived in Hope Falls and was engaged to Easton Bishop. The two of them had entered a reality home renovation show and won. They were continuing to flip houses while he worked on a book he was writing, and she worked as a real estate agent. Audrey could not be happier for her sister.

Ava, the second oldest and the one who was set to get married on Valentine's Day, was the most nurturing of all the sisters. She had long, light brown hair and gorgeous blue-green eyes. She was kind and caring and it didn't surprise Audrey at all that her sister had gone into the mental health profession. Ava was a psychologist who was focusing her specialty on childhood trauma and early development.

Her soon-to-be husband, Asher Ford, worked in law enforcement and had recently joined the Hope Falls force after leaving New York homicide division. He moved himself and his teenage daughter across the country so that he could focus on being a parent to Blake, who was having some behavioral issues. Audrey knew that Ava was going to be an amazing stepmom.

Viv was third in the lineup and probably the most opposite to Audrey. She had long vibrant red hair and huge green eyes. Whenever she was stuck for a Halloween costume, she'd throw on a red dress and go as Jessica Rabbit, who she was a dead ringer for. Viv was the wild child. Growing up their mother had endearingly nicknamed her 'Troublemaker.' She was flirty, fun, and free spirited. She loved adventure and new challenges. She had a phobia to commitment and loved meeting new people. She was blunt, brutally honest, and bold.

Viv was unapologetic in her pursuit of happiness. If she wanted to do something, she did it. If she wanted to say something, she said it. If she wanted something she went after it. No hesitation. No overthinking. No shame. Audrey had always envied Viv's fearlessness.

Audrey was the youngest Wells sister and well, the plainest in the bunch. Where her sisters all had stand out features, she just had dark brown hair and her eyes were sometimes green sometimes light brown, which she supposed made them hazel. Even her eyes couldn't make up their mind as to what they wanted to look like. She was the only Wells girl to inherit their father's olive complexion which her mother always commented on, saying how much she looked like him with a hint of sadness in her voice.

Audrey loved organization, lists, plans, and keeping everything in order. If Viv was a fly by the seat of her pants type, Audrey was a wear the same pants every day and never go anywhere type. She was shy, quiet, and the bookworm of the bunch. She blended into the background and was an observer.

"Do you need a ride home?" Viv adjusted her purse strap on her shoulder as the sisters made their way out of the rec room.

"I came with you so...yes." Audrey would have thought that would have been obvious.

"Okay, well I just have a few people I need to talk to. I'll be back."

With that declaration, Viv was gone. Audrey was left alone in the lobby surrounded by people who were all making small talk. Feeling out of place, she did what she always did when she found herself in situations like these. She moved to an out of the way spot, took a book out of her purse, and put her head down.

She did, however, make sure she had a plain view of the door so she'd be able to see Josh when he came out. If he saw her, there was a good chance he'd come over and at least give her a hug and maybe a kiss on the forehead which he did about fifty percent of the time when they said goodbye.

It might not be a kiss on the lips, but she treasured those sweet moments of physical contact probably a lot more than she should. No, *definitely* a lot more than she should.

As THE MEETING came to an end, Josh stood and offered Nonna his arm. She used it as leverage as she stood. These days it took her a little while to get out of a chair if she'd been sitting for a while. She said her bones got stiff so it was a process. He hated seeing her growing physical limitations because it was the evidence that her age was finally catching up with her.

When he was a kid, he had honestly believed that Nonna would outlive everyone, including his father and himself. He'd been right on one count.

Nonna continued using him to brace herself after she

was on her feet as he leaned over and picked up her coat. He then held it out so she could put one arm through at a time, making sure to keep hold of him with the other. He'd bought her *three* canes, one for her house, one for the auto shop and one that he kept in his car so she would always have one at her disposal. So far, all they'd been used for was collecting dust.

His mind was still stuck on this singles week thing and he wanted to press her for more information but he knew that she would say it was none of his business. Maybe it wasn't but he was very concerned about her taking on a project of this scale. She was already doing too much, and he'd noticed that she was getting tired and needing to rest a lot more often than she had been even six months ago.

If she was taking this on, he would need to step in and help. Which meant he was going to have to deal with people. Which was his worst nightmare.

Being in the garage, fixing cars, was his safe place. He did okay dealing with customers one on one but only when it was under his own roof on his terms. When he knew exactly what needed to be said and there was a structure to the conversation it was fine. Small talk, however, was his personal hell. He'd never been a huge fan but growing up in a town of this size where everyone knew everyone, he'd gotten good at faking it. But that was when he was younger before he'd been diagnosed with depression, generalized anxiety disorder, and PTSD. Now he wasn't so good at faking it.

"If you scowl like that for so long your face is going to look like a bulldog, il mio tesoro." Nonna reached up and patted his cheek, using the Italian nickname she'd given him when he was a child which translated to, my treasure. She had a special name for each of her grandkids and great grandkids. Josh's name had always made him feel special, which he was sure was the point. Her hand was freezing, as always, and her skin was soft and smelled like Vaseline Intensive Care hand lotion. His grandmother had been using the same lotion since he was a kid. He'd never smell that smell and not think of Nonna.

"You ready to go?" He asked after her coat was buttoned up.

"No, no, no." She tsked at him as she shook her head. "Always in a hurry. I need to talk to my Vivi first. We have the big plans. You wait for me? Yes." Without sticking around for his response, she shuffled away.

As he watched her go, he noticed that she looked thinner than she had before the holidays, which made her appear even more frail than she already did. The woman was barely one hundred pounds soaking wet and could not afford to lose even a pound. At her last check-up, Dr. Mills had made it a point that she needed to incorporate some more calories into her diet. Josh had researched the best protein shakes and healthy snacks for her to have on hand. He filled her cupboards weekly with the nutritious snacks, but she insisted on her regular diet of Ritz crackers, black licorice bites, and Shasta soda.

"Hey J."

Josh looked up and saw Davis Brown walking toward him. Davis was a retired NFL player who owned Davis Construction. Josh worked on Brown's personal vehicles and his business trucks from time to time. Nonna was going to be upset that she'd gone off to talk to her Vivi and missed seeing Davis. She had a big crush on the man. Every time she saw him, she told him that he reminded her of her hall pass Denzel Washington. Josh had to admit the two men did resemble each other, they definitely shared the same megawatt smile. Davis, for his part, was always a good sport about Nonna's flirting, and even encouraged it by making claims of how he would wine and dine her if he wasn't a married man.

Josh lifted his chin in greeting. "Hey, man."

"Hey, I've got a couple of trucks that I need to bring in. One of them is leaking coolant and the steering wheel is shaking; the other needs new brake pads and the engine light is on. You gonna have time this week to look at them?"

Josh nodded. He had a few oil changes scheduled and he was working on the mayor Henry Walker's transmission in his classic '66 Ford Bronco but he could definitely fit a couple of Brown's trucks in. "Yeah, bring 'em by tomorrow morning."

"Thanks, man." Davis shook Josh's hand and gave him a one-armed man hug. "I appreciate you," he said before heading out of the rec room.

That was a great example of the sort of interactions Josh was comfortable with. Short. Sweet. And to the point. They had a purpose, a beginning, middle, and an end.

He waited for a few minutes but as the crowd dwindled, he figured he might as well head in the direction Nonna had gone.

A quick search out in the hallway and courtyard proved fruitless. There were no signs of either Nonna or Viv, and Viv was hard to miss. She had fire engine red hair and a lot of curves that she showcased proudly. A lot of people around town, and even tourists, referred to her as Jessica Rabbit because she was the epitome of that cartoon coming to life.

He doubled back and walked into the lobby thinking the two might have gone out there. He didn't find Nonna or Viv but he did find Audrey. She looked up from her book at the same time he came out of the rec room.

He smiled automatically. He couldn't help it; it was just what his face did when he saw her. "Hey."

"Hi." Audrey dipped her head and her long dark lashes brushed against her high cheekbones. She smiled as she looked back up and his heart expanded in his chest.

She always had that effect on him. He was convinced that her smile could cure cancer, could solve world hunger, and bring world peace.

"I was looking for Nonna," he said as he looked around. "She said she needed to talk to your sister."

"Viv took off a few minutes ago, she said she'd be back." Audrey explained.

Josh assumed they would have to come back this way, so he could just hang with Audrey until they did. Which was no hardship on his part. Being near her was like feeling the sun on his face after a dark, cold winter night. "I'm guessing you didn't know anything about this singles week thing?"

"No." Audrey shook her head.

He'd figured that she hadn't. He was sure that she would have mentioned something to him if she had. He and Audrey were friends. Good friends. At least, as good of friends as he could be with someone whose clothes he wanted to rip off every time he saw her.

"What do you think they're up to?" Audrey asked as she put her book back in her purse.

He shrugged as he put his hands in his pockets. He did that a lot around Audrey to stop himself from reaching out and brushing a stray hair back behind her ear, or cupping her face just to feel the softness of her creamy skin…

Josh cleared his throat as he shook his head, trying to stop the direction his mind was headed. "I have no idea. But I guess if you think about it, they are sort of experts on being single."

"That's true." Audrey chuckled.

"Excuse me."

Josh looked over his shoulder and saw Gladys Hines, who was in a wheelchair after her hip surgery, wheeling by.

He took a step forward so that she had plenty of room. When he did, he ended up about an inch away from Audrey who lifted her chin, tilting her head back so she could look at him since he was more than a foot taller than her.

Josh was six foot four and Audrey was only five foot two. She was petite in frame but had curves in all the right places. His mind flashed back to two summers ago when she'd worn a bikini because she'd lost a bet to Viv. He'd spent plenty of time imagining what her hourglass figure would look like if it wasn't hidden behind her usual baggy clothes, but nothing could have prepared him for what the reality was. Her flat belly and tiny waist were accented by the flare of her generous hips and she'd had every guy down at the riverside drooling over themselves.

As he stared down into her amber gaze, he felt himself being pulled by an invisible force as his heart rate increased. He was lowering his head closer and closer to her, only stopping when he felt her breath on his face. That's when he realized what he was about to do and he stopped up short. Instead of following through, he put his arms around her and gave her a hug and a quick kiss on the forehead. It had been his go to move whenever he got caught in the gravitational pull that only she had over him.

"I need to go find Nonna. It's late. I need to get her home."

Audrey grinned and nodded, but he could see the confusion in her hazel eyes at his abrupt departure. As he walked away from her, he wanted nothing more than to turn back and erase that confusion by telling her exactly how he felt about her and how it took every ounce of self-restraint he had not to kiss her full red ruby lips, but he couldn't do that.

He would never risk what they had. It was too special, too important, and she just meant too much to him to take the chance of losing her. So, there would probably be a lot more forehead kisses in their future, and he was okay with that. He had to be.

3

Audrey locked the door to Brewed Awakenings and turned in the direction of Pine Auto Shop to check and see if the garage door was up and Josh was working.

Seeing Josh under the hood of a vehicle was one of the sexiest things in the world. He was just so...capable. The way the white T-shirts he always wore clung to his chiseled tattooed arms and pulled taut across his broad, muscular back, highlighting his impressive frame always caused butterflies to begin to flutter low in Audrey's belly. Every time she saw him working on a car or truck, he looked like he could be posing for a women's calendar of mechanics. He oozed sex appeal.

But the eye candy wasn't the only reason Audrey loved seeing Josh in his garage. Whenever he had a vehicle to fix, he looked happy. Content. Like he was in his element. It was one of the few times she'd noticed that he didn't have any stress in his face or body. It was strange to her because, even though she loved her job, loved the people she served, and loved working with her sister, it did stress her out sometimes.

But when Josh had his music playing and had a wrench or whatever else mechanics used in his hand, he was in his bliss. Which was somehow even sexier than his outward appearance which was what Viv referred to as four-alarm-fire-hot.

Unfortunately, Audrey wasn't going to get a Josh sighting tonight. The bay door was rolled down and the lights at the shop were off.

She wondered where he was.

Was he on a date?

Over the past eight years that she'd lived in town, he'd never had a girlfriend. Not an official one, anyway. He'd dated a few women that she knew about off and on, but as far as she knew nothing had ever been serious.

He could be with one of them now. She wondered what they were doing. Were they out to dinner? Playing mini-golf? Going to a movie?

She knew two things they absolutely were not doing. One, they weren't going for a ride on his motorcycle. And two, they weren't spending the night at his house. Those were two hard and fast rules he had when it came to dating.

She'd asked him if women liked going on rides on his bike, it had been her sad way of trying to open up the conversation and hint that *she'd* like to go on a ride with him. But it had backfired. He'd told her he'd never taken anyone for a ride. When she asked him why he explained that bike rides were sort of like therapy for him, they were his escape. And he didn't want to have anyone on the back that would threaten to ruin that for him.

As far as the no overnight guests rule went, she wasn't exactly sure what that was about. He'd mentioned it once when Viv asked how many women had done the walk-of-shame from his house and he'd told her zero because he never let anyone stay the night. Viv had gotten distracted and not asked a follow-up question so Audrey didn't know why that was, but she assumed it might be because he just didn't like people in his space, or maybe it was because he didn't like the morning after awkwardness of getting the person to leave.

She wouldn't really know since she'd never spent the night at anyone's house or had anyone spend the night at hers. She'd never even been on an actual date.

The sun was beginning to set as she made her way past the fire station which sat on the corner of the street that Brewed Awakenings was on. She'd worked the afternoon shift, which was bittersweet. She loved the extra sleep that not having to be up at four in the morning provided. But Josh only came into Brewed Awakenings in the mornings so working the afternoon shift meant no Josh.

As she turned onto Main Street and walked along the wooden sidewalk along the downtown area lined with mom-and-pop shops, she was filled with a sense of rightness and belonging. It was the same feeling she'd always gotten when she'd come here as a child for summer vacations.

Hope Falls had always felt like home.

String lights crisscrossed above the street and hung between the black lampposts giving the entire downtown area a magical glow. There was a river that flowed beside the town that had a bridge that spanned across it which was also lit up with twinkle lights which only added to the quaintness.

As she approached Sue Ann's Café where she was meeting her sisters, she heard the rev of a motorcycle and her breath caught in her throat. She saw the singular headlight coming toward her and it wasn't until the bike pulled to the four-way stop sign that she exhaled.

The rider wasn't Josh.

Days that she didn't have a Josh sighting were just not as sweet as days that she did. Not just because of her romantic feelings for him, but also because over the years he'd become her best friend. If something good or bad happened, he was the first person she wanted to tell. If she was having a good or bad day, he was the one she wanted to share it with. It just made things a little complicated because she was also madly in love with him.

They had gotten into the habit of having movie nights once or twice a month. Usually on Sundays after he ate at his grandmother's house, he would stop by. She had a tradition of baking on Sundays, so she'd always have fresh brownies, cupcakes, cookies or other goodies ready or just coming out of the oven. They would curl up on her couch, separately not together, sadly, watch a movie, usually a comedy and enjoy whatever treat she'd prepared. Inevitably by the time the credits rolled there would be one goody remaining which they would fight over. Not physically. Although she wouldn't mind tussling with him.

Unfortunately, their resolutions came in the form of either quick draw, where they would both put their respective hands on their knees, count backwards from three and the first to grab it won. Or they'd go with the classic, rock-paper-scissors. But her favorite way of settling the score was a good old-fashioned staring contest.

That one was her favorite because she got to brazenly stare into Josh's deep brown eyes. She'd get so lost in them sometimes, that she would forget why she'd been looking at him in the first place. He always broke first. He said that he couldn't look at her and *not* smile. She wasn't sure if that was because he knew what a dork she was or if it was because he just found her funny, or if she made him happy. She really hoped it was that she made him happy.

As she walked under the bright yellow awning and entered the café, she immediately saw that her oldest sister Grace was already seated with Viv at the sisters' favorite table; the table sat right in the front of the café, centered under the picture window that overlooked the downtown area.

Audrey had always loved the eclectic décor at the small eatery, and it hadn't changed in the over two decades she and her sisters had been coming here. There were a dozen tables sitting at comfortable angles around the dining floor. Each was covered with eclectically mismatched tablecloths. Shelves lined the back wall and displayed local crafts and personal mementos. Photos dotted the walls, which featured residents of Hope Falls and many of the events hosted by the town. It had such a homey feeling and whenever she was here it felt like a hug.

"Hey!" Audrey smiled as she approached the table and took off her scarf and gloves. "Where's Ava?" Audrey asked as she took a seat beside Grace across from Viv. She thought she would have been the last one here because she had to close up Brewed at five and that's when the sisters were meeting.

"She's in the bathroom," Grace explained.

Audrey noticed Viv was smirking at her as she lowered down.

"What?" The second she asked the question she regretted it. If her sister was looking at her like that, it had something to do with Josh, a subject Viv teased her about mercilessly.

"I saw you outside, before you walked in. You thought that was Josh on the motorcycle, didn't you?"

Unrequited love was difficult enough without people, people who were supposed to love you, pointing it out all the time. Talk about salt in a wound.

Before she had to respond to her sister's accurate assumption, Ava returned. As she took a seat next to Viv she said, "Oh, I heard you are doing something with the singles for Valentine's Day."

"Yep." Viv nodded proudly as she made her hands in the shape of a heart. "Project Valentine."

Beside Audrey, Grace choked on her soda.

Audrey patted Grace's back. "Are you okay?"

Grace nodded. "Yep, just went down the wrong pipe."

Audrey noted that while Grace explained her choking, she was giving Viv a strange look. She figured her oldest sister must be thinking the same thing that Audrey had been. There was no way that their sister could take on such a huge project. Especially with Ava's wedding scheduled the same week.

Which reminded Audrey why they were there.

"So, the wedding. Where are we at with plans?" Audrey asked as she pulled out her notebook to take notes. She and Grace were definitely the two type-A personalities in the family, but Grace's tended to come out more in needing control, whereas Audrey just needed to be organized.

"Right, so far we know it's going to be at the church," Ava explained happily.

Audrey smiled. Ava had always wanted to get married at the church in Hope Falls. The wedding she'd planned last year was going to be outside, because her fiancé hadn't wanted a church wedding. Audrey was happy that her sister was marrying the right man and she was going to get her dream wedding.

"What about the reception?" Grace asked.

Her sister's eyes squinched. "I don't know yet. It's Valentine's Day so a lot of the venues are taken. When

Blake suggested the day, I didn't really think about finding a venue for the reception."

Ava's fourteen-year-old soon-to-be stepdaughter Blake had thrown out getting married on Valentine's Day when Ava and Asher were discussing possible dates on Thanksgiving and the couple had decided it was as good a day as any.

"We could have it at Brewed," Audrey suggested.

"Yeah." Ava nodded and Audrey could see that she had probably already thought of that as a possible solution but wasn't really sold on the idea. "It's just...I mean, I know I've only lived here for less than a year, but I have *really* fallen in love with the whole town, and I sort of didn't want to put a limit on the guest list for the reception. Not that everyone will want to come, but I just don't want to leave anyone out. I sort of wanted the reception to be a big party that everyone was invited to."

"I get it." If Audrey ever got married, she wouldn't want anyone to feel excluded in her celebration and Brewed would max out at seventy-five people or so, and even that would be pushing capacity to the limit.

"What about the ballroom at Mountain Ridge?" Viv asked. "I'm sure Amanda and Justin would figure out how to make it work."

Ava cringed slightly. "Yeah, I thought about that, too, but that was where mine and Ian's reception was supposed to be. I just want this to be totally separate."

All the sisters were silent for a moment before Viv's face lit up. "What about the Riverside Recreation Area? The Valentine's Day Festival will be down there. We could put up a tent. That way even if people were working the festival they could stop by and celebrate."

Ava smiled widely. "That's actually a *really* good idea."

Audrey wrote down that she needed to speak to

someone about what permits they would need and also get pricing on tents.

"Okay, enough about me." Ava said. "What about you, Grace? Have you and Easton set a date yet?"

Grace shook her head. "Let's just get through your wedding first."

Audrey could see that Grace was still a little shell-shocked from all the changes in her life. Just a few months ago she'd been living in Los Angeles as a lawyer. Then she'd decided to move to Hope Falls and she'd ended up falling in love with Easton, who she met when she was stranded on the side of the road during a snowstorm. And now she was getting married, something she'd always said she had no plans on doing.

The conversation turned back to the plans Viv had for singles week when Kelly King, a server at Sue Ann's and Viv's friend came over and took everyone's orders. Before she left, she shook her head. "Damn, two Wells sisters with rings on their fingers. If it weren't you two, I'd be pissed that you took such prime male real estate off the market."

"There's still plenty of good men out there," Grace reasoned.

Kelly picked up Grace's hand. "Easy to say when you've got a rock the size of Gibraltar on your left hand, and it was given to you by the hot one."

Grace grinned. "He is hot."

Grace's fiancé Easton was one of four brothers who were all extremely good looking and two of which were firefighters in Hope Falls. But out of the bunch of Men's Health cover models, Easton had been deemed "the hot one."

Kelly sighed as she released Grace's hand when another table called her over.

As the sisters' conversation turned to Ava's new

practice and the real estate market in Hope Falls, Audrey's mind wandered back to Josh and what he might be doing tonight. She also wondered if she'd ever get over the crush she'd had on him since she was four years old. Or if she was ever going to get the nerve to do something about it.

4

———

JOSH PULLED UP TO HIS GRANDMA'S HOUSE AND PARKED HIS truck out front. He looked out the windshield and saw Matt and Amy Kellan with their twins Peyton and Paige building a snowman in their front yard while their Great Dane Scooby Doo, ran around in circles barking and trying to bite the snowman's head.

It was like watching a scene right out of a movie. One that he'd never have.

His half-sister Claire, who he shared a father with, had twins as well. Bridgette and Bethany were turning five this summer. She also had a one-year-old son named Braydon. Being a kickass uncle was the closest he'd come to having kids of his own. Fatherhood was not in his future. Even if he hadn't got in a dirt bike accident at fifteen that caused him to be sterile, he didn't think it was responsible of him to reproduce considering the shitty genes he had.

His mom Lori had serious mental health issues. She'd been in and out of his life since he was a baby. He hadn't seen her in a few years, but that was nothing new. His entire life it had been the same pattern. She'd show up on their doorstep out of the blue after being gone for months, sometimes years, promising that she had changed, and things would be different this time around. His dad would always welcome her back into their home and their lives. She would stick around for a while, and then disappear without any warning. No note. No explanation. No promise of when or if she was going to return.

It used to stress him out when he was a kid and even a teenager. But now that he was in his mid-thirties, he no longer allowed himself to give a shit about it.

So as far as his maternal gene pool, it was safe to say he was swimming in murky water. And his dad was not that much better. Angelo Bianchi was a drunk that cared a hell of a lot more for the bottle than he ever had about having a kid. His dad ended up dying from liver failure due to his alcoholism. Not exactly prime genetic material.

Growing up wasn't all bad, though. The one constant in his life had been the woman he was going to see now. Nonna. She'd raised him. She'd been the one who was home after school. She'd been the one who showed up to his parent teacher conferences. She'd been to every baseball and football game. Every dirt bike race. She was always in the bleachers cheering him on.

He stepped out of the truck and waved at Matt, Amy and the twins before heading in through the back door, which was unlocked. He'd tried to convince Nonna that she needed to start locking her doors, but she just ignored him. Which was another reason he wanted her to move into Golden Years. Her safety. Nonna was old school and hadn't ever locked her doors in the sixty plus years she'd lived in Hope Falls. She said that she didn't see any reason to start now. But things were different now. Especially with the influx of tourism.

Thankfully, Matt and Amy were right next door, and

they kept an eye on her. They came over and checked on her when Josh couldn't get a hold of her which usually ended up being because her hearing aid wasn't turned on so she couldn't hear her phone. And she went next door when there were any emergencies, like when her pipe burst at three in the morning. As much as he appreciated Matt and Amy's help, he didn't like that responsibility falling on their shoulders.

"Nonna, you need to lock your door." Josh knew that he was wasting his breath, but he still had to try.

Nonna completely ignored his comment as she stood at the stove stirring the sauce. "Did you see Audrey today?"

Josh checked his watch. "Wow."

"Wow?" Nonna's brow furrowed. "What is wow?"

"That's a record for you."

"What record for me?"

"It took you less than *three seconds* to bring up Audrey."

Nonna loved Audrey and was convinced that she and Josh would end up together. It was her favorite topic of discussion. That and which Kardashian she liked best on any given day; the top spot changed on what felt like a weekly basis. The last he'd heard it was Kim. Nonna was impressed by the fact that she was working on prison reform and pursuing her law degree.

He had to admit, he was too.

"Well?!" Nonna's skinny arms flew in the air. "Did you see her?"

"No, I didn't." Josh bent down and kissed Nonna's cheek.

That wasn't completely true. Josh had seen her this afternoon when she'd arrived at Brewed Awakenings, but he hadn't talked to her. He'd almost gone in for an afternoon coffee, but he did his best to limit exposure to her. The more time he spent with her, the harder it was not to do something stupid. Something that he couldn't take back. Something that might ruin the most important relationship he had in his life, besides Nonna.

Audrey Wells was one of his closest friends. He wasn't sure exactly how it had happened. When he'd gotten medically discharged from the Army and came back to Hope Falls, he'd been in a dark place. A very dark place. And the death of his father hadn't helped. Then, within six months of moving home, Audrey had moved to town with her sister and opened Brewed Awakenings.

He would never forget the first day he saw her, she was standing in front of the empty storefront that would end up being Brewed Awakenings with Lauren Harrison, who was his friend Caleb's cousin and was a realtor in Hope Falls. He remembered he was in excruciating pain that day from his injuries, and he'd just untangled the financials of the business and realized just how badly his father had run Pine Auto Shop into the ground. He was in crippling debt and in crippling pain physically, emotionally, and mentally.

He'd been having some pretty dark thoughts when he'd walked out of the garage and saw *her*. Her long silky dark hair was shining in the sun and her full ruby red lips drew him like a moth to a flame. He'd stood there completely awe-struck by her beauty. He forgot where he was or what he was doing. Nothing else existed in that moment but the dark-haired goddess standing on the corner. Obviously, he'd been attracted to women before, but he'd never had such a primal, visceral reaction to one like he had that day.

When Lauren left, he watched as the brown-haired beauty lifted her hand over her eyes to shield the sun as she turned her head in his direction. He'd never forget the moment their eyes met. There'd been a spark of recognition in her gaze and then it happened. Those full, ruby red lips of hers pulled up into a wide smile and his entire world shifted on its axis. But instead of it being off balance, her smile made everything feel right. For one glorious moment, he didn't feel the searing pain of his back. The world wasn't closing in on him in crushing anxiety. He felt light. He felt free. He felt safe.

His first thought was that she must be an angel. A heavenly being. He'd grown up in church and he'd heard of people seeing celestial creatures.

He never expected the angel to walk toward him and say, "*It's Josh, right. Do you remember me?*"

He was sure she must have mistaken him for someone else, because he would never have forgotten the stunningly beautiful woman who was standing in front of him. He opened his mouth to speak, but no words came out.

But then she continued, "*I'm Audrey Wells. I used to vacation here with my three sisters and mom. You fixed my mom's flat tire the last summer we were here. But that was like fifteen years ago.*"

Then it all came back to him. He remembered Audrey and her sisters Grace, Ava, and Viv and their mom Mrs. Wells. But would never have expected the cute little girl in pigtails that had followed him around like a puppy to end up being this goddess with pinup worthy curves and a smile that caused his heart to expand in his chest to twice its size.

He'd spent months recovering from his injuries and battling a fairly serious depression. He'd suffered from a lot of flashbacks, especially at night. Night terrors his therapist called them. Then his dad died, and he inherited a business he'd never wanted in the first place, and to add insult to injury it was in a dire financial place. He'd felt like he'd been living his own personal hell. Seeing Audrey that day was the first ray of sunshine he'd seen. She was like his own personal angel and still was.

Once they got reacquainted, he'd found out that she truly was an angel. She was the sweetest, kindest, most honest and caring person he knew. And she was his friend. He didn't have very many of those.

The last thing he would ever do was jeopardize that relationship by doing something stupid like telling her how he felt about her. That he couldn't go one day, one hour, even one minute most of the time without thinking of her. That she was the light in his darkness. That she'd saved him when he thought that there was nothing left to save.

"That girl isn't going to wait around for you forever." Nonna wagged her finger up at him.

Josh grinned and turned on the charm in a way that never failed to make Nonna smile. "Why do I need a girl when I have you, Nonna?"

"Pssh." She waved him away, fighting the smile he saw was pulling on her lips. "I'm not going to live forever, you know."

He hated when she talked like that, even if he knew it was true.

Josh walked over to the pantry and checked Nonna's pill box to make sure that she'd been taking her medication. He refilled it every Sunday for the week ahead but if he stopped by midweek, he liked to double check that she hadn't missed any days.

She'd called him over tonight because she said that her internet wasn't working so she couldn't watch her shows. "I'm going to reset your router."

"You need to ask that girl on a date." Nonna ignored what he'd said and returned to her original topic. Audrey.

Josh wasn't blind and he wasn't an idiot. He knew that Audrey had a crush on him. And as much as he'd love to do something about that, he couldn't. Not only because he was scared to risk their friendship, but also because she deserved better than him. She deserved someone who didn't have the demons he had. She deserved someone who could give her the world. A man who could give her a family, like Matt and Amy had.

He wasn't that man.

And more than anything, he wanted Audrey to be happy. Even if it killed him to see her with someone else. Which he thought there was a pretty good chance it would.

For the past eight years, he'd waited for that shoe to drop. But as far as he'd known, she hadn't dated anyone since she'd lived in Hope Falls. She'd told him about a boyfriend she'd had in high school named Chris, but other than that, she didn't really talk about guys with him.

This damn singles week was probably going to mean an influx of men. Men who would be an idiot not to see how amazing Audrey was. He knew that she wasn't going to stay single forever, but he was going to cherish the time he had with her until she did find her prince charming.

After making sure Nonna was up and running again, he walked back into the kitchen.

"Okay, you should be all good to watch your shows."

Nonna had become obsessed with reality television over the past few years. Her favorites were *The Bachelor*, the *Housewives* franchise, and the *Kardashians*. He had no clue what she found entertaining about the reality shows, but she loved them. She always had them on at the shop and thanks to streaming services she had them playing on a constant loop at her house.

It reminded him of when he was growing up and she watched soap operas: *Days of our Lives*, *General Hospital*, *The Young and the Restless*, and *The Bold and the Beautiful*. All of them. She used to record the episodes on VHS tapes so she could re-watch them later. He guessed the reality shows were just updated soap operas.

"Sit. Sit." She waved her hand towel at him. "I feed you."

Josh's back was killing him and since Nonna refused to let him upgrade her dining set, the wooden chairs absolutely wrecked his back. She didn't know that, of course. If she did, she'd probably let him buy her a new dining set.

Knowing that he couldn't refuse his grandmother's cooking, Josh sucked it up and sat down. What was excruciating pain in comparison to a good home-cooked meal with his number one lady? It was definitely a fair trade off.

5

"BIRTH CONTROL?" AUDREY REPEATED WHAT HER SISTER Ava had just said as she wrote the specials of the day on the board. It was barely six in the morning and even though Audrey had been up for an hour and a half, she still wasn't firing on all cylinders.

She'd had a dream about Josh last night. A very sexy dream that she wished she'd never woken up from. But her damn alarm had interrupted things just when they were getting good.

"Yeah." Ava nodded. "Jenna's going to talk to her today."

Jenna was Blake's mom. She and Ava's fiancé Asher had been divorced for quite a few years, and she'd even remarried. But unfortunately, her second marriage hadn't worked out either. So, she was newly single. And apparently going to be speaking to their teenage daughter about going on birth control.

Ava continued, "Blake says that nothing is happening with her and Noah, but they've been together for a while now. And they're teenagers."

Noah Barnes was such a good kid. Well, a good teenager. He was a good student, a star athlete, and worked two part-time jobs. When Asher and Blake had moved here last summer Blake hadn't been happy about the move. Thankfully, she made friends and met Noah and that had eased the transition. The two teens had been pretty much inseparable for over six months.

A funny side note to that story was that Asher and Blake had *coincidentally* moved to Hope Falls the exact same day Ava got left at the alter and decided to stay in Hope Falls.

It wasn't a coincidence, it was fate, Audrey heard her mother's voice in her head.

Maybe it was fate. If that was the case, Audrey wanted to put in a formal request for *fate* to start working on her behalf with Josh.

"Mom put me on birth control when I was Blake's age, since Ian and I had already been together for two years." Ava said as she hopped down from the counter where she'd been sitting while Audrey got things ready to open.

"Yeah, me too." Their mom had put her on birth control after she'd gotten a steady boyfriend in high school and she'd been right around Blake's age. "I just can't believe that Asher is okay with all of this." Audrey said as she hung up the board displaying the specials.

"He's not. Not really. What father wants to think about their fourteen-year-old daughter going on birth control. But Jenna made some good points. One of which was that *he* had been sexually active at that age. Which she knows because they were together then. She also reemphasized that it's just a *talk*. That's all. Jenna's not putting her on anything. She just wants Blake to know that if that's something she wants, then Jenna will support her. Not like

44

Mom who didn't really give us a choice because she wanted us—"

"Us to have choices in our future," Audrey finished their mom's mantra in chorus with her sister.

That was what their mom would always say was the reason any of them should be on the pill, so they could have choices in their future. Looking back and thinking about how young their mom was when she was left to be a single parent to four girls under the age of five, it made sense.

"Thanks for this." Ava held up her iced caramel latte with two shots of espresso. "I have back-to-back clients all day and I'm going to need it."

Ava gave Audrey a hug and headed out of the coffee shop. As Audrey looked around, she couldn't help but be proud of what she saw.

When she'd envisioned opening up a coffee shop in her mom's honor, this was exactly what she saw. Her mother loved Old Hollywood, which was why all of the girls were named after starlets from that era. Grace's namesake was Grace Kelly. Ava's was Ava Gardner. Vivien's was Vivien Leigh. And Audrey had been named after Audrey Hepburn. All of their middle names were Christmas themed, which was another one of Cora Wells' obsessions.

Black and white portraits of each one of the girls' namesakes hung on the walls, along with James Dean, Marilyn Monroe, Bette Davis, and Cary Grant, who were some of her mom's other favorites. The décor had a vintage Hollywood theme, there was a large black chandelier hanging in the center of the room, there were a half dozen bistro tables arranged throughout the room, a farm table on one side, and two oversized couches with coffee tables in front of them lined the opposite wall.

As she wiped down the counter and got ready for the

morning rush, the conversation she'd just had with her sister replayed in her head. She had two takeaways from it. One, she was so proud of Asher, Jenna, and Ava for the way that the three of them were co-parenting. They truly put Blake first. And second, teenagers in this town were getting more action than she was.

Audrey was a virgin, which had never bothered her before she turned thirty. She honestly hadn't really thought about it that much before then.

She didn't need to have Ava's degree in psychology to know that her father "peacing out" when she was two had to have affected how she felt about men. It wasn't just the trauma of her father abandoning them, either. It was that their mother never moved on. She never got over him. Until her dying breath, she maintained that Mason Wells was the love of her life. That sort of blind devotion in the face of total abandonment had definitely shaped the way that Audrey viewed relationships.

Then there was watching her sisters in their romantic entanglements which she'd had a front row seat to as she grew up. They were all different and equally dysfunctional, from what Audrey had observed.

Grace dated people, but nothing was ever serious. She kept men, well, men before Easton, at arm's length. No one she dated actually knew who Grace was beneath the mask of cold indifference she put on. Sometimes they didn't even know her name. Audrey had lived with Grace all through college and she remembered one time some dude had come to pick her sister up and had asked if Tracy was home when she answered the door. If it was a first date, Audrey would have understood, but it was their third date and he didn't even know her name. Grace hadn't cared at all. She went and enjoyed a very expensive dinner at Spago in Beverly Hills. She then proceeded to date the guy for the next three months.

Audrey couldn't ever imagine being intimate with someone who didn't know her at all.

And then there was Ava who started dating Ian when they were both twelve. Ian ended up dumping her on her wedding day, which was honestly the best thing he could have ever done for her sister. Audrey grew up watching the two of them. They went from preteens, to teens, to adults and their relationship never changed. It was almost like they were *too close* to each other to even see who the other person was. They'd been together so long that they took for granted that they actually knew each other, but the truth was they didn't.

Audrey knew that wasn't the case with the man Ava was set to walk down the aisle with on Valentine's Day. Asher saw her sister. They saw each other.

And then there was Viv. Viv loved men but was terrified of commitment. Part of the reason Hope Falls had been such an easy sell when Audrey had asked her sister to move here the tourist nature of the town. It always cycled through what she referred to as "fresh meat." Guys that were in town for a week or two was what she considered a perfect amount of time to spend with someone. Long enough to have fun, not long enough to get bored.

Audrey was the opposite. She was sort of scared of men but loved the idea of commitment. When she was a preteen, she'd seriously considered becoming a nun. She loved helping people and had no desire to ever get married or even have a boyfriend. But that hadn't panned out, mainly because she wasn't Catholic.

She'd had the same boyfriend all through high school, but besides some heavy petting nothing happened. They broke up when Chris went back East to college. Not long after he left, she saw on his social media that he was Facebook official with someone else and, plot twist, it was a guy. It hadn't surprised her to find out that he was gay. It actually made a lot of sense considering how little had happened between them physically since they'd been together for four years.

As the morning progressed Manny arrived for his shift and there was a steady flow of customers to keep them both busy. But not even her work could distract her from the glaring fact that she was going to be thirty-three in a few months, and she was still a virgin.

How had that happened?

And, more importantly, what was she going to do about it?

THE BELL DINGED over the door as Josh stepped inside of Brewed Awakenings. This was his favorite part of the day. The twelve steps that it took to get to the counter that Audrey stood behind. He loved watching the smile spread wider on her beautiful face with each step he took closing the distance between them. Her smile still had the same effect on him that it had the first time he'd seen it. It was a balm to his soul, it soothed him.

This morning Audrey's long dark locks were pulled up in a ponytail. As much as Josh loved her hair when it was down, he had to admit he was partial to when she wore it up. It showcased the smooth, slope of her neck. Every time they hugged; he was tempted to press a kiss to the soft skin just below her ear. He'd wanted so badly to run his fingers along the gentle curve of the back of her neck. There'd been so many times, so many moments when he'd almost crossed a line with Audrey. So far, he'd been able to resist the temptation, but he could feel his resolve slipping with each interaction that they shared.

"Morning," she chirped brightly.

"Morning" He grinned.

"Two chocolate croissants and a tall black coffee?" she asked tilting her head adorably to the side.

His order never changed. He always got a chocolate croissant for himself and one for Nonna and a tall black coffee for himself. He nodded.

"It'll be a minute for the croissants. I have a batch in the oven." She motioned over her shoulder toward the back wall where the industrial oven was located.

"Sounds good."

Josh stepped to the side as she turned and headed the direction of the oven when out of the corner of his eye, he saw Manny walking toward him. It was hard to miss the guy. He was a retired professional sumo wrestler who stood six foot two and weighed three hundred pounds plus. When Manny started working at the coffee shop, Josh had to admit it had seemed like an odd pairing, but it only took one visit in the shop to see Manny's passion for java. The man lived and breathed coffee beans.

As a native of Hope Falls, it fascinated Josh how people like Manny ended up in the small town. He was of Samoan descent and had been born and raised in Hawaii, which was arguably one of the most beautiful places in the world to live. He'd spent over a decade and a half traveling to countless countries competing in sumo and for some reason he'd chosen to settle in Hope Falls.

Josh knew that a lot of people thought the town was magic. Audrey's sister even liked to say that there was something called the 'Hope Falls Effect.' Josh had never known exactly what she was talking about when she said it, but he knew he sure as hell had never experienced it.

"Nice shirt," Josh commented on the floral button up shirt with the Brewed Awakenings logo on the right chest pocket Manny was wearing.

"Oh, you like?" Manny looked down. "It's new, it's an Aloha shirt."

"Looks good."

Josh loved that Audrey and Viv let their employees express themselves by choosing their own uniforms as long as they put the Brewed Awakenings logo on it. Their other part-time employee Carly, who had a more punk rock style, had put the logo on shirts with mesh arms and faux leather jackets.

"Hey brudda, you have to try this." Manny handed him an espresso glass filled about halfway to the top. "I just brewed it with beans I got in this morning from Zimbabwe."

Manny was a master mixologist, except he didn't specialize in alcohol, he dealt in coffee beans. He was always so excited to share his creations with Josh. And while Josh appreciated the enthusiasm and his passion for his craft, Manny's talent was wasted on him. He was not what you would call a coffee connoisseur. Josh wished that he had a more discerning palate, unfortunately he didn't.

Josh brought the glass to his mouth and was about to throw it back when Manny stopped him.

"No, brudda, you gotta smell it first." He mimed bringing the glass up to his nose and inhaling.

Josh mirrored Manny's gesture and then drank the java in one gulp.

"Mmm." Josh grinned as he set the glass down. "That's good."

Manny's expression was expectant. "Do you taste the notes of berry and hazelnut?"

Nope. He just tasted sweet coffee.

Josh nodded. "Yeah, man. Really good."

Manny smiled widely, clearly proud of his creation.

"Ahh, brudda." Manny gripped Josh's shoulder, easily able to reach him across the counter. "You make my day."

With that, he grabbed the glass and went back into the back room probably to continue working on his next brew.

Josh looked around and saw that there were only two other people in the coffee shop. Mr. Jenkins, the high school principal and Mary Higgins who owned Say Cheese, the photography shop downtown. The two were huddled together in the corner and his first thought was wondering if there might be something going on there.

Damn, he'd been back in Hope Falls too long. This is what the town did to people and how rumors started.

He shook off that thought and looked around the rest of the shop which was empty. He specifically came at this time of the day because it was after the morning rush when most people were at work and Audrey was usually working the front by herself. He never stayed long. Just got his order and left. But those few minutes of just being in her presence kept him buzzing for hours. She was that potent. Which was why he did his best to limit the amount of time he spent around her.

Audrey stepped back up to the counter with his order in hand and a smile on her face. Her eyes were twinkling as she asked in a whisper, "Did you *really* taste berry and hazelnut?"

He grinned down at her as he shook his head slowly.

Her smile grew even wider and Josh's heart swelled at the sight. "Thank you, for saying you did."

He reached into his back pocket to grab his wallet, but she put out her hand. "It's on the house."

This was the same song and dance they did every time he came in, which was three to four times a week for the past eight years, so they'd done it approximately fifteen hundred times. From the first time he'd come in on opening day, Audrey had never let him pay. He always tried, she always refused.

"Audrey—" he started to argue but she cut him off.

"So, the next time I need to get my oil changed, you'll let me pay for it? Or if my air conditioning goes out again then you'll let me—"

"That's different. Those things happen a few times a year, if that. I'm in here a few times a week."

"Yes, but this is a few bucks as opposed to hundreds, even thousands of dollars."

The bell rang above the door and Audrey looked past Josh and smiled to welcome the new customer in. When she was distracted, he put a twenty in the tip jar. Whenever she wasn't looking, he always snuck twenties in the tip jar.

"Thanks." He lifted his bag of croissants and his cup of coffee.

"You're welcome." She grinned, seeming pleased with herself that she'd been able to get him to accept the goods without paying.

He smiled and turned to leave. Twelve steps. That was how long it would be until he'd be outside the coffee shop. Those twelve steps he took away from her were the least favorite part of his day.

6

"Hey, Audrey!" Cindy Brown smiled from behind the desk at Golden Years Senior Living. Last time Audrey had seen her friend, she'd had gorgeous long braids down to her back, today her hair was in tight curls framing her perfect heart shaped face. Cindy was in her fifties, but she didn't look a day over thirty-five. The woman never aged.

"I love your hair!" Audrey handed Cindy a peppermint macchiato with extra whipped cream, which she brought her every time she came to Golden Years.

"Oh, you are truly a saint." Cindy took a sip and closed her eyes, when she finished her drink, she set her cup down before patting the bottom of her curls. "And thanks. I love my braids, they are basically no maintenance, but sometimes you just gotta let your hair breathe and go natural."

"You look great!" Audrey enthused.

Cindy gave her a wink before smiling widely as she peered over the countertop. "And who do you have with you today?"

Audrey glanced down as she introduced the dachshund and golden retriever. "This is Duchess and Barkley."

Every Tuesday evening Audrey brought in shelter dogs to the retirement home. It was a program she'd started after volunteering at both the shelter and the senior home. Dogs needed to be socialized and the residents at Golden Years loved the interaction. She also ran a program where kindergartners and preschoolers in after-school care came for a few hours every month and did art projects together. The kids and the seniors loved it. They thrived off the interaction.

That program had started after one day when she was volunteering at the library as part of a reading program. She couldn't get through one page without one of the kids interrupting her. She realized that all they really wanted was for people to listen to them. And all the seniors at Golden Years wanted was company. She figured it would be worth a shot.

She'd contacted the school and worked with the principal to make it happen. So far, it had been a roaring success. The kids looked forward to it, as much if not more than the seniors.

"Hello, Duchess and Barkley." Cindy rounded the counter and knelt down and gave each of the pups a good scratch behind the ears. "What's their story?"

"Duchess was part of the hoarding case in Jasper County. And Barkley was picked up out at King's Pond," Audrey explained.

Cindy reached out and petted Barkley's head. "I would take them both home if I could."

"So would I," Audrey concurred whole-heartedly.

Cindy, like Audrey, was a huge animal lover. She had four cats, three dogs, two rabbits and some chickens. The two women had bonded over their shared love of rescues and Cindy's great appreciation for caffeinated beverages.

Audrey had two rescue cats, Liza and Frank. But since they were both special needs, and she was so busy with the coffee shop and volunteering she didn't think it was responsible to take on more pets. If that wasn't the case, she would have a zoo.

"Oh, I've been meaning to talk to you!" Cindy's face lit up as she stood.

Audrey knew that particular brand of face-lighting-up all too well. Her friend was going to try to set her up in three, two, one…

"Davis just hired a new foreman. He's forty, divorced, *no* kids, and he used to play in the NFL, that's how Davis knew him. He's just moved to Emerald Creek and Davis is going to bring him to JT's on Friday night. You should come. It could be like a double date."

Cindy's husband Davis had played professional football for ten years and now owned a construction company. He and Cindy had been childhood sweethearts who had broken up in college. They'd both gone on to marry other people, have kids, raise those kids and then subsequently divorce their significant others. They'd reconnected at their twenty-five-year high school reunion and they'd been together ever since. Cindy was blissfully happy, and from Audrey's experience, blissfully happy people who were in relationships, were always trying to recruit people into their club.

Audrey smiled sweetly. "I'm actually helping my sister out with wedding plans on Friday night."

She was lying through her teeth. She hated lying. But more than lying she hated being set up on blind dates. She'd never actually gone on any of them, because it honestly sounded like her worst nightmare.

"Okay, well what about next Friday?" Cindy asked hopefully.

"This month is going to be crazy. We have Ava's wedding, and I'm helping Viv with the singles week."

Technically, Audrey *had* told Viv to let her know if she needed any help. So far, she hadn't asked her to do anything, but Audrey considered herself on call.

Cindy clapped her hands together. "That's right. We're having a singles week. Well, you better snap that man up before that. Because let me tell you he is *not* going to stay on the market long if you know what I mean?"

"I do." Audrey humored Cindy the same way Josh had when Manny asked him if he could taste berry and hazelnut flavors. "So, is everyone in the game room?"

"Yep." Cindy went back behind the counter. "They've been waiting for you all day. You really make a difference here, Aud. I hope you know that."

Audrey smiled feeling uncomfortable accepting the recognition. She didn't really do anything except bring some kids and animals to visit with people that were lonely. That didn't exactly make her a hero.

She walked down the wide hallway and when they reached the double doors, she looked down at her four-legged companions. "Okay, I need you both to be on your best behavior."

Both animals looked up at her, their tails wagging. Duchess was wearing a sweater that Mrs. Davenport, one of the residents there, had knitted and donated to the shelter and Barkley had on a bow tie. She tried to dress all the shelter animals in cute clothes, and she took pictures with the residents to put on the website to try and bolster adoptions.

As soon as she walked through the door Mrs. Davenport's face lit up and she clapped her hands. Audrey wasn't sure if it was because she recognized the sweater or she was just excited that they were here.

"What did you bring us today? A rat?" Mr. Wilson teased as he leaned down to pet Duchess who had hopped up onto the chair next to him and was demanding his attention.

"That is Duchess, Mr. Wilson."

"Oh, aren't you a fancy girl," he cooed at her.

"And who is this?" Mrs. Davenport asked as Barkley walked up and put his head beneath her hand.

"This is Barkley."

"Oh, Mr. Barkley. What a handsome name for a handsome boy." Mrs. Davenport scratched behind his ears.

"Don't hog him, Gladys!" Mrs. Campbell, who was sitting on the other side room shouted.

"I'm not. He walked over to me!" Mrs. Davenport shot back.

Audrey made her way around the room making sure each one of the residents got a chance to pet either Duchess or Barkley. She had just finished her first round when her phone vibrated in her pocket.

She picked it up when she saw it was Viv calling. "Hey."

"Hey, I'm stuck in traffic on 80 and I'm supposed to meet the Dining in the Dark people in ten minutes."

"The who people?" Audrey held her finger to her ear.

"Dining in the Dark. They want to come for singles week. It's going to be like speed dating, but you won't know what each other looks like. It's a popup restaurant that you eat in the dark, and I think you have a blindfold. The guests will have a different date for the appetizer, main course, and dessert. They are here in Hope Falls to do a demonstration, but I'm not going to make it back in time."

"I'm at Golden Years wit—"

"Please, sissy! I don't want to flake on them. Ava had clients and Grace is doing some online real estate course thingy. Help me, Obi-Wan, you're my only hope."

Audrey looked around the room at the residents. Normally, she did four rounds with the dogs so each person each got plenty of time. But she could let them know that something came up and tell them she would be back on Thursday. And she had said that she would help.

Audrey sighed. She could never say no to her sister, and she did appreciate that she hadn't been her sister's first call and the Star Wars reference. "Okay. Text me the address."

———

JOSH POPPED a can of cat food and dumped it in the bowl. Then he repeated the task opening another jar and dumping it in another bowl. He set both bowls down on the cement floor and whistled. Within seconds both Bullet and Batman appeared.

They were strays that had shown up a few years back. Bullet was the first to start hanging around. Josh named him that because he was gray and fast as fuck. He'd almost named him Houdini because he was there one second, gone the next, but he thought Bullet fit him better. Batman showed up about a week after Bullet, he was a white cat with a black mask that looked exactly like the superhero of the same name.

As he watched the cats eat their dinner, he heard Nonna's voice in the back of his head. "*If you keep feeding them, they'll keep showing up.*"

She talked a big game, but he'd seen her sneak them tuna fish when she thought he wasn't looking.

He washed his hands, turned up the volume on the

nest speaker that Audrey had gotten him for his birthday last year and got back to work. He'd made an offhanded comment about how the radio in the garage needed an upgrade. Then two months later, on his birthday, she'd given him the nest.

She always got him such thoughtful gifts. Which shouldn't surprise him, she was a thoughtful person. But he did have to be careful what he said around her. If he mentioned that he needed to get some new white shirts, she'd show up with a packet of Hanes and say that she picked them up when she was shopping for one of the charities she volunteered for. If he said that he was going to get the next Grisham novel when it came out, a hardcover copy would show up on his door on release day.

As much as he appreciated her paying attention and being so thoughtful, it made him feel bad that she spent her time and money on him. He didn't deserve her friendship and he sure as hell didn't deserve anything more than friendship, which was what he really wanted to have with her.

He was finishing up replacing an alternator when he felt his phone vibrate in his pocket. He pulled it out and saw that it was a text from Pricilla.

He'd casually dated Pricilla off and on for years. They'd met at JT's a month after he got home after being injured. She lived several towns over and had never pressured him for anything more than a hookup every few months. Neither of them were looking for anything serious. It was sort of the perfect situation. Or at least it had been. It had been over a year since he'd seen her last and things had not really gone as planned. When it came time to get down and dirty, he hadn't been able to…perform.

If it was just the once, he would have thought it could be a fluke. But it wasn't. And it wasn't just her. She was one of three women that he saw on a casual basis. He also hooked up with Jenny who was a divorced single mom from Sacramento. And Sabrina who ran a wellness center in Lake Tahoe and didn't believe in labels. None of the relationships were anything serious. They all knew that he wasn't exclusive and didn't want anything serious. The women would usually hit him up when they were between relationships or getting over a break-up or looking for some no strings fun.

Except, for a while now, there'd been no fun to be had thanks to his equipment not working. Every time things had gotten heated in the past two years, his body refused to cooperate. It was really starting to fuck with his head.

He'd talked to his doctor about it, thinking it had to do with the medication he was on for pain and anxiety, but since everything worked just fine when he was alone, the doctor said it was probably more mental than physical. Josh wasn't completely convinced that was the case.

Pricilla: *Hey stranger. It's been a while. I'm going to be passing through Hope Falls. Do ya wanna grab a drink at JT's?*

He wondered if maybe he should meet Pricilla and give it another try. It's not like she hadn't been understanding about his performance, or lack thereof. Just like Jenny and Sabrina who had both been very sweet about the situation. And he'd made sure they were taken care of and hadn't left frustrated. He didn't need his dick to satisfy a woman, he just wished it was an option.

And maybe if things did go better, and everything worked the way it was supposed to, it would take the edge off. If he was with someone, maybe he'd be able to stop obsessing about Audrey so much. He'd had it bad for her for years, but lately it felt like his feelings for her were at critical mass. Every interaction they had, he worried that he was going to do something stupid like declare his undying love for her or kiss her.

If he saw Pricilla tonight, maybe then he could be around Audrey without wanting to rip her clothes off of her.

Even as he thought it, he realized that it was a bad idea. Did Pricilla use him? Sure. She'd been very upfront about that fact. She called whenever she got dumped, and when she had been going through a divorce. But seeing someone because you were lonely or trying to get over someone was different than seeing someone to try and numb your very active feelings for someone else.

He texted back that he was working and wouldn't be able to meet her. He was putting his phone back in his pocket when it vibrated again.

Pricilla: *Are you seeing someone else? It's totally okay if you are. I just…you've seemed distant lately.*

He wrote back a short response.

Josh: *No.*

As soon as it delivered, he watched as bubbles appeared on his screen, but then they disappeared. Then they came back and disappeared again. It was obvious that Pricilla had more to say to him, but she wasn't sure how to say it.

He knew then that their relationship had run its course and he knew that he owed her an explanation.

Josh: *I'm not seeing her, technically, but there is someone else.*

Pricilla: *Okay…thank you for your honesty. I hope she makes you happy. I really mean that. I'm not being sarcastic. You are a really great guy and you deserve to be happy.*

Josh wasn't sure he agreed with that. He was a broken and very damaged man in every way possible. But she didn't need to know that. He sent back a sincere reply.

Josh: *So do you.*

He'd put his phone away and slid back under the Mustang to try and forget about the fact that he'd just confessed to someone that he had feelings for Audrey. Not that he'd named names but still, he'd admitted it.

He was just starting to get back into the flow of work when he felt something hit his knee. He didn't have to look to know that it was Nonna's slipper. She took it off and swatted him when she wanted to get his attention.

He rolled out and Nonna was staring down at him holding her shoe in her hand.

"I thought you went home already," he said before he realized that she must have gone home because she was wearing her house shoes. Her house was only around the corner from the shop. He walked her home when it was dark outside, but today she'd left well before sunset.

"I was home. I came back. I forgot that I need you to do something tonight."

"What?" Josh sat up and wiped his hands.

She made a shooing motion with her hand. "You need to go eat without the lights on."

Josh stared at Nonna, sure that he'd either heard her wrong or that she was going to explain what she'd just said. Her accent was thick, and she mixed up phrases, but normally he understood what her point was. Tonight, he had no clue.

"Did your electricity go out?" he asked, trying to decipher her statement. "You want me to have dinner with you in the dark?"

"What? No! Not me. You don't eat with me. You need to go to downtown and eat without the lights on. It's for the singles week. Viv can't go. She's in the car. You need to go and tell me if it is good for singles." She shoved a printout at him.

He looked down at the flyer.

Dining in the Dark

Come and join us for an evening you'll never forget. Originated in Europe, dining in the dark is a concept that has been enjoyed for years. This unique culinary experience heightens your other senses, sharpening your sense of taste and enhancing the enjoyment of your meal.

"You want me to go eat in the dark?" He looked back up at her, still not quite sure what that meant.

"Yes, that's what I say! Go!"

"What time am I supposed to be there?"

"Now. Go, now!"

"Nonna, I need to shower. I have grease on my shirt."

"No, no, no! It's fine. It's dark. You go!"

Josh sighed knowing that this was a losing battle. He had no clue what this was going to be like but he also knew that there was no way he could say no to Nonna. She said go, so he went.

7

AUDREY WAS HAPPILY SURPRISED WHEN SHE PULLED INTO the parking lot next to the Riverside Recreation Area. When she asked Viv to text her the address her sister's reply was simply Riverside Rec. Audrey thought she must have been mistaken but sure enough there was a tent that resembled a small wedding tent set up on the far end of the expansive grass area next to the picnic tables.

She got out of her car and looked around as she walked toward the tent, she honestly had no clue what she was in for. She'd never heard of eating in the dark, but she figured she'd just go into it with an open mind. Audrey had gone to dinner by herself plenty of times, but usually she brought a book with her and read while she ate. That wouldn't be possible since the room was going to be, she assumed from the context clues of the name, dark.

Guilt niggled in her chest, but she was trying to put her abrupt departure from Golden Years out of her head. She felt bad for bailing on the residents, they'd been very disappointed when she'd said that she had to go but she told them she'd be back Thursday. But that hadn't been as bad as having to take the dogs back to the shelter. The looks on the dogs' faces when they had to go back in their kennels broke her heart. But she knew that it was better to get them out and socialized and getting pictures of them to put up on the website interacting with the residents. It was a good thing, but sometimes there were hard parts of good things.

As she stepped inside of the tent, she was greeted by an attractive woman who looked to be in her mid to late twenties. She was stunning with bright blue eyes and dark brown hair on the roots that gradually got lighter as it went down the length of the strands and was nearly blonde at the tips. She was pretty sure the style was called ombré. She'd thought about doing it, something to switch things up. But she'd never actually pulled the trigger.

She'd never dyed her hair in her life. The last time she was getting her hair cut at The Last Tangle, her stylist Brianna told her that her hair was what the industry called virgin hair because it had never been treated with color.

Even her hair was virgin.

"Welcome to Dining in the Dark. I'm Kenna, it's Vivien, correct?"

"No. Actually, I'm Audrey. Vivien is my sister, but she got stuck in traffic. So, I'm here instead."

"Oh, okay. And have you ever dined at a blackout restaurant before?"

"No." Audrey shook her head.

"Do you want to wait for the rest of your party, or would you like to be seated?"

"It's just me, so I guess seated."

"Oh, I have a reservation for two."

"My sister was probably going to meet someone," Audrey guessed. "But now it's just me."

Kenna smiled and went through the menu that had been preselected to make sure that Audrey didn't have any allergies or dietary requirements. She asked Audrey to place her cell phone in a small locker and explained what she could expect from the experience. "Guests find that dining in the dark can feel a little overwhelming at first, but once you get acclimated it's actually very enjoyable. When you take away one of your senses the others compensate, your sense of taste, touch, smell, and sound enhances, creating a unique and pleasurable experience."

Audrey nodded with a grin that dropped when she saw Kenna pull out a long piece of black material. "What's that?"

"It's a blindfold. I'll put this on you and then place your hands on my shoulders and I'll lead you inside the dining room, sort of like a conga line."

"Oh…I thought…I just assumed the room would be dark."

"It is, but we also blindfold our diners just to ensure that they have a completely blacked out experience."

"Oh, okay."

For some reason a blindfold made things feel much more serious to Audrey, even though she knew that at any time she could take it off. Her heart was beating a little faster as Kenna wrapped the material around Audrey's eyes and secured it behind her head.

"Does that feel comfortable."

"Yes."

The next thing she knew her hands were on Kenna's shoulders, and she was escorting her to her seat. Audrey lowered down carefully, making sure that she could feel the seat beneath her as she did, so she didn't fall on the floor. When she was safely in her chair, she put her hand on the table and felt the prongs of her fork press against her fingers as a clanking sound of silverware bumping together sounded.

She pulled back her hand like she'd touched a hot stove. "Sorry."

Audrey wasn't sure what she was apologizing for, but she felt very out of her element.

"No, that's good. You should get familiar with the landscape of the table. Where your plate and silverware are and your glass of water. And there is a bell in the center that you can ring if you need me. Normally staff would be in the room, and you would be able to call them over but since this is a private dining experience, just ring the bell and I'll come in. Would you like a drink before I bring out your salad?"

The way Kenna asked the question made Audrey think that it was more of a suggestion to take the edge off since she was jumpy. If she couldn't read, she might as well have a glass of wine. "I'll take a glass of wine."

Kenna listed Audrey's options and she went with the house white. "Great, I'll be right back with your drink."

Audrey tried to put herself in the shoes of one of the singles who might be coming to this experience. She wondered if it would be more or less nerve-wracking to not be able to see your dates. As she sat waiting in the dark for what felt like a lot longer than it should take to get a glass of wine, especially considering she was the only guest in the popup restaurant, she did notice that her sense of smell seemed to be heightened. There was a faint aroma of something floral in the air. Maybe there were floral arrangements as centerpieces.

Would there be centerpieces in a restaurant that you couldn't see?

She heard the sound of the curtain that led into the

dining room being opened and she sat a little straighter expecting to be receiving her wine.

"Okay, right this way."

Audrey heard Kenna say, obviously leading someone into the restaurant and what sounded like two pairs of footsteps. It was so strange not being able to see who had entered.

"Here we are. You can sit."

"Here?"

Before her brain caught up with the information her ears were telling her, her entire body responded to the familiar baritone voice. A tingling sensation spread from the top of her head to the tips of her toes, her heart sped up and she found it difficult to breath. She started to reach up and take off the blindfold but stopped herself as she said, "Josh?"

"Audrey?" Josh sounded just as surprised to hear her voice as she'd been to hear his.

"What are you doing here?" she asked.

"Nonna asked me to come because Viv was in a car."

"Yeah, she's stuck in traffic." As soon as she said it out loud, she realized this was a setup. It had to be.

Kenna went through the same spiel that she had with Audrey and took Josh's drink order. "I'll be right back with your drinks."

Audrey couldn't believe that her sister had done this. Actually, yes, she could. She absolutely believed that her sister did this.

"I thought you would be at Golden Years tonight."

Audrey smiled to herself. She knew it was silly, but she loved the fact that Josh knew her schedule. "I was. Viv called and said it was an emergency."

"Ahh."

Audrey's heart was pounding in her chest. She'd eaten with Josh a lot of times before. They had movie nights where they ordered pizza. They'd had lunches at Sue Ann's. And shared wings at JT's.

But this felt different.

And not just because she was wearing a blindfold. Although, she had to admit, she did like the element of the blindfold. It definitely heightened things. She wondered if it would do that in the bedroom as well. She remembered seeing a movie, that she was much too young to see, with Kim Basinger called *9½ Weeks* where she was blindfolded by Mickey Rourke. And she'd read quite a few romance novels where blindfolds were incorporated in the bedroom. It had always intrigued Audrey and been something that she hoped, if and when she ever had sex, she could try.

"So, this is...different," Josh voiced exactly what she'd been thinking before her mind trailed off in a more adult-themed direction.

"Yeah, it is."

"I bet you've never been on a date like this before."

"I've never been on *any* date before," she chuckled. Audrey wasn't sure why she'd revealed that to Josh. Maybe it was because he'd referred to what they were doing as a date, and it had made her nervous.

"You've never been on a—"

The rustle of the curtain moving, followed by footsteps, cut off Josh's question.

"Okay, here are your drinks." Audrey heard the sound of the drinks being set down on the table. "They are on your left and I'll be back with your salads."

Audrey carefully lifted her hand and felt along the table for the wine glass, scared that she might bump it and knock it over. When she felt the base, her fingers gingerly moved up the stem and she lifted it to her mouth. She tipped the glass up and allowed herself a generous drink. Now more than ever she needed to take the edge off. As she set it back down, she licked her lips, tasting the sweet tang of the wine.

"So, you said that you've never been on a—"

Again, Josh was interrupted by the sound of the curtain being pulled back. Within seconds she heard the clank of a plate being set down. "Okay we have your spinach salads with poppyseed dressing. Would either of you like crushed pepper sprinkled on top?"

"No, thank you," Audrey replied as she felt for her fork, to make sure she knew where it was before Kenna left. She did.

"Sure," Josh responded.

Audrey heard the gears of the pepper grinder as Kenna twisted it several times. When she finished, she said, "Remember, just ring the bell if you need anything. Enjoy."

Audrey waited until she heard the rustling of the makeshift door before she lifted her hand to try and find her glass once again. It was easier the second time, her hand went right to it. Then she picked up her fork and took her first bite. Once she had her bearings, eating wasn't actually that difficult.

After a few moments of eating and drinking in silence, Josh asked, "You weren't serious about the date thing, right?"

She finished chewing her bite and swallowed before answering. "No. I mean, yes. Yes, I was serious and no, I've never been on a date."

"What about in high school? I thought you had a boyfriend."

"I did. We went to the movies and to play mini-golf but it was always with big groups of friends. We never went anywhere just the two of us." He always wanted to be with people, never alone with her, which made a lot more sense in hindsight.

"What about when Viv signed you up on Bumble?"

"I chatted with a few guys, but never met anyone."

A couple of years ago, Viv had decided to take Audrey's personal life, or lack thereof, into her own hands and had created profiles on several different apps. Josh was in the coffee shop when Audrey found out about her sister's plan because she started receiving messages from matches.

At first, she'd been mortified when he'd discovered what her sister had done. She didn't want him to think she was so pathetic she needed people to make fake accounts for her. But then she'd sort of liked how protective he'd been about her.

He'd told her not to meet anyone without telling him or Vivien where she was going. He said that she should try and google the guys' names just to make sure that they were who they said they were. He also told her that she should only meet them in public places in the daytime. He specified that they should be places that she was familiar with and he even offered to go with her and be close just in case things got sketchy.

She'd thought about setting up a date, just so she could have him go along, but then decided that wasn't fair to whatever guy she was meeting. Just because her personal life was a mess didn't mean she needed to drag unsuspecting people into it.

"What about college?" Josh asked, apparently not able to let the subject drop.

"I didn't date anyone," she answered honestly.

Josh and Audrey had been friends for eight years. Well,

longer if you counted the summers that Audrey used to spend in Hope Falls. Of course, they weren't really friends then, although she had a *huge* crush on him. Josh being four years older than her when she was four to ten was a much bigger age difference than it was when she'd moved here in her twenties.

But in all the time they spent together, they never talked about relationships or who they were dating. Audrey knew that over the years he'd seen a few women, none of whom lived in town. Pricilla lived in Crescent River, which was a few towns over. Sabrina lived in Lake Tahoe. And Jenny was from Sacramento.

She only knew about the women because it was Hope Falls, and everyone knew everyone's business. Also, Viv seemed to make it her mission in life to know who Josh was seeing and give Audrey play by plays. She knew her sister was trying to make her jealous. She wasn't subtle about the fact. Especially when Viv said that she was trying to, "*light a fire under her.*"

And it worked. Sort of. She was jealous of the women Josh spent time with in some ways. But not in others. He might be having sex with Pricilla, Sabrina, and Jenny, but did they have Sunday movie nights together? Did they do quick draw, rock-paper-scissors, or staring contests to determine who would get the last baked good? Had they been in a bowling league together? Did he bring them leftovers of Nonna's cooking?

She doubted it. Even though she and Josh weren't romantically involved, she did feel like they had a special relationship. Which was part of the reason she'd never been honest about how she felt. She never wanted to ruin that relationship.

"I can't believe you've never been out on a date." Josh

said, clearly not being able to wrap his head around her lack of experience.

"Yeah, and I've never had sex either." Audrey froze. She wasn't sure why she'd just made that confession.

Was it the dark that gave her the courage?

Was it because she was sick and tired of her status, and she knew that if she didn't do something drastic it would never change?

Or was it because she just wanted him to know?

She wasn't sure what had prompted her to say what she had, but she'd done it. The cat was out of the bag. The milk was spilled. There was no going back. Josh knew she was a virgin. And she really hoped that he'd volunteer to do something about it.

———

JOSH'S FORK slipped from his hand and there was a loud clank as it landed on his plate. Thankfully, he was able to retrieve it and it didn't fall on the floor. When he once again had a firm hold on his utensil, he heard himself ask in a hoarse whisper. "What?"

Audrey cleared her throat, and he heard her chair move as if she was sitting up straighter in it.

He expected the next words out of her mouth to be telling him that she'd been kidding. That it had been a joke. It was so strange not to be able to look in her eyes and see if she was serious. Or if she'd been kidding. She had to have been kidding, right?

"I've never had sex. I'm a virgin."

Okay, maybe not.

Wait. She was thirty-two.

There weren't thirty-two-year-old virgins, were there?

Apparently, there were. Josh's mind was officially

blown. He honestly could not believe what he was hearing. He thought it was unbelievable that she'd never been on a date, but now this…

He opened his mouth to say something, but nothing came out. He tried to think of what the appropriate response to hearing that information would be, but he was at a total loss.

"Sorry, I shouldn't have said that. Talk about TMI," she laughed, but it was a forced laugh. He could tell that she felt uncomfortable with what she'd just revealed. He didn't want her to feel uncomfortable with him ever.

"No don't apologize. You can tell me anything I was just…I don't…" He felt like such an asshole but he didn't know the right words to say. He was in shock. Maybe he shouldn't be. Maybe that information shouldn't surprise him. But it did.

The curtain rustled and he heard Kenna walking into the room. "Okay, we have your entrées here. Are you finished with your salads? Do you want me to clear?"

"Sure," he responded automatically even though he hadn't finished his salad.

At the same time Audrey said, "Yeah."

Kenna went into detail about their main dish, explaining the sauce that was dripped over the chicken, how the veggies were blanched before they were sautéed in herbs and oil, and how the potatoes were hand whipped and drizzled with a garlic butter before saying, "Do you have any questions, or do you need anything?"

"No." Josh replied.

"Nope," Audrey answered.

"Okay, just let me know if you do."

With that she left and they were alone again.

"This smells delicious," Audrey said.

"It does," Josh agreed.

They both began eating their main dish and Josh was still trying to think of something to say to address the virgin elephant in the room.

But Audrey let him off the hook when she asked, "So how did you get roped into this?"

He told her that Nonna had told him he needed to go eat without the lights on, which she chuckled at. Then she explained that Viv had called her while she was at Golden Years because she was stuck in traffic and couldn't make it.

The conversation then turned to the work she was doing at the senior living facility and how badly he wished that Nonna would move there. The rest of the meal and dessert continued, and they easily fell into their regular pattern of joking around and talking about everything and nothing. But in the back of his mind all he kept thinking about was that she was a virgin.

Audrey's a virgin, was playing on a constant loop in his head. He knew that his brain shouldn't be stuck on that, but it was.

He'd noticed when he was feeling anxious that would happen a lot. He would repeat things over and over in his head and get stuck on a certain thought, almost to the point of obsessing over it.

There was one moment between them when they both reached for their glasses and their hands brushed one another's. The graze of skin on skin caused tingles to spread from his fingers up his arm and through his body like a wildfire. He had no clue if it had affected her the same way, but it took him a moment to recover from it. He had to take a few deep breaths and a large drink of cold water to get his body under control.

He'd touched Audrey before, but never when they were both blindfolded in the dark. There was something about those circumstances that made an innocent brush of hands feel much more intimate.

The rest of the meal went by without any further accidental grazes. And when they were done, Kenna escorted them out of the room the same way she'd escorted them in. As they walked out single file, Audrey's hands were on Kenna's shoulders and his were on Audrey's. Josh tried not to pay attention to how soft her skin felt beneath his touch, or how silky her hair felt as it brushed against his fingers.

He heard the curtain being pulled back. They went a few steps and then stopped. "Okay, you can remove your blindfolds. You may want to shield your eyes or look down; the light can be a little jarring."

Josh's heart was pounding heavily against his ribs as he lifted his arms and pulled the material off his head. He squinted when he opened his eyes and saw that Audrey was doing the same. They both handed the blindfolds back to Kenna and she gave them back their phones.

The entire exchange Josh kept sneaking looks at Audrey. Every time he did, she was looking straight at Kenna, not in his direction. It was as if she was avoiding looking at him altogether.

Which she might be. She'd just revealed something very intimate and personal about herself and he hadn't exactly handled it well. The more he thought about how he'd responded the more anxious he felt, and that just made the entire situation worse.

As they said their goodbyes, Audrey raved about the food and told Kenna that she'd let Viv know she'd had a great time. He smiled and nodded, but if he were being honest, he hadn't even tasted the food after she'd dropped the virgin bombshell on him.

When they walked out to the parking lot, he noticed

that she'd parked on the opposite side of the picnic area from him which was why he hadn't seen her car when he rode up.

"Do you need a ride?" she asked when she didn't see any other vehicle but hers.

"No, I have my bike." He motioned to the other lot.

"Oh, okay." She nodded and smiled. "Well, see ya later." She lifted her hand in an awkward wave before turning on her heel and heading toward her car.

He took a step and caught her wrist, pulling her back toward him. "Audrey, wait."

When she turned back around her lips were parted as she looked up at him with so much raw vulnerability shining through her golden eyes, he could barely stand it. His mind was racing with the right words to say.

Should he thank her for trusting him enough to share something so personal? No, that somehow sounded weird and sort of creepy.

Should he tell her that he thought it was cool that she was a virgin? No, that sounded patronizing.

Since he didn't have the right words to say, he fell back to his default. He pulled her into his arms and hugged her. Tightly. He held her for much longer than he normally did, not wanting to let her go. Then he pressed his lips to her forehead. Just like the embrace, his kiss was not brief, it lingered.

Finally, he let her go, stepped back putting his hands in his pockets so he wouldn't reach out and touch her. She looked a little dazed and both of their breathing was a little more labored than it normally was.

"Goodnight," he rasped.

"Night." With that she turned and walked to her car. He waited and watched as she drove out of the parking lot. When her taillights disappeared, he ran his hands through his hair and took a deep breath as he had a feeling of déjà vu.

It was the same feeling he'd had the first time he'd seen Audrey and his world had shifted on its axis. He felt like tonight's dinner had caused a seismic shift in the plates of their relationship, and he had no clue what to do about it.

8

"THANKS FOR COMING IN!" AUDREY WAVED AT MR. AND Mrs. Brooks, who owned the old-fashioned ice cream parlor downtown, as they walked to the door to leave with their granddaughter Beth.

Beth had visited the doctor that morning and had to get shots. They'd asked her what treat she wanted for being brave and she'd said a chocolate croissant from the coffee shop. The couple thought it was hysterical and ironic that, of course, their granddaughter had chosen something other than ice cream as her treat when so many other kids chose Two Scoops as the place they wanted to go for a treat.

As the door shut behind the trio, Audrey's mind played the same sentence that had been running through it on repeat all day.

I can't believe I told Josh that I was a virgin.

She still had no clue what had possessed her to make such a personal confession. For some reason having the blindfold on had given her the boldness to make the intimate declaration.

And he'd said…nothing.

But, then again, what could he say? There wasn't really a good response to that. Sure, she would have loved it if he'd offered to help change her status, but that wasn't really Josh's style. He was quiet. He processed things.

There'd been so many times when she'd said something and then he'd commented on it days later. He didn't say much but when he did speak, it was usually insightful and profound. She wondered if he was processing what she'd told him. Or if he even cared.

Maybe she was making too much of this. Maybe he'd forgotten she'd even said it.

"Aud?"

Audrey turned and saw Carly standing in the doorway that led to the back of the store where the employee break room and storage rooms were, she was holding her jacket and had her backpack on. It was clear by her expression that she'd been talking but Audrey had no clue what she'd said.

"Sorry, what?"

"I was just saying bye."

Audrey looked up at the clock. She saw that Carly's shift ended five minutes ago. Wow. The day had really gotten away from her.

"Oh, right. Bye. See you Friday." Audrey was proud of herself for remembering when Carly was scheduled next. She'd been so scatterbrained all day she'd take the small victory.

"Babe, you've seemed…distracted all day. Do want me to hang out until Viv gets here? I totally can," Carly offered.

"Sorry, no I'm good. I just… have a lot on my mind."

Carly smiled widely, causing the deep dimples on her left and right cheeks to appear, both of which were pierced. "Have you read *The Boy, The Mole, The Fox and The Horse*?"

"No." Audrey shook her head.

Carly walked up to the counter beside her and set her jacket down. "That book changed my life. It taught me a lot of important lessons, but three in particular that I keep with me. And when I see someone is going through something, like you seem to be, I share those lessons with them, and it usually helps."

Audrey was all ears. She would take all the help she could get.

Carly lifted her hand that was covered in henna tattoos and held up her pointer finger tipped with a bright pink nail. "The first is when the horse and the boy are in the forest and there is like a bunch of fog all around them. The boy tells the horse that he can't see his way through. The horse asks him if he can see his next step and the boy says yes. And the horse tells him to just take that."

She raised her middle finger to join her pointer. "The second is when the boy asks the horse what the bravest thing he's ever said is and the horse answers with one single word, help. He tells the boy that asking for help isn't giving up, it's refusing to give up."

Her ring finger joined her middle and pointer. "And the third is when the horse tells the boy when things get difficult, he needs to remember who he is. And the boy asks him, 'Who am I?' And the horse tells him 'You are loved.'" Carly stared at her for a moment before lowering her hand and picking up her jacket. "Just some things to think about."

"Thanks." Audrey said as Carly pulled her into a hug before heading out the back of the store.

Audrey wasn't sure if the things Carly had told her helped but she did think there were good lessons in them.

Sometimes you just need to take the first step even if you can't see your way out of a situation. That asking for help is a really brave thing to do. And that, no matter what else you are, you are loved.

She'd guessed she'd done the first one last night. She might not be able to see a way out of the virginity forest, but she'd definitely taken the first step. She'd told Josh that she was a virgin.

Audrey returned to her task of inventory and was trying to concentrate, but her mind was a scrambled mess thinking about the dinner the night before.

It had felt…intimate. Not just because she'd revealed something so personal, but also because of it feeling like a real date.

Not that she actually knew what that felt like. As she'd disclosed the night before, she'd never been on a date. But that's what she'd imagined it would feel like. She'd had butterflies, although in fairness, the winged creatures always seemed to show up when Josh was around.

A long sigh fell from her lips as she dropped her head back. When they'd finished dinner, Josh had walked her to her car, and he'd hugged her and kissed her on her forehead. It was where he always kissed her. But just like the dinner last night it felt different.

Maybe it was her imagination, but she would swear his lips lingered longer than they usually did. Just like she was certain the hug had lasted longer than normal. She'd almost asked if he was okay because he'd been holding her so tight, when he dropped his arms and took a step back from her. Then, he put his hands in his pockets, which always made her insides swoon. The position showcased his biceps and forearms like he was posing for a men's health magazine. It highlighted every chiseled-toperfection curve, dip, and bulge. She noticed he did it a lot around her and she wasn't sure why.

Since she could see his garage out the side window of the coffee shop, she'd seen him interact with a lot of other people and she'd never seen him put his hands in his pockets when he was talking to anyone else. He crossed his arms sometimes, but he never put them in his front pockets.

Not that she was complaining. She was a huge fan and always enjoyed the gun show. She just wondered why he only did that around her.

She'd also never seen him kiss anyone's forehead like he did hers. The first time he'd done it, she'd been so excited. She'd thought for sure that was the first of many more kisses to come in other, more intimate, areas. She figured it was just his warmup. She'd figured wrong.

He'd been doing the forehead kissing for about, oh let's see, six years now and it had never progressed past that innocent area. Now she feared it was more familial than anything else. She'd noticed that he always kissed his grandmother on the cheek. Maybe he kissed her on the forehead because he thought of her as his sister.

That was a very real possibility. It would explain why he'd been so protective of her when Viv had set her up on dating sites. And why he'd even offered to go with her to the dates and be there just in case anything went wrong.

Her mind was going a million miles a minute racing around the what-if track when the bell dinged above the door and Audrey's heart skipped a beat thinking for a split second that it might be Josh.

Her heart sank just a little when she saw Sue Ann Perkins and Renata Blackstone enter the coffee shop. Today Sue Ann's long floral skirt had a baby blue base and was covered in iris flowers that perfectly matched the cardigan sweater combo she wore. Her cheeks were especially rosy and round and when she saw Audrey a wide smile spread on her face. Beside her, Renata's waist length, salt and pepper hair was pulled tight in a braid that started at the base of her neck. Her olive complexion was complimented by her forest green turtleneck. Her expression remained stoic as she entered the coffee shop.

"Hello there, Miss Audrey," Sue Ann beamed as the duo approached the counter.

"Hi, ladies. How are you doing today?"

"We stopped by to speak to Vivien about the singles week events. She has some out-of-the-box ideas that we need clarification on."

Renata Blackstone did not suffer fools or engage in small talk. She got right to the point.

When Audrey and Viv first moved to Hope Falls, Audrey was certain the woman just didn't like her at all. Over the years, however, she'd come to realize that Renata just wasn't a warm and fuzzy person. But she cared about Hope Falls and all the residents in it. She was kind, generous, and Audrey suspected had a soft side that she just didn't reveal to too many people.

"Oh, she's not in yet. But she should be here any minute. If you take a seat, I can get you ladies a tea and coffee while you wait."

"That will be fine." Renata's chin dipped in a nod.

"The regular?" Audrey's eyes bounced between both women.

They both nodded in agreement and then moved to a bistro-style table that sat in front of the floor to ceiling glass front of the shop.

Audrey prepared Sue Ann a peppermint tea and Renata a coffee with two sugars and a pinch of cinnamon. Part of what she loved about living in such a tight-knit community was having regulars and knowing those regulars' orders. Just like Luke from Gilmore Girls knew his regulars' orders. She really was living out her childhood dream.

She dropped off the drinks and went back behind the counter and texted her sister. Viv took advantage of the fact that she owned the shop and viewed her start times as flexible. Very flexible. Normally, on Wednesday's she was on time, though because she knew that Audrey volunteered at the animal shelter in the afternoon, but not always.

After shooting off a quick text to her sister to let her know that Sue Ann and Renata were waiting to speak to her, Audrey continued to help the few customers that trickled in. Each time the door opened she looked up hoping that it was Josh. Each time, she was disappointed.

She wouldn't classify herself as a paranoid person, but in the back of her head she kept thinking that Josh's no show today must be because she'd revealed her virginity to him. It must have made him uncomfortable. Especially if he did, in fact, think of her as a sister.

But the forehead kiss. It was definitely longer than they usually were. And there'd been a different look in his eyes when he'd said goodbye.

"Hey chickadee!" Viv smiled as she walked in from the back of the shop wearing a Brewed Awakenings sweatshirt and holding a notebook in her hands. "Sorry, I'm late. I hurt my back this morning."

"How?"

"I don't know." Viv shrugged. "I was just getting up out of a chair and I felt it tighten up. I tried to foam roll it out, I iced it and put heat on it but nothing's helping."

"Do you want me to stay?"

"Nah, I'm good. Wednesday afternoons are pretty slow. You can save the world, I'll be fine."

Viv always referred to Audrey's volunteer work as 'saving the world.'

"Oh, did you get my text? Renata and Sue Ann are waiting to speak to you." Audrey motioned to the women seated at the bistro seat.

"Yep. That's why I brought this." Viv lifted up the white three ring binder she was holding, and Audrey saw that the words Project Valentine were written in black marker across the front.

Audrey had to admit, she was impressed. Viv seemed to be taking this a lot more seriously than she did most things in her life. She didn't think Viv had ever had a notebook for anything, even when she was in high school.

Viv gave her a cheeky wink before grabbing a croissant, taking a bite, and heading over to Sue Ann and Renata.

Audrey was still trying to shake off the disappointment that Josh had been a no show today as she removed her apron and grabbed her purse from beneath the counter and put on her jacket. He rarely missed a morning shift she worked.

Maybe he was just busy, the angel on her shoulder said.

Or maybe he just didn't come in because you made things weird, the devil on her other shoulder, who sounded a lot like Viv pointed out.

She shook that thought off as she grabbed her purse and was just about to head out the back when Viv called out to her.

"Aud!"

Audrey checked her watch. If she didn't leave now, she'd be late to her shift at the shelter. Yes, it was volunteer, but still. She made her way to the table where now all three ladies were seated.

"I was just telling Sue Ann and Renata about the

Dining in the Dark experience," Viv explained. "And they have questions."

"How do you eat in the dark?" Sue Ann asked, looking genuinely curious.

"It's not actually as difficult as you'd think," Audrey smiled. "It's easy once you get acclimated to the environment."

"I was telling them that it is supposed to enhance all of your other senses. Smell. Touch. Taste. Hearing. Did you find that your other senses were enhanced?" Viv asked.

Audrey flashed back to when Josh brushed his hand over hers when he was reaching for his glass, the tingles spread from her fingers, to her wrist, up her arm, and down between her legs.

"Yes." Audrey nodded.

"And apparently, it's easier to connect with your date because of that," Viv explained.

Sue Ann's eyes lit up. "Oh, you went on a date?"

"No." Audrey shook her head. "It wasn't a date. Josh was there because Nonna asked him to go and I was there because Viv got stuck in traffic."

"Did you two have a *good time*?" Sue Ann asked hopefully, completely ignoring Audrey's explanation.

Audrey smiled and she could feel her cheeks burning with embarrassment as Sue Ann, Viv, and even Renata looked up at her expectantly. She hated any attention directed at her and especially attention that had to do with her personal life. "It was…different, for sure. But I think it will work really well for singles week. I'm actually running late. I'll see you all later."

Wanting to make a quick escape, Audrey didn't go out the back door to the parking lot where she was parked. Instead, she left out the front of the shop. As she walked around the corner to the back of the building, her eyes automatically scanned over to Pine Auto Shop.

Josh was in the garage working beneath the hood of a classic car. It looked like the car he'd inherited from his dad, but she couldn't be sure. He was wearing a long-sleeved thermal shirt that hugged his chiseled arms. His blue jeans were worn in all the right places, showcasing his firm rear end. Her mouth watered at the sight.

Her phone buzzed in her purse, and she pulled it out as she felt something wet on the corners of her mouth. She lifted her hand and realized that it was drool. She had literally been standing there drooling over Josh.

Embarrassment washed over as she rushed to her car and got in. As soon as she shut the door she looked down and saw it was a message from Pete who worked at the shelter.

Pete: *Just got a new pit mix in who is terrified of men. Are you on your way?*

She shot a quick message back.

Audrey: *Be right there.*

As she pulled out of the back lot pride prevented her from sneaking one more peek at Josh. She couldn't believe she'd *actually* drooled. If Viv knew that, her sister would have a field day.

9

JOSH SAT ON THE BLEACHERS THAT LINED THE GYM AT THE community center with a notebook on his knee and a pen in his hand. He'd felt…*off* all day today. He knew why. He'd skipped his morning run to Brewed Awakenings because after the night before, he was trying to put some distance between himself and Audrey. He hadn't taken his favorite twelve steps toward her smiling face behind the counter which meant he hadn't got his Audrey or caffeine fix for the day, which was making him a little bit irritable.

After leaving Dining in the Dark, he'd spent a restless night tossing and turning. All he'd thought about was Audrey's confession last night.

She was a virgin. How in the hell was that possible? He had so many questions but the main one was why? He knew that it wasn't because she didn't have options.

Over the years, he'd witnessed a ton of men ask her out. He'd watched quietly on the sidelines as they pretty much lined up to shoot their shot with her. He'd been a silent bystander as guys hit on her and threw out pickup lines at her, some were decent most were cringy. And it wasn't just the men that approached her, either. There was a network of matchmakers all over town trying to set her up. This was just a rough guestimate, but if he had to put a number on it, he'd bet that at least seventy percent of the town had tried to set her up with "this great guy they knew."

He couldn't count the number of times he'd heard someone say that she had to meet their brother or cousin or son or grandson. And it didn't stop at familial setups, he'd listened as people pitched the new guy at fill-in-the-blank job, or the recently divorced single dad that won't stay on the market too long, or the guy who is "perfect" for her with qualities such as funny, charming, smart, successful, hardworking who she'll absolutely "love."

Audrey was basically Hope Falls unofficial town sweetheart, and everyone wanted her to settle down with the 'right guy.'

Now that he thought about it, though, he'd never actually heard her agree to go out with any of the potential suitors that were being offered up on a silver platter. Normally, she made an excuse about having a prior commitment. He had seen her take a few numbers from particularly aggressive wannabe cupids, but he'd never followed up to see if she'd called any of them. Mainly because he didn't want to hear about it if she had.

He shifted on the bleacher and tried to turn off his brain. He didn't think his caffeine withdrawal was the reason for his restlessness and neither was his back pain, which he was used to living with. His discomfort was emotional and mental. He wanted to crawl out of his skin and escape. It was like the walls were closing in on him.

All day he'd done his best to ignore what was building up inside of him like a pressure cooker. But not even blasting music and working on the car his dad had left him, a cherry red '67 Chevy Nova which he was almost finished restoring, had been able to occupy his mind. If he hadn't promised Caleb he'd be here tonight for a pickup game, he would be on the back of his bike. Sometimes, when all else failed a ride was the only thing to get his mind right.

After he got injured he'd gone to therapy for his PTSD and depression. One of the tools that his therapists had given him was that when he was feeling anxious, to get a pen and paper and write whatever came into his head.

Over the years he'd amassed several notebooks filled with random thoughts, usually in the form of poetry, not that he would ever claim that he was a poet. He absolutely was not. His ramblings were just articulations of whatever was going on in his head. And 99.9% of the time they were about the one person who occupied his mind and soul.

As he sat on the metal bench and put pen to paper his muse once again guided his way.

Lighthouse
In my darkest days and nights
Beneath the crushing midnight sky
The waves of pain crash
The currents of turmoil surround me
I am drowning
I am lost in an ocean of despair
And then I see you
My lighthouse
My safe place
My serenity

"Hey Pastor Harrison!"

Josh lifted his head and saw his childhood friend Caleb speaking with Lily Maguire, a dancer and choreographer who taught classes at the community center. She was married to Eric Maguire who was the chief of police.

Caleb and Josh were there to play a pickup game with Eric and his brother Jake who was the fire chief. Amy, who lived next door to Nonna and kept an eye on her with her husband Matt, was Eric and Jake's sister. They also had another sister named Nikki who had married a senator. Josh had grown up with the Maguires, but since he was a few years younger than the youngest sibling, he'd never been that close to any of them.

Truth be told, he'd never really been that close to anyone, except Caleb, growing up. He'd always sort of felt like an outsider looking in when it came to this town.

As his friend chatted, Josh closed his notebook, and stuffed it back into his gym bag.

When Caleb finished talking to Lily, he made his way to the bleachers.

Josh shook his head at his friend. "It's still weird hearing people call you *Pastor Harrison*."

"I know, right? Every time I hear it, I look around for my dad."

Caleb's father, who happened to be named George Harrison, had been the pastor at Hope Falls Community Church for nearly forty years before retiring right around the time Josh had come back home. Caleb stepped into the role as senior pastor at the church. Unlike Josh who had never wanted to follow in his father's footsteps, that had always been Caleb's dream, or as he put it his calling.

Caleb and Josh had grown up living next door to each other. They'd bonded at an early age over racing big wheels and skipping rocks down by the river. Their friendship continued all through their school years.

On the outside looking in, the two men had nothing in common. Caleb was likeable, sociable, he loved to read, he'd been a straight A student, his dad was the pastor and his mom was the Sunday school teacher and choir director.

Josh kept people at arm's length, he was a loner, he rode dirt bikes, he'd almost flunked out of high school, his father had been a raging alcoholic, and his mom was crazy and gone most of the time.

Thanks to his less than desirable home life, Josh ended up at Caleb's several nights a week for dinner. If he wasn't with Nonna, he was at the Harrisons. Caleb was more like a brother to Josh than a friend.

"I keep telling people to just call me Caleb, but…I don't know… it's not sticking." His friend shrugged as he sat down and changed his shoes.

Josh didn't think of Caleb in a pastoral way. While the rest of the town had appeared to seamlessly accept his new role and treat him with the same respect, reverence and regard they'd treated Caleb's father, Josh had never quite made that leap.

When he saw Caleb, he saw the kid that had talked him into smoking behind the bleachers when they were twelve. He saw the brace-faced teenager that he'd broke into their rival Lakeside High's football field and spray painted "losers" on the field when they were sixteen. He saw the guy that he'd spent a wild weekend with in Daytona Beach to celebrate their twenty-first birthdays.

He'd never gone to Caleb for any real advice before, but the rest of the town lined up for his wisdom. They also lined up to try and set him up. Caleb might even get setup more than Audrey, but unlike her, he actually went on some of the dates. Usually just one, though. He hadn't had anything serious for a while now.

Caleb had always been a somewhat nerdy guy growing up. Girls liked him well enough, but he never garnered the attention he did these days. Once he stepped into the role of town spiritual leader, he skyrocketed to what was damn near rock star status. Most of the single women had made it clear they were interested and nearly all of the grandmothers, mothers, aunts, and sisters had tried to set him up with every available woman between the ages of twenty and forty.

He dated somewhat regularly, definitely more than Josh did. So, there was a chance he might have an insight on the situation with Audrey. Obviously, Josh wasn't going to name names, of course, but his friend might shed some light on things.

"Can I ask you something?" Josh turned to his friend.

Caleb finished tying his shoe and looked up at Josh. "What's up?"

He could see the concern in his friend's eyes. Josh's MO had always been to hold things inside. He never shared what he was feeling with anyone or asked for help. Nonna accused him on more than one occasion of being an island unto himself.

But Caleb could usually tell if there was something off with him. When he returned to Hope Falls Caleb had been a huge reason he'd gone to see someone about his mental health. If it weren't for his friend, he would probably still be white knuckling his way through it, or he might not even be here.

Josh took a breath and tried to figure out the best, most delicate way to phrase his question. "If someone is a virgin, in their thirties, could that be for a religious reason?"

Josh knew that Audrey attended church any Sunday she wasn't working at Brewed Awakenings. But so did most people in Hope Falls. It was just sort of what they did.

Caleb nodded. "Sure."

"Are there other reasons someone might be?" As soon

as Josh asked the question, he knew that he was grasping at straws. His friend counseled people as part of his job and went out on a ton of first dates, but that didn't make him an expert on virginity.

And even if he was, that didn't mean he had any insight into Audrey's situation.

Caleb leaned forward, resting his elbows on his knees. It was the position he got into when he was about to drop knowledge or speak about something that interested him. The few times Josh had gone to church since Caleb had taken the reins from his old man, Caleb had ended up sitting on the steps of the altar with his elbows resting on his knees by the end of the sermon.

"It's funny you mention that because I was just reading a study that said there is a growing trend of people waiting longer to have sex. One in six millennials and Gen Zers are still virgins at twenty-six as opposed to twenty years ago when that statistic was one in twenty. They think it might have something to do with everyone being so disconnected due to all of the devices. The theory is twofold, first that the availability of porn is causing a decrease and fear of intimacy with an actual person. Second that since everything is at their fingertips, including social approval, shopping, and ordering food, that people's brains are getting constant dopamine spikes just by being on their phones which decreases their libido.

"There's another theory that has data showing that all the processed food that people consume is the culprit because it's lowering sex drives.

"As far as religious reasons, there are definitely still people that want to wait until they're married to have sex, but it's not as common as say, thirty years ago."

"Are the women you date mostly virgins?" It was

another stupid question, but apparently Josh was full of them tonight.

Caleb grinned as his brow wrinkled. "I don't ask, but if I had to guess I would say no. Why?"

Before Josh had to answer, Eric and his brother Jake walked into the gym and interrupted the conversation. The four men played a pick-up game and Josh did his best to put Audrey and her virginity out of his mind. But it was like one of those pictures that once you see it you can't unsee it. It was all he could think about.

10

AUDREY POURED A GLASS OF MERLOT AS FRANK WALKED along the edge of the kitchen island and sniffed the air, his tail flicking with each step he took.

"Hello there, old man." Audrey reached out and ran her hand along his back as a grin tugged at the corners of her mouth.

She'd adopted Frank, short for Frank Sinatra who was another one of her mom's favorites, and had given the black and white tuxedo cat the name because of his bright blue eyes that rivaled the late crooner who was known for his baby blues. She'd also adopted a mini ragdoll cat, who she named Lucille after Liza Minnelli's character Lucille Austero who suffered from chronic vertigo or what she called "the dizzies" on *Arrested Development*.

When she adopted the cats, she was sure that Lucy was going to be the princess or the diva of the duo, but boy oh boy, was she wrong. Frank was whatever the male version of a diva was. A divo?

Both cats had special needs. Frank was diabetic and Lucy was diagnosed with cerebellar hypoplasia, or wobbly cat syndrome, which was the reason she'd named her after the character on one of her favorite shows.

She'd had the cats for nearly seven years now and Lucy ended up being the sweetest most loving appreciative cat Audrey had ever known. She always greeted Audrey at the door. When she called Lucy, she came right to her. She snuggled on command and had a lot more dog-like characteristics than feline.

Frank was the opposite. He only graced Audrey with his presence on his terms. He would only eat his food if she warmed it up for him, otherwise he'd go on a hunger strike. Every night she had to fluff his blanket and lay it out over the end of the bed, or he wouldn't settle down and go to sleep. And she'd gone through about a dozen different types of cat litter before Frank deemed one worthy enough that he'd relieve himself in it.

They say that rescues are supposed to be grateful because they somehow know that you saved them, but Frank acted as if he was doing her a favor by allowing her to serve him. Which she found ridiculously adorable.

She grabbed her wine glass and lowered onto her overstuffed couch. Her butt hadn't even hit the cushion before Lucy was beside her. She gave her little girl some love and was reaching for the remote when she got a text from Viv.

Viv: *Heading over to the new yoga studio. They are opening on February 1st and they want to offer a special for singles week. The owner offered a demo class but it's AcroYoga and I need a partner, can you come?*

Viv added about ten prayer hand emojis to the end of the text.

Audrey sighed. She'd been looking forward to relaxing and having her glass of wine all day. She was exhausted because the last few nights she'd spent tossing and turning thanks to her embarrassing confession. She hadn't seen Josh since. He hadn't come in for his usual coffee and chocolate croissants since the night they'd dined in the dark.

She was also about to start her period, which she was sure was adding to her emotions about Josh being MIA and was having cramps. The last thing she wanted to was to be bent into a pretzel so she messaged her back that she was tired.

Audrey: *I'm really tired.*

She'd barely sent the text when she heard a horn outside at the same time her phone vibrated with another message from Viv.

Viv: *I'm really outside. Let's go!*

Audrey knew that resistance was futile. Her sister wasn't going to let this go. And maybe a class would be good for Audrey. Maybe it would clear her head. And who knew, maybe it would actually help her cramps.

Audrey: *Be out in 5*

Audrey bent down and kissed Lucy on the top of her head before heading into her room and grabbing a pair of yoga pants she'd inherited from Viv who got them off some TikTok ad. They were supposed to make your rear look great, but Audrey just liked them because they were a pretty pink color. She pulled on a sports bra, and a loose-fitting tank top. She threw on a sweatshirt, puffer jacket, two pairs of socks and Ugg boots. Layers were the key to living in Hope Falls. She'd learned that lesson the first winter she'd spent here. She'd bundle up to go somewhere, but then be so hot once she got inside.

She was out the door in less than five minutes and when she got into Viv's Jeep she noticed that the back seat was filled with boxes. She didn't remember having any big shipments for Brewed coming in. And even if they had, she wasn't sure why they'd be in Viv's backseat.

"What's all this?"

Viv's face lit up. "It's singles week swag, baby!"

Viv reached behind her and pulled open a box and then grabbed a shirt and sweats and handed it to Audrey. She held them up and saw that on the front of the shirt was a tiny cupid with an arrow and on the back the words Hope Falls Effect. And on the sweats, along the leg were the letters HFE and a tiny cupid.

Audrey was impressed. "These are so cute!"

"Look at the back of the shirt!" Viv instructed excitedly.

She turned it around and saw that in the center of the back of the shirt she'd put her sister Ava's definition of the Hope Falls Effect in tiny writing similar to how tour dates are listed on a band T-shirt.

HOPE FALLS EFFECT

Hope Falls:

noun (place)

1.   a small, picturesque town tucked in the Sierra Nevadas with an idyllic landscape backdrop of lush deep green pine trees and dotted with colorful aspens. The heart of the town, Main Street, is a five-block stretch of small storefront businesses, lined on each side with wooden sidewalks filled with a cast of colorful characters sure to enrich your life.

Effect:

verb (action)

1.   someone who never thought they would ever fall in love or fall in love again and suddenly they meet their soul mate

2.   a person who thought that their career was over

suddenly gets a new opportunity that changes their life forever

3.   someone who is running from something bad in their past, or has issues with their family, they move here and the situation resolves itself

4.   those who are lonely, find support from the community

5.   things magically fall into place in the following areas: love, career, friendship

6.   saves people

7.   heals people

8.   is the missing puzzle piece in people's lives

"These are amazing!"

"I also ordered pens, mugs, wine tumblers, and PopSockets with The Hope Falls Effect on them. I'm trying to make it a thing."

Audrey was so impressed, as always, with Viv's creativity. She'd been the one who'd come up with the logo and swag for Brewed Awakenings. She designed mugs and pens for the coffee shop for each season, and they usually sold out.

"I'm thinking of adding some of these to Brewed's swag collection."

Audrey looked at her sister who was clearly in her element. When Viv was excited about something, she came to life. Her brain was an endless idea factory.

"What?"

"Nothing, I'm just really impressed with how your brain works."

Viv smiled widely. "Thanks, most people are horrified at how my brain works."

JOSH PULLED up to Om Sweet Om, which wasn't opening for another week, and saw Viv's SUV parked out in front. He wasn't sure if he was relieved that Viv was the one who was here or disappointed. When Nonna had asked him to come by and get some information about a yoga class for Valentine's week his first thought was that it was another setup and Audrey would be there just like when she asked him to go to Dining in the Dark.

But she wasn't. Viv was here. He recognized Viv's Jeep Cherokee right away.

He hadn't gone into Brewed Awakenings the last few days because he'd been trying to figure out why Audrey revealing that she was a virgin had been affecting him so much.

They weren't together. They could never be together. He loved her but he knew there was absolutely no future for them.

He was broken. Physically and emotionally. She deserved someone who didn't have night terrors and get anxiety attacks. She deserved someone who didn't have to take medication for constant back pain. She deserved someone who could give her a family.

Over the years, he thought he'd come to terms with her being with someone else. He loved Audrey, he was in love with Audrey and because of that, he wanted the best for her. He wasn't the best, plain and simple.

But for some reason, knowing that she'd never been intimate with someone had brought up a lot of feelings for him that must have been simmering under the surface. Feelings that he'd been able to ignore before now. Primal me-Tarzan-you-Jane feelings that he wasn't sure he could disguise if he saw her.

So, he'd stayed away. But when Nonna had asked him

to come to the yoga studio, his pulse raced at the thought of Audrey being there.

He knew that he was being ridiculous. She was his friend, one of his best friends. If he wanted to see her, all he had to do was stop by her house. Or the coffee shop.

He hadn't been in counseling for a few years, but if he didn't get this straightened out in his head in the next couple of days, he thought he might need to call Dr. Lowe.

Josh got out of his truck and made his way up to the studio. On the short walk, he noticed that there was a heaviness in the air and the clouds overhead looked dark and ominous. All day he'd known that a storm was coming. Ever since the explosion, his back was more accurate than any meteorologist. It had been aching since he woke up this morning, not the usual pain but the bone deep gnawing ache that only happened when there was a storm coming in.

When he reached for the door, he realized it was actually convenient that Nonna had asked him to stop by because he'd been planning on checking this place out once it opened. His PT had suggested incorporating yoga into his therapy and it had made a difference. It wasn't a cure-all by any means, but it had helped with his core strength and also flexibility, which in turn helped with his back pain.

As he pulled open the glass door and walked in, it took his brain a second to catch up to what his eyes were seeing. Viv was standing in front of him, but she wasn't alone. Audrey was there.

"Hey, J! What are you doing here?" Viv asked, seeming to be surprised to see him there.

"Nonna sent me to pick up some paperwork."

"Oh, crap. I forgot to tell her that I was covering this. She did say she would check it out but I figured AcroYoga wasn't her thing. Sorry it was a wasted trip, and you came by for nothing."

Josh looked over at Audrey who smiled at him. It wasn't a wasted trip, and he hadn't come by for nothing because he got to see her smile. That was everything to him. She was everything to him.

When a blush rose on her creamy cheeks he wondered if she could read his mind. He needed to get out of here before his thoughts turned less PG, which they always did when Audrey was around.

"No worries. See ya." He lifted his hand and was turning to go when Viv stopped him.

"Actually, if you have some time would you mind taking the AcroYoga class with Audrey? I hurt my back the other day and I just don't think I'm up for it." Viv put her hand on her lower back.

Josh had no idea what AcroYoga was, but it was an excuse to spend time with Audrey so he didn't care. There was only one problem.

He glanced down at his jeans, boots, and hoodie. "I would but I don't think I'm dressed for it."

"No worries! I have just the thing!" With that Viv rushed around him and out the door leaving him and Audrey standing alone in the lobby of the yoga studio.

Concern etched her face in the form of a wrinkle on her forehead. "Are you sure you can do it with your back? I don't want you to hurt yourself."

"Yoga is good for my back. I was actually thinking of picking up a class schedule once it opened."

"Oh, okay." Audrey shifted from one foot to another and that's when he noticed her reflection in the mirror she had her back to.

Fucking hell, her ass looked amazing in those yoga pants. They were scrunched in the center and he got a semi-chub just from a reflection. Beads of sweat broke out on the back of his neck. If she did downward dog in front of him he might cream his pants.

"Are you okay?" she asked as she tilted her head, her concern returning.

"Yep." He diverted his eyes just as Viv rushed back inside and thrust a pair of sweats and a shirt at him.

"You can be my guinea pig and tell me if they're comfortable."

Josh looked down at the garments he was holding. "What are they?"

"They're swag for singles week."

Just as he was looking around for somewhere to change a woman walked out from the back. He recognized her as the owner, Tiana. She'd moved to town about a month ago and he hadn't met her yet, but this was Hope Falls so, of course, he knew her name and most of her life story. She was going through a divorce with a high-profile athlete and had moved to Hope Falls for a new start.

When she saw him, she smiled, "Oh, hi. We're actually not open yet."

"Oh, no," Viv interrupted her. "This is Josh. He's going to be taking the class with Audrey."

Tiana looked surprised but she rolled with it. "Oh, okay."

"Do you have somewhere I could change?" Josh asked.

"Oh, yes, of course. Right down the hall, second door on the left."

Josh walked past Audrey and as he caught a whiff of her sweet, floral shampoo he wondered what in the hell had he just gotten himself into? And, more importantly, how in the hell was he going to hide his reaction to Audrey while wearing gray sweats?

11

"ARE YOU SURE YOUR BACK IS GOING TO BE OKAY?" Audrey heard herself ask for probably the tenth time as she took a sip of water. As much as she was enjoying this, the one thing that was stopping her from completely allowing herself to fully bask in the glory of having Josh's hands all over her was because she was so scared that she was hurting him.

The past hour had arguably been the best hour in her life. She and Josh'd had full body contact, but it was more than just the touching. They'd had to work together and use their body weight to balance each other. They'd managed to do every pose that Tiana had shown them and hold each one, which she was proud of considering the last time she'd worked out her age started with a two and not a three.

"I told you, yoga's good for my back."

It was the same answer he kept giving her, and she wanted to believe him, but she feared that he might just be white-knuckling through the pain for her. He seemed a little bit...tense.

"I know but this isn't regular yoga. This is…I mean… all my body weight is on you."

The look that flashed in Josh's eyes heated Audrey from the inside out. But as fast as it flared, it was extinguished. It was replaced by a guarded look as he grabbed his own water bottle and took a sip. "You weigh a hundred pounds soaking wet."

"Okay, next pose is supported back bow," Tiana said, indicating their water break was over. "Josh you are going to be the base partner. I need you to lie down on the floor on your back and bend your knees in close to your ribs. And Audrey you are going back up to him and sit into the bottom of his feet, reach down and grip his ankles."

Audrey moved into position and listened to the instructions as Tiana walked them through each step. When Josh straightened his legs Audrey's feet lifted off the ground and she was in the air as Josh cradled her backside with his size fourteen feet. She'd never been so happy that he had big feet since she was packing a lot of junk in her trunk thanks to her mom. Just like the song, she got it from her mama.

"Okay, as soon as you feel steady, you can release Josh's ankles and grab your own. Josh you can hold Audrey's shoulders to help balance her."

Before Tiana was able to finish getting the instruction out, Audrey felt Josh's large hands on her shoulders. With his support she was able to release her left hand first and move it to her own ankle and then she repeated the same thing with her right.

"Breathe in and out." Tiana demonstrated the breaths as Audrey held the pose. "Great job. And now Audrey, you can transition into dancer's pose or backfly by releasing one of your legs and extending it in the air."

Almost every time Tiana asked her to go into another

pose it sounded impossible in Audrey's mind, but Josh made it easy. He was the best base anyone could ever ask for. The second Audrey would start to feel shaky, or off balance, Josh would grip harder, change the position of his hands, or shift beneath her to steady her. If she hadn't known any better, she'd be sure that he'd done this a million times before.

"Okay, breathe," Tiana instructed when Audrey was in position. "And now we're going to release the pose. Audrey you can lower your leg as Josh bends his knees lowering his legs and setting you gently on the ground."

When her feet hit the mat, she grasped onto Josh's ankles again for leverage so she could straighten to a standing position.

"Alright, guys we have one more pose to end class. This pose both of you will be standing so Josh if you can rise to your feet."

Disappointment washed over Audrey that the class was over. She felt closer to Josh after this past hour than she had in the eight years they'd known each other as adults. It was amazing how much physical touch created bonding feelings between two people. Not just the touch, but also the breathing, the eye contact, it all worked together.

She would definitely be telling her sister that she should include this activity in the singles week itinerary. Although she wouldn't personally feel comfortable doing this with a stranger, she could see how it would be a good experience to get to know someone, and at the very least see if there was chemistry in a safe environment.

Josh stood to his feet and Audrey looked up to check and make sure that there weren't any hints of pain in his expression. As much as she wanted nothing more than for this class to never end, she would call it immediately if she saw any evidence that this was hurting Josh.

He grinned down at her, and she knew she'd been caught.

"I'm fine, worry wart." He lifted his thumb and brushed it over the wrinkles that she hadn't known had formed between her eyebrows.

A thrill chased down her spine. Josh's hands weren't just big and strong, they were also calloused thanks to his days spent doing manual labor. She loved the way the roughened pads of his fingers felt against her smooth skin. There was something innately sexy about his touch.

"Okay, we're going to do a standing straddle bat. Josh, I'm going to need you to place your hands on Audrey's hips."

Josh stepped forward, closing the space between himself and Audrey and did as instructed. The second his hands gripped her sides, a tingle exploded between her legs.

"And now Audrey, lift your hands and place them around Josh's neck." Audrey felt her breathing grow shallower as she lifted her arms. She knew this wasn't dancing, per se, but she'd always loved to dance and had fantasized about Josh pulling her out on the dance floor one of the hundred nights they'd hung out at JT's bar. He never had. She'd actually never seen him dance with anyone.

Once her hands were in place Tiana continued," Okay now Josh step your feet past hip distance apart and bend your knees." When he did Tiana said, "Now Audrey you're going to hop up and straddle him wrapping your feet around his waist."

Audrey felt her cheeks flush as she felt Josh's hands squeeze on her hips as she hopped up and wrapped her legs around him. She'd never been in this position with anyone before and it felt intimate to be hanging on him like this. Her breathing was coming in short pants, and it had nothing to do with the energy that she'd expended over the last hour.

"Okay now Josh you're going to lean forward slightly as Audrey you relax your neck as you lean back and release your legs opening them up and straightening them out into a wide split. Once her legs are outstretched, Josh you can release her hips lift your arms out to the side and hold her ankles."

They both followed the instruction and when Audrey's head fell back, she was able to see their reflection in the mirror. Her eyes met Josh's gaze in the mirror and for a moment, the world around Audrey disappeared. All that she saw was the two of them, in a very intimate looking pose. Heat swirled low in her belly causing a tingling sensation to build between her legs.

"Okay, great. Josh you can straighten back up, grip Audrey's hips once again and gently lower her to the ground."

When Audrey's feet hit the ground, Josh didn't release his hands from her waist immediately and Audrey didn't lower her arms from behind his neck. She stared up at him as their breaths both came in short pants. If they weren't in a yoga class, Audrey would have thrown caution to the wind, lifted up on her toes and pressed her lips to his, consequences be damned. She was getting to the point that she would risk the awkwardness for the slim possibility that he might kiss her back.

"Okay, great now let's both step to the edges of our mats and take a deep breath."

Tiana started taking them through the cooldown when Audrey heard her phone vibrate in her bag several times, but she ignored it as she focused on her breathing at the end of class. But as soon as they namasted she went over and pulled it out.

She opened the text and Josh must have seen her reaction to what she saw because he asked, "What's wrong?"

"Um, it's the shelter. We had a dog come in the other day, Thor, who is terrified of men and apparently, he's not doing well with the storm. Pete can't get near him to get his thunder vest on. I need to go." She quickly threw on her layers and pushed her feet into her Ugg boots. "Thank you, Tiana! The class was great! I'm sure that Viv will be in touch to get you on the schedule for singles week."

Audrey flew out the door before she remembered that she'd come here with Viv.

"Shit," she cursed under her breath.

Normally, she would just run home and get her car. But it was pouring rain.

The next thing she knew, there was something over her head and she heard Josh's deep voice say, "Come on."

She glanced up and saw that he was using his jacket as a make-shift umbrella for her. She walked beneath the cover and Josh was able to open the driver's side door and let her in while still keeping his coat above her.

When she climbed inside the truck she inhaled, and warmth spread through her. The truck's cab smelled like Josh. He started the truck and headed in the direction of Hope Falls Animal Shelter instead of toward her house.

"Oh, you don't have to take me to the shelter. You could just run me home to get my car."

"It's fine."

A flash of light lit up the inky night sky before there was a crash of thunder. Audrey checked her phone to see if Pete had sent any more updates. He hadn't.

"Everything okay?" Josh asked.

"Yeah. I was just checking to see if Pete messaged me again." Audrey took a deep breath. She needed to calm herself before going into this situation. Dogs reacted off of energy and if she was stressed and tense then Thor would pick up on it.

When he'd come in the other day, it had taken her a couple of hours to build trust with him. He came from an abusive situation. A neighbor had called the police to report it. He was such a sweet boy and she hated thinking of him having to endure any more trauma. If she didn't have Frank and Liza at home, she would have adopted him the day he was brought in.

The truck had barely come to a stop in front of the shelter when Audrey jumped out. She didn't wait for Josh as she rushed to the front door. Pete opened it before she made it up the walk.

"Thanks for coming. He's having a really rough time." Pete must have noticed Josh behind Audrey because his eyes widened. "Hey, J."

"Hey," Josh greeted him.

As Pete handed Audrey the thunder jacket, his eyes widened giving her a what's-this-all-about look. Even though Pete was not what Audrey would classify as a gossip, this was Hope Falls. She was sure that the entire town would know Josh had come with her to the shelter by tomorrow. She wouldn't be surprised if it made the front page of the paper.

Pete buzzed the trio into the back room where the kennels were. Some of the dogs started barking when they entered from excitement. Pete hung back and Audrey turned to Josh who was following her. "He's scared of men, so you should probably stay here."

Josh nodded.

Audrey walked between the gated kennels and when

she got to the end, she saw that Pete had put up towels over the sides of Thor's kennel. It was something they did to try and lessen the stimulants around the dogs to keep the environment calm.

She moved the towel, lifted up the latch and opened the door.

Thor was huddled in the corner shaking uncontrollably.

"Hey, sweet boy. It's okay." Audrey took deep breaths as she entered, making sure that her energy was calm and confident.

The closer she got to him the more audible his shallow breathing was. He was panicked. She crouched down and ran her hand over his head. His panting continued and his eyes darted wildly.

"You're okay, buddy." She continued speaking in a calming tone, doing her best to assure him. "You're safe. Everything is okay."

His breathing had just started to even out when there was bright flash in the room followed a few seconds later by a deafening crack of thunder. Thor let out a heartbreaking yelp of fear and he started shaking even worse than he had been a few moments before. She wanted to get the jacket on him before the next crack of thunder.

"Shh, shh, shh," she shushed him as she ran her hand down over his head. She placed the thunder jacket on his back and tried to connect it around his chest and belly but the position he was in made it impossible.

She'd just managed to get her arms around his chest when there was another flash and booming crack. This time when Thor yelped it sounded like a dying animal.

"Okay, it's okay. You're okay, sweet boy."

She heard footsteps behind her, and she turned to see Josh standing in the entrance of the kennel.

Audrey held out her hand The Supremes stop-in-the-name-of-love style. "Don't come in, he's scared of men."

Instead of entering Josh just crouched down so he was closer to Thor's level and spoke in calming, soothing tone. "It's okay, big guy. You're okay. It's just a little thunder. Nothing to worry about."

Audrey turned back and saw that Thor was sniffing the air toward Josh. His eyes didn't appear to be as wild and panicked, it's like his brain had switched to being curious about Josh.

"Yeah, that's a good boy." Josh reached out his hand making his wrist limp and Thor stretched his neck to sniff him.

After a few minutes Josh shuffled slightly on his feet and then lowered onto his butt so his back was leaning against the cement block of the kennel wall. He was no longer facing Thor head on; he now had his side to him. As soon as Josh changed positions Thor took a tentative step in his direction.

Audrey couldn't believe what she was seeing. Thor wasn't cowering, or crying, or yelping. He was still shaking but he didn't seem terrified.

Josh remained perfectly still, just speaking in that same soothing, low, calming voice and within ten minutes Thor had crawled onto his lap, curled up, and had fallen asleep as Josh petted his head.

"His name is Thor and he's afraid of thunder?" Josh asked in a teasing tone once Thor was snoring peacefully.

Audrey honestly could not believe what had just happened. If she hadn't seen it with her own eyes she wouldn't have. "How did you do that?"

"I worked with bomb sniffing dogs when I was in

Beirut. Dogs respond to energy. You just have to stay calm and almost telepathically tell them that they are safe and that everything is okay."

The left side of Audrey's lip curled as she let out a tiny huff of air. She knew all of that and had been trying to put it into practice, but she'd failed miserably. "You make it sound so easy."

Josh's shoulder lifted in a tiny shrug. "It is once you learn how to stay in a calm and authoritative state. It works with humans sometimes, too."

It sure as hell worked on Audrey. She wanted nothing more than to crawl up into Josh's lap, curl up in a ball, and fall asleep as he stroked her hair. But right now, that position was occupied.

12

"Seriously? Another one?"

Josh pulled what was left of the shredded rag from Thor's mouth. He'd thought that he'd Thor-proofed the garage but every time he turned around the dog had found something else to destroy.

He'd had Thor for three days and he was a completely different dog than the petrified animal he'd seen in the shelter. When he'd come around the corner to check on Audrey after he'd heard the high-pitched yelp, his heart had broken at what he saw.

Growing up, he'd always wanted a dog, but his dad had never let him get one. When he got home from the Army, he'd thought about getting a dog, his psychologist had even suggested that he get one to help with his PTSD and night terrors, but he felt guilty getting an animal when he could barely take care of himself.

But having Thor had shown him that Dr. Lowe was right. He'd felt happier and calmer these past few days than he could remember ever feeling.

Thor looked longingly in the direction of the oversized

dog bed Josh had gotten for him which was currently inhabited by Bullet who was snuggled up in the center. The tiny cat looked even more miniscule due to the scale of the bed.

"It's your bed. You can lay on it, too," Josh told Thor whose only response was to flop down on the concrete floor and let out an exaggerated sigh.

For all the years that Bullet and Batman had been coming around they only ever showed up when it was feeding time. But the past three days that Thor had been at the shop, the cats had been hanging out all day and staying in the shop when Josh closed at night. Sleeping on Thor's bed.

At first, Thor seemed to like the company. Both cats would snuggle up next to him on the bed and Josh had gotten some adorable pictures. Now, it seemed that there must have been a shift in the relationship dynamic because if Batman or Bullet were on the bed first, Thor didn't go near it.

It was so funny to Josh that Thor could literally eat the cats as snacks, but he was nearly as scared of them as he was of thunder, at least when it came to claiming his bed as his domain.

"They get on the bed when you're sleeping on it. You can get on it when they are," Josh pointed out as he lowered down onto the creeper and laid down with barely any pain in his back.

Having Thor hadn't been the only change the past few days. Since the AcroYoga class his back had felt markedly better. He'd only had to take pain medicine twice. He felt stronger and more flexible.

His tertiary blast injuries had mostly been in his back. He'd broken his arm and fractured his ribs but those both healed. His back was the only physical ongoing injury he dealt with and the AcroYoga had been the most effective form of therapy he'd found. He'd seen the benefits from doing yoga by himself, but they were nothing compared to the difference he experienced from the class with Audrey.

It was sort of the difference between jerking off and having sex. There was something to be said about practicing with another person. The balance, stretching and strengthening was exponentially better. He was tempted to ask Audrey if she'd take more classes with him, which he was pretty sure she'd agree to, but he knew that was playing with fire and he would definitely get burned.

The class with her had not only affected his physical body, it had also affected him both emotionally and mentally. The way she looked at him with complete trust as he'd held her above him. The way the curves of her body fit perfectly in the palms of his hands. The way they moved together in perfect harmony as if they'd done it a thousand times before. Even Tiana had commented on how intuitive their movements were with one another.

His dirty mind had immediately filled with other things they could do together where their bodies would be in sync. If they were that intuitively synchronal with one another with their clothes on how much better would it be if they didn't have any barriers between each other.

Those thoughts were not appropriate to be having about Audrey, especially considering the fact that she'd never shared any naked time with another person. Since he'd found that out it had only made him want her more, which was something he didn't even think was possible. He wasn't sure what that said about him as a person.

His mind was a million miles away when he felt the familiar swat of Nonna's shoe on his leg.

Josh rolled out from under the car. "You could just say my name to get my attention."

"Who can hear with all this racket?!"

The music wasn't that loud, but Josh pulled out his phone and turned the nest speaker down.

"Oh, what a handsome boy you are," Nonna talked in baby talk as she lavished attention on Thor who was standing beside her eating it up. "You are the most handsome boy there ever was."

"Thanks, Nonna," Josh teased.

Nonna ignored him and kissed her hand then put it on the top of Thor's head before turning her attention to Josh. "I need to call Pastor Harrison."

"Okay," Josh wasn't sure why she was telling him that.

She held out her hand. "Give me your phone to call his number."

He handed his phone to her even though he wasn't sure why she needed his phone to call him.

She looked down at it and back up at him. "Where is it? Where is his number?"

"I don't have Pastor Harrison's number." Josh could get it from Caleb, but he didn't have it in his phone.

"What are you talking about?!" Her voice rose as her hands flew up in the air. "He's your best friend."

"Oh, do you mean Caleb?"

"That's what I said, Pastor Harrison."

Oh, for the love... This was ridiculous. "Nonna, you've known him his whole life. You caught us smoking behind the bleachers at the football game when we were twelve. You can call him Caleb."

She wagged her finger in Josh's face. "No, no. He's a pastor. Pastor Harrison. You show respect."

Josh still couldn't get used to people calling him that. Pastor Harrison was Caleb's dad and forever would be.

He took his phone back and scrolled through until he

found his friend's contact then pressed the call icon and handed it to her.

"Hello, Pastor, this is Nonna. I have a favor I need for you. You need to go to the community center tonight to dance with Audrey. My Vivi hurt her back, *povera bambina*, and now Audrey needs you to dance with her."

Audrey?

Dance with her?

"Okay, you call me back."

Nonna handed the phone back to Josh. He opened his mouth to say something but was stunned speechless. Why hadn't Nonna asked him to go to the community center? Why had she asked Caleb?

An image of Caleb and Audrey dancing together flashed in his head and an emotion dangerously close to jealousy filled him. In the back of his mind, he'd always been a little scared that the two of them would end up together. And if Josh was being honest, they deserved each other. Most of the time that phrase was being used it had a negative connotation. But not this time. Caleb was the best man that Josh knew. He was kind, funny, caring. He spent his free time volunteering and serving the community. Just like Audrey did.

The two of them would actually be perfect together. Which was probably why the thought of Caleb showing up at the community center tonight made Josh want to puke.

"Why did you ask Caleb to go and not me?" Josh blurted out.

"I already ask you too much." Nonna waved her hand dismissively. "You eat with no lights on and have to go and do the yoyo."

"Yoga," Josh corrected her as his mind raced to figure out how he could fix this. "Caleb's busier than me. I'll go."

She looked over her shoulder and looked at him like

he'd just escaped a mental institution. "You want to go to the dance? You don't do the dancing."

It was true. He didn't "do the dancing." The only time he'd been on a dance floor was with Nonna when she'd guilt tripped him into dancing with her by saying things like, *"I'm not going to live forever?"* and, *"When I die, won't you be so sad you didn't want to dance with me?"* and, *"I wish I had a grandson who wanted to dance with his Nonna, but I guess he's too embarrassed because she is too old."* Or some other guilt trip. But those occasions had been few and far between, and ninety-nine percent of them had been at family members' weddings.

Josh looked down at his phone and sent his friend a quick text.

Josh: *Don't worry about the message Nonna just left. You don't need to go to the community center. I'm going.*

As he typed the message he noticed that his hands had grease stains on them and he probably smelled like a grease trap as well.

"What are you doing?" Nonna asked as he hit the button to lower the bay door.

"Closing up."

"Why? You're not finished working." Nonna motioned to the parts that were laid out on a rag on the cement floor.

"I'll finish later."

"Why? Why you don't finish now? Where are you going?"

He didn't know if she was being intentionally clueless to prove some point or if she really didn't know what was going on. If he had to guess, he'd go with being intentionally clueless to prove a point.

"First, I'm going home to take a shower. Then I'm going to the community center."

"First you get a scowl and make bulldog face when I

ask you for help, now you go when I don't ask you. This is what is wrong with young people. You are all crazy people." She threw her hands up in the air.

There was a very good chance he was crazy for what he was doing. In his sane mind he would never volunteer to go take a dance class. But that's what Audrey did to him. She drove him crazy.

───────────

AUDREY PUSHED OPEN the door to the community center excited for her evening. Out of all the events that Viv was considering for the singles week this was the only one Audrey had actually volunteered to attend.

Tonight, she was meeting with the dance instructors of a program called Show Her Off that taught basic dance moves, no dance experience necessary, for couples. The spin for singles week was that they were going to teach these basic steps at the beginning of the night and then each of the singles would switch partners with every new song that came on.

She wasn't sure who her dance partner would be this evening, but she didn't even care. She was basically like Sarah Jessica Parker in *Girls Just Want to Have Fun* when she's standing up in front of the class at her new school and her teacher asks her to tell them all a little about herself and she says, in a very dreamy way, *"I love to dance."*

That was Audrey. She'd always loved to dance; she'd just never had a partner to dance with. Since she was a kid, she'd romanticized dancing with her significant other. Whenever she was a little girl imagining what her life would be like when she got older, she had never seen herself having babies or kids but she had envisioned herself being married and madly in love. There was one scene that was a recurring daydream.

The setting was the kitchen, she was standing in front of the stove cooking with music playing in the background. Her husband would walk in, see her, wrap his arms around her and they would start slow dancing. She'd tell him she was going to burn the chicken or the rice or whatever was on the stove, and he would just spin her out and then in again and tell her it could burn, the only thing he wanted to taste was her, or some other equally cheesy-slash-sexy retort.

She knew dancing was a silly thing to fantasize about, and she had no clue why that was where her brain always went. But for better or worse, that was her reality.

When she walked into the rec room, where she was meeting the instructors, she had to admit that she was a little disappointed that Josh wasn't there. In the back of her mind, she'd thought that for sure Viv would take this opportunity to try and set them up again, like she was sure her sister had done with the Dining in the Dark and the AcroYoga.

Unfortunately, he wasn't there, and neither were the instructors. She walked over to the bleachers and sat down to wait and her mind drifted back to a few nights ago at the shelter. She honestly didn't think that she could love Josh any more than she already did but seeing him with Thor had caused her to fall even deeper.

Pete took off once Thor was calmed down, leaving her and Josh alone in the shelter. She and Josh stayed in the kennel and waited for the storm to pass. Thor slept on Josh for about an hour before the weather cleared up and she said that they could go.

Josh looked up at her and said, "*I'm not leaving without him.*"

Her heart had exploded into a million pieces. He adopted him on the spot. It was the most romantic thing he could ever do.

Now that she thought about it, the fact that she fantasized about dancing and thought the most romantic thing a man could do was adopt a dog may be two reasons she was still a virgin.

The double doors opened and when she looked up and saw a man and woman walk in who she didn't recognize her heart sank. Josh wasn't coming. She was kicking herself for not texting him to see if he would come with her. She should have taken matters into her own hands instead of just assuming that Viv would be playing matchmaker. If she'd asked him to come, he probably would have agreed.

For the past eight years, she'd just been waiting for something to happen between them and where had that gotten her? Smack dab in the friend zone. After that yoga class, after experiencing what it felt like for Josh to touch her, she wanted more and she was tired of waiting. Audrey had always hated any sort of confrontation and was more comfortable just letting things happen, but this was too important to remain passive.

If she wanted to get out of the friend zone, then she was probably going to need to step out of her comfort zone.

She forced herself to smile as she stood and walked over to meet the instructors. The man introduced himself as Hunter and his partner as Junie. He went over the basic idea of the program and asked if she was ready to start.

"Yep."

"First, we'll show you what you'll be able to do by the end of the night."

"Great!" Audrey agreed enthusiastically.

He turned the music on and she watched as he and

Junie did what looked like a fairly difficult dance sequence, complete with dips, holds, spins, and a few moves Audrey had never seen before.

She had no clue if she'd be able to remember all the steps, but she was excited to find out. When the song ended she clapped and a deep voice sounded behind her causing the tiny hairs on the back of her neck to stand up on end.

"Fancy seeing you here."

She was already smiling before she turned around and lifted her chin to meet Josh's deep brown stare.

"You got roped into this, too, huh?" Her voice was a little breathy as she did her best to sound unaffected by his arrival. But she was affected. Very affected. Inside she was jumping up and down like she'd just won the lottery.

"Nonna mentioned that you were going to be here and needed a dance partner and I volunteered."

Had she just heard him right?

Did he say that he volunteered to come down here?

"Oh." Audrey was trying not to let herself read too much into what that meant, but her inner romantic had fallen onto the swoon couch with the back of her hand pressed to her forehead.

Hunter walked over and introduced himself to Josh and explained what they would be learning.

Audrey was doing her best to tamper down her excitement at least on the outside, because on the inside she was freaking out. So many nights they'd been at JT's, not together but they'd both been there, and she'd dreamed of him walking across the bar and asking her to dance with him. In eight years, it had never happened. But now, now her dream was finally coming true. Sort of. This wasn't exactly the same as him crossing the room and asking her to dance but beggars couldn't be choosers.

"Okay, let's get started."

They slowly walked through the first few steps and while they did she realized why Josh had never asked her to dance, he had two left feet. Which made him showing up tonight even sweeter and caused her to fall even more in love with him.

13

Josh had never seen Audrey smile as much as she had the past hour. She'd glided around the dance floor the entire time grinning from ear to ear. He watched as she said goodbye to the instructors and waited for her to put on her coat and gloves.

"Thanks again for doing this. I hope you at least had fun," she said, still grinning from ear to ear as she joined him and they started walking to the exit.

"I did." And he was damn glad *he* was the one who was here and not Caleb. Especially now that he knew just how much contact the dancing had entailed. The thought of his friend's hands on Audrey's lower back, of his arms wrapped around her as he dipped her, of his forearm grazing her shoulders as he spun her out, evoked a feeling dangerously close to irate jealousy.

Audrey loved dancing, that much was obvious even if she hadn't told him that she did. Her face had glowed the entire night. And when she thought of this night, of the fun she'd had, it would be Josh that would be in her memories, not Caleb.

By the end of the night Josh wasn't doing half bad, if he did say so himself. Once he got the moves down, it was actually pretty simple. There were five steps and they were all interchangeable and worked with any song that came on. The program really did work for people who had zero dancing skills and had no idea what they were doing. He wasn't going to be auditioning for *Dancing with the Stars* anytime soon, but he definitely thought he could hold his own on the dance floor and not make a fool of himself.

"Do you think Viv and Nonna are going to include this in the itinerary?" he asked as he pushed the door of the rec room open and held it for her as she walked into the lobby.

"Definitely. I think the singles will love it and if they do meet someone then it could be something they continued doing together." She stopped walking and turned to face him. "Did you see the documentary *What is Love?*"

He grinned down at her. "Yep, right after I binged Sex in the City and Gilmore Girls."

"Hey!" She pointed her finger at him. "Gilmore Girls is a really good show!"

He knew she loved that show which is why he loved to tease her about it. Because she would get a fire in her eyes and her lips would pucker in a really adorable way, just like they were doing now. His eyes dropped to her much too kissable mouth. She rolled her eyes as a grin tugged at the corner of her perfect ruby lips.

Fuck, had her lips always looked so damn kissable? He had a feeling that they were becoming more kissable by the day.

"I thought you *might* have watched it because part of it was shot in Hope Falls."

Now that she mentioned that he did remember Nonna talking about the filming crew coming to town. "I haven't, why do you ask?"

"Oh, because there was one segment that featured a man named The Colonel. He'd been married to his wife Marie for sixty plus years and when he was asked what the secret to their successful relationship was, he said it was slow dance Sundays."

"Slow dance Sundays?" Josh had never heard of that.

"Yeah, he said that over the years life brought with it a ton of distractions like work, kids, having company visiting from out of town. But no matter what, before the clock struck midnight, they would slow dance in the kitchen. And he said that even if they'd been upset about something or had a disagreement, the second she stepped into his arms all that would melt away.

"When they were together, they would switch up the songs they'd play but when they were apart, they would always play their song. So, when he was overseas during the war, no matter where he was in the world, she knew on Sunday that he was dancing with her to their song and he knew she was dancing with him. That way even when they weren't physically together, they both knew they were with each other in spirit."

Josh noticed that Audrey's eyes got a little misty.

"That's really sweet." Josh had never thought of dancing as a way to stay connected, but he could see how it would work. And if there was some alternate universe that he and Audrey could be together, he hoped they had slow dance Sundays.

Her forehead scrunched. "I don't know why I thought of that."

He loved when she did that. When she got so excited about a topic, she forgot how she arrived at it.

"You were talking about couples being able to keep dancing together after they learned these steps."

Her face split in a smile. "Oh, right."

As they continued walking through the lobby, he realized that he might be a glutton for punishment, but he didn't want the night to end.

"Did you walk here?" He figured she had because he hadn't seen her car out in front when he got there.

She nodded.

"Do you want to go for a ride?"

He'd never taken a woman on his motorcycle before. It was a sacred thing for him. He'd gotten the bike during his rehab and his rides had helped him as much as his therapy.

She blinked up at him, clearly surprised by his request. She'd asked him before if the women he dated liked going for rides and he'd told her his rule. He'd shared with her that he didn't take people out on it because riding was his therapy, it was transformative, it was damn near a religious experience, and he never wanted that to be tarnished or cheapened.

"On your motorcycle?" she clarified as her eyes widened to the size of half-dollars.

"Yeah."

"I don't have a helmet."

He could lie to himself that this was a spur-of-the-moment invitation, but the truth was he'd bought another helmet almost two years ago. And he never had any intention of anyone other than Audrey wearing it. "I've got an extra."

Confusion clouded her golden eyes and then she shook her head. "Oh, I thought you said that no one ever—"

"No one has ever used it before."

A flush covered her cheeks as the corners of her mouth curled up at the edges. She licked her lips nervously and he suppressed a groan of male appreciation. He wanted so badly to lean down and press his lips to hers and run his own tongue along the seam of her mouth.

Unaware of his innermost desires, she blinked up at him with total trust. "Oh, um okay. Yes. I'd love to."

His chest bloomed with warmth as they walked in silence out of the community center. He held the door open for her and as she walked past him the faint floral scent of her shampoo drifted up as he inhaled. All night he'd been catching whiffs of the intoxicating aroma. Just like Audrey it was delicate and gentle. And every time he smelled it, it was just enough to tease his senses and he wanted more, which was the same way he felt about Audrey herself. He wanted more.

As they stepped outside the inky sky above them was dotted with bright stars. If there was one thing he'd always appreciated about Hope Falls it was the sky at night. During his time in the Army, he'd traveled to and visited a lot of different places, he'd seen the sky from a variety of locations, but there was nothing like the sky at home. Its magnitude was rivaled only by its majesty.

His heart was racing as they approached his bike. He'd fantasized about taking her out on his bike, but he'd never allowed himself to do it before. For years he'd worked diligently to keep Audrey at a safe distance. But these past couple of weeks had made that impossible. They'd shared too much together and now he wanted more. He just wasn't sure how much more he would allow himself to take.

When they reached his bike, he took off his leather jacket. "Put this on."

She was wearing her puffy jacket, which was adorable on her, but he knew that the cold air would cut right through it.

"No." She shook her head. "I have a jacket."

"That jacket's not enough." He started to put his jacket around her shoulders, but she moved away in protest.

"But then you won't have a jacket."

"I'll be fine. Put the jacket on."

He could see a battle going on behind her hazel eyes as she decided whether or not she was going to continue arguing with him. He knew that she could be stubborn, but so could he. All anyone had to do was meet Nonna and they would know he came by it honestly.

Finally, she sighed, lifted her arms and threaded them through his coat. Once she had it on and zipped up, he pulled out the extra helmet from his storage compartment and put it on Audrey's head. He clasped it beneath her chin and made sure that it fit securely. He could feel her wide eyes watching him and it took every bit of self-control he had not to lean down and kiss her perfect lips.

"Does that feel good? Is it too tight?" he asked.

She lifted her hand to her head and patted it. "It's good."

He put his own helmet on, threw his leg over his bike and then instructed her how to get on behind him. Her arms wrapped around his waist and her chest pressed against his back. He wondered if she could feel his heart pounding through his back.

The motorcycle roared to life, and he felt Audrey's arms tighten around his waist. He turned his head and asked, "Are you ready?"

"Yes!" she shouted to be heard over the engine as she nodded her head vigorously.

He pulled out of the parking lot and an overwhelming sense of rightness, of calm, of everything in his world being exactly what it should be washed over him. Every time he got on his bike, he felt hints of those things which was why he'd protected his sacred riding time. But this was more than a hint, this was all consuming peace.

Josh wasn't going to worry about the next time he got

on the bike and Audrey wasn't behind him. One of the quotes Dr. Lowe had told him that had really resonated with him was from Lao Tzu, it said that if you are depressed, you're living in the past. If you are anxious, you're living in the future. If you are at peace, you're living in the present.

Tonight, he wasn't going to allow his brain to think about the past or the future. He was just going to be in the present because for the first time in his life, his present was perfect.

AS THEY RODE through the mountain roads, Audrey was sure that she must be dreaming. First, she'd got to dance with Josh and now she was on the back of his motorcycle. And that's not all they'd done, in the past couple of weeks, she'd dined in the dark with him, taken a yoga class and gone to the animal shelter where she'd been impressed, once again, by just how amazing Josh was.

Over the past few days, she'd caught glimpses of Josh and Thor in the garage. She noticed that Josh talked to Thor *a lot*, which she thought was adorable. Audrey didn't understand people who had pets and *didn't* talk to them.

Josh took a corner and her grip tightened around his waist. The wind whipped in her face and adrenaline raced through her. This was probably one of the most daring things she'd ever done.

Viv was the risk taker. She'd gone sky diving, bungee jumping, and even swam with sharks. And she'd invited Audrey to join her on all of those activities, but Audrey always said *no, thank you*. She would rather experience those things in the safety of a book than in real life.

The risk/reward was not worth it for her. But when

Josh asked her if she wanted to go for a ride, she knew immediately that the risk/reward was worth it. She'd spent years imagining what it would be like to be on the back of Josh's bike and the reality was far exceeding her fantasy.

It was thrilling. Her entire body was infused with adrenaline, and she felt more alive than she ever had before. Yes, there was an element of danger to it, but that's what made it so exhilarating. But she would only ever feel safe enough to do something like this with him. If there was anyone in the world that she'd trust with her life, it was Josh. She knew implicitly that he would protect her at all costs and never do anything to harm her.

Which was one of the reasons that she wanted Josh to be her first. Besides being the sexiest man she'd ever seen and the fact that she was in love with him, she knew that with him, she would be safe. He would always take care of her.

When she saw that they were heading back to town, she made herself a promise. She was going to tell Josh that she wanted to be with him. That she wanted him to be her first. Tonight was the night that she was going to lay her cards on the table.

She heard her mom's voice in her head, *If not now, then when?* It was something she'd started saying after she got sick. Basically, it was a mantra to live each day like it was your last. Something that Audrey had not practiced, at least in her personal life.

As they turned onto her street her pulse sped up and she felt like she was going to be sick but she knew that she had to tell him how she felt. She couldn't let this moment pass her by, like she had so many others.

They pulled up to her house and he slowed to a stop and put the kickstand down. She got off the bike and as she was taking off the helmet he dismounted as well. As she handed the helmet back to him, she saw that her hands were shaking. She wasn't sure if it was from the adrenaline that was still coursing through her body or the nerves of what she was about to say.

"Thank you, that was amazing."

He smiled and her insides turned to mush. "I'm glad you liked it."

All of her self-protective instincts were screaming for her to turn around and go inside of her house, but she wasn't going to give in to that impulse. Playing it safe had gotten her nowhere. It was time to take a risk because if she did and it went her way, the reward would be more than worth it.

Her mouth suddenly went dry as she attempted to swallow over the large lump of anxiety that was clogging her throat. "Um, do you remember when we were at dinner...at the dining in the dark?"

He nodded.

She could feel her cheeks heating but she knew that if she didn't blurt this out, then she would never forgive herself. "And I told you that I was a virgin," she continued.

His expression remained unreadable as he nodded again.

She took a deep breath. "Well, I don't want to be one anymore."

Damn it. That sounded like something a little kid would say. What was she doing?

Her eyes shot down to her feet as she shifted her weight from her left to her right foot. This was coming out all wrong. She'd never been good at flirting. If Viv was standing here, she'd know exactly what to say. Let's be honest, Viv wouldn't be standing here because she would never have waited eight years to make a move.

Screw it. If she and Josh were really as close as she

thought they were, then even if he rejected her their relationship would survive. And that was, truly, the most important thing to her.

She lifted her head back up and said calmly and firmly, "I want my first time to be with you. I want you to be my first." She said it two ways just so there wasn't any room for interpretation of her meaning.

She waited for him to respond, but he just stared at her, and she realized that he probably needed time to process what she was asking. Josh was a processor and this was a lot of data to intake at once.

"You don't have to say anything now. In fact, I'd rather you didn't answer. But I just wanted you to know. I don't want to be with someone to just do it for the sake of doing it and to get it over with. I want to be with someone who I know will take care of me. Who I trust." *Who I love*. She kept that last part to herself. She figured that asking him to deflower her was enough revelation for one night.

"Nothing would have to change between us. We would still be friends just like we are now." She ducked her head suddenly feeling embarrassment swamp her. The high from the ride was apparently wearing off. "And I totally understand if you don't want...I mean, if you're not attracted to me that's totally—"

"I'm very attracted to you." His voice was so deep she felt it vibrate through her from head to toe.

Her eyes shot up to meet his and when their gazes met, the intensity in his stare stole her breath. She opened her mouth to speak, but there were no words there. He wasn't saying yes, but he wasn't saying no.

She didn't have a clue what he was thinking behind his milk chocolate stare. But she was scared if she stayed there a moment longer the next word out of his mouth would be *but*. I'm very attracted to you *but*...

Since that *but* would ruin what would otherwise be the most perfect night of her life, she figured it was best to end things now.

"Just think about it. And thank you again…for tonight." She lifted up on her toes and pressed a kiss to his cheek before turning and practically running up her front steps.

When she got inside her house and closed the door her heart was pounding so hard she was sure it was going to beat right out of her chest. She fell back against the door and slid down to the ground just as Lucy wobbled up and crawled into her lap. Audrey picked her up and cuddled her little snug bug against her chest as she tried to catch her breath.

For most people, telling someone they'd known for eight years that they wanted to have sex with them and then kissing them on the cheek would be a fairly tame thing to do. For Audrey, it was downright scandalous.

14

JOSH OPENED THE FRIDGE AND STARTED TO GRAB A BEER but decided against it so he put it back. His anxiety was at an all-time high and he'd made a promise to himself a long time ago that he'd never use alcohol to escape. He'd seen his father do that. And he assumed that's what his mother did when she was using, although he hadn't witnessed it personally because she was absent for so much of his life.

He closed the fridge and ran his hands through his hair. He felt like he was crawling out of his skin. His anxiety hadn't been this severe in years. Most of the time he was dealing with this level of anxiousness it was due to his PTSD or his night terrors or the pain that he was in. But what he'd been feeling the past two days could not be attributed to his past. His anxiety was because of Audrey's proposition.

"I want my first time to be with you."

"I want you to be my first."

Those statements had been repeating over and over and over and over again in his head.

"I want my first time to be with you."

"I want you to be my first."

He still couldn't believe that she'd come right out and said that to him…and he hadn't said anything. Well, that wasn't strictly true. He'd told her that he was attracted to her, but that was about it.

For the past two days, he'd thought about every possible outcome in this situation and none of them were good. What was he supposed to say to her?

I want to be with you more than anything, but I'm too fucked up. Hell, he wasn't even sure if he could physically perform. He hadn't been able to in over two years.

And his ED wasn't the only flashing red light to this situation. He couldn't be anything more than just a friend with benefits because she deserved a hell of a lot better than him. She deserved someone who wasn't a mental case, who wasn't in pain all the time, and who could give her a family. So then what options were they left with? Friends with benefits? Maybe if they were just acquaintances, sure. But if they were just acquaintances like Pricilla, Jenny or Sabrina then they would have already had sex.

But they were more than that. They were more than friends. They cared about each other in a deep, meaningful way. There was no way to add no strings sex to that sort of relationship. Especially considering Audrey had never had sex with anyone.

That fact made him want her more and know that he couldn't have her in equal measures.

This entire situation had gotten out of hand, and he had no clue how to deal with it. The most important thing was that he didn't lose Audrey. But he was scared if he kept being distant because of his anxiety over not knowing how to handle the situation that is exactly what would happen.

Not knowing what else to do, he grabbed his

notebook out of the cabinet next to his dining table and sat down and just wrote the first things that came to his head.

The Dance
Two people
One motion
Circling to rhymes
Connection so strong
Their breaths collide
Heart beats sync
Their bodies glide
Moving together
Suspended in time

He was so lost in his memories of the dance class that the knock on the door startled him. He closed his notebook and stuffed it back into the cabinet. Caleb had mentioned that he might stop by tonight and hang out if he got done with the annual bake off which he was MCing before eight. He still couldn't believe that was his friend's life. Hosting the annual Hope Falls Bake Off.

Josh shook his head and Thor's nails clicked on the floor as he followed Josh to the door. When he opened it, Josh was expecting to see his friend but instead was surprised to see his sister standing there with her three children and a lot of bags.

"Uncle J, Uncle J!" His twin nieces Bethany and Bridgette wearing identical turtlenecks with overalls and scarves hopped up and down with their hands in the air. The only way he could tell them apart was that Bethany's hair was blonder than Bridgette's.

"Hey munchkins!" He bent down and they both launched themselves into his arms.

Mid hug both girls started screaming, "A puppy! A puppy!"

"You got a dog?" Claire asked, her brows lifting high toward the heavens.

His sister had *strongly* suggested, several times, that he get a therapy animal, just like Dr. Lowe had. Part of him wished he'd listened to them and had gotten a dog sooner but then he might not have Thor. And Josh would gladly endure the eight years he'd spent white knuckling through his trauma to have the dog he truly felt was meant to be his. Thor.

"Yep." Josh nodded as he set the girls down and scratched behind Thor's ears. "This is Thor."

"Princess Thor!" Bridgette exclaimed.

"I love Princess Thor!" Bethany threw her arms around Thor's neck.

Thor's tongue was hanging out the side of his mouth as he panted, and Josh could swear he was smiling. The corners of his mouth were tilted up. He was in hog heaven receiving all that attention.

Josh stepped back and held the door open for his sister who walked in with his nephew Braydon on her hip. "Sorry to just show up like this. I tried to call but it went straight to voicemail."

Shit. Josh had been so distracted by the bullshit in his head he must not have charged his phone. What if Nonna had needed him? Or what if Audrey had called? What if she'd texted? He thought she hadn't reached out to him since he'd dropped her off at her house, but what if he was wrong? He pulled his phone out of his pocket. Sure enough, it was dead.

"What's up?" He asked as he plugged it into the charger in the kitchen.

"Um, well…"

146

"I have to go potty." Bethany was hopping back and forth from her left foot to her right doing the pee pee dance.

"Me too!" Bridgette threw her hand up in the air.

Both girls started running down the hallway in what looked to be a serious race.

"I'd better go supervise. They've been having fun flushing things down the toilet lately." Claire handed Braydon to Josh and disappeared down the hall after the girls.

"Hey little man, you're getting big," he said as he tossed him up in the air and Braydon giggled.

Josh hadn't seen his nephew and nieces for about four months because his sister and the kids had spent the holidays back East with Claire's husband's family. He was realizing that was too long to go. This guy was significantly heavier, and the girls looked like they'd both grown at least an inch.

Since these munchkins were the closest he'd ever get to having kids of his own, he didn't want to miss any of it. He resolved to get back to his schedule of heading down to Sacramento at least once a month. Nonna loved the visits and so did he.

He was already planning when he'd head down there next when his sister returned. She took a deep breath and tried to take Braydon back.

"I've got him," Josh assured her.

"Okay, um, I have a *huge* favor to ask."

"What's up?"

Claire had never asked him for anything in his life. They hadn't been that close growing up, since Claire was nearly a decade older than him and had always lived with her mom. They hadn't actually had any real relationship until after their dad had passed. Oddly enough, when they planned the funeral, they'd sort of bonded over what a shitty father he was, something they'd never really talked about when he was alive.

After that, they kept in touch more regularly. And then she'd asked Josh to walk her down the aisle when she got married. It had been such a huge honor that he took very seriously. Once the twins were born, they got even closer.

"The kids and I are on our way to Tahoe; Martin is there for business." Claire's husband worked in marketing and had clients all over the world. He travelled a lot for his job. "We were going to head up there and spend the weekend. I had a babysitter lined up. She was supposed to come with me, but when I went to pick her up, she was too upset to go because she'd just found out her boyfriend was cheating on her. I guess she looked through his phone and saw plans he was making because she was going to be out of town.

"Anyway, I figured I would just bring the kids with me, we could have a mini family vacation. And we still *can*. But as I was driving I got an idea, and I tried to call you but you didn't answer. So, I figured since I was driving this way anyway, I'd stop by and see if the kids could stay here for two nights. I know it's a long shot and I'm sure you're busy and I *totally* understand if it's too much."

"Of course," Josh agreed easily. He'd love to spend a few days with his munchkins.

Claire didn't seem convinced by his answer. Her head tilted to the side and a wrinkle appeared on her forehead. "Are you sure? You've never had all three of them at once. You're gonna be seriously outnumbered."

"It's not a problem. We can go visit Nonna and if it gets to be too much, I'll call in reinforcements." The last time he'd babysat it was just the twins, they were three and Claire and Martin went on a babymoon, which Josh had never heard of but apparently was a thing. He'd had them for three days and both Caleb and Audrey had stopped by and helped him out.

"Are you really sure?"

"Yes," he assured her.

His sister's face relaxed and she threw her arms around both him and Braydon. "Oh my gosh! I owe you! Big time!"

"It's no problem, really. We'll have fun."

The girls came back into the room, Thor trailing behind them. Bridgette had taken off her scarf and wrapped it around his neck. They'd also found a tiara, which they must have brought in their bags, and had placed it on his head.

"Come on, Princess Thor." Bethany instructed as the girls ran to the front room and opened the trunk of toys he kept for them. "We have to find you a dress for the ball."

Princess Thor happily trailed behind the girls, proudly wearing his hot pink scarf and tiara.

Claire looked at him once more, her face etched with concern. "Are you absolutely sure about this?"

"Well, I wasn't before, but now that I know we're having a ball how can I say no?" he teased.

AUDREY GRIPPED Josh's jacket as she walked up the steps to his house.

She'd had it for two days. Her plan had been to give it back to him when he came into the coffee shop, but...he hadn't come in.

The last forty-eight hours had been a roller coaster of emotions. She'd felt embarrassed and stupid and regretted saying anything to Josh about what she wanted one minute; but then the next minute, she'd get irritated and mad that he hadn't even come in to talk to her about it.

They were *friends*, first and foremost and she wasn't going to let him get away with avoiding her. He didn't want to have sex with her? Fine. But they were at least going to have a conversation and clear the air.

And yes, she was using returning his jacket as an excuse to show up at his house unannounced. But honestly, why did she need an excuse? She didn't. He'd shown up on her doorstep countless times for movie nights and vice versa.

This was normal behavior for them. Just because she'd said that she wanted him to take her virginity didn't negate the eight years of friendship they'd shared. Right?

She'd worked herself into a healthy indignation by the time she reached the front door. As she lifted her hand to knock, she heard a high-pitched giggle and her boldness shattered like a glass bottle under a steam roller. There was a woman in there. He was with someone else.

She was turning around when she heard another sound. This time it was clearly a child's voice. She stepped back up to the door and pressed her ear to it. When she did, she heard what sounded like a stampede of horses.

Was his sister there? Maybe Claire had come to visit with the kids. She knew Josh had been missing them since he hadn't seen them over the holidays.

Okay, so maybe tonight wasn't the night for them to have their talk.

She turned to leave and smacked right into Noah Barnes who was wearing a Slice of Heaven ball cap holding a red, insulated delivery bag. Noah was dating Audrey's soon to be niece, Blake. She'd always liked Noah and was usually happy to see him, but right now she wished he would disappear.

"Hi, Miss Wells!" he said loudly.

And keep his voice down.

"Hey, Noah," Audrey said weakly feeling embarrassed that he'd caught her with her ear on the door like a creep. She sidestepped him and started toward the stairs. She'd made it down two steps when she heard the doorbell ring and a second later the door opened behind her.

"Audrey?" She heard Josh's deep voice.

Crap on a cracker. She'd been caught. Twice. First, by Noah who'd seen her eavesdropping and now by Josh who'd seen her trying to sneak away. This is what came of trying to assert herself and take control of her life. And people wondered why she was content being at home with her books and cats.

"Hey!" She turned around and smiled. Noah was taking two pizza boxes out of his bag as she said it. When her gaze lifted, she saw that Josh was holding his nephew on his hip. She never wanted to have kids, her biological clock had never ticked, but she couldn't deny there was something innately sexy about a man holding a baby.

Josh took the pizzas with his free hand and thanked Noah, who smiled and waved as he hopped down the porch taking two steps at a time leaving Audrey and Josh alone. Well, not totally alone. Braydon was there, too.

She'd thought she was ready to face Josh, but suddenly she felt shy about being here. All of her I-am-woman-hear-me-roar righteous indignation flew right out the window. She just wanted to go home, put sweats on and have a date with Ben, Jerry and a romance novel.

"I was just coming to drop this off." She lifted her arm, holding his jacket out in front of her and realized that he had his hands full. She looked around the porch. "Um, I can just leave it…"

"Are you hungry?" Josh either didn't notice or he

gracefully ignored Audrey's awkwardness. Either way, she was grateful.

"I don't want to intrude." She knew that Josh didn't get to see Claire that often and she didn't want to interlope on their family time. The two of them had only become close since they were both adults.

"I'm babysitting three kids under the age of five. You wouldn't be intruding. You'd be helping."

"Oh, okay. Sure." Audrey nodded and stepped inside and saw that the twins were camped out in front of the TV totally engrossed in the movie *Shrek*. Thor was sitting between them wearing a beautiful sparkly ballgown and a tiara on his head.

"Actually, Thor has been doing most of the work." Josh said as he set the pizzas down on the side table.

"I see that." Audrey grinned.

Josh shifted Braydon on his hip. "Hey girls, do you remember—"

"Audrey! Audrey!" Both girls screamed and ran over to her; Thor was right behind them.

As she hugged both the girls and said hello to Thor, she was actually relieved that tonight had turned out how it had. Maybe what she and Josh needed was just a normal night, hanging out, no pressure.

"Who's hungry?" Josh asked.

"Me!" Bethany shouted.

"I am!" Bridgette lifted her arm high in the air.

"Go wash your hands and I'll get your plates." He told them.

Both girls scrambled out of the room, racing each other to see who could make it to the sink first.

Audrey looked at Josh. "How long do you have them?"

"Two nights."

"You look tired already," she grinned.

"I am, but I love it."

She could tell that he meant that. He'd mentioned to her before that he didn't want to have kids. At the time she remembered being happy about him saying that because it was a commonality they shared. But seeing how amazing he was with his nieces and nephew she wondered if he really did but he just hadn't found the right person. If that was the case, then they really didn't have a future, because as much as she loved kids, she did not want to be a mom.

"Uncle J! Bridgette flushed your toothbrush down the toilet!" Bethany yelled.

"I did not! It fell!" Bridgette shouted back.

Yeah, her biological clock was definitely *not* ticking.

15

Josh bent over and gently laid Braydon down in the porta-crib that Claire had set up in his room before she left. When he moved his hands from under him, his nephew stirred so Josh patted his back gently until he was sound asleep again.

When he straightened up to standing his back protested shooting a sharp pain down his spine and through his right leg. Chasing two four-year-olds and carrying around a one-year-old was a young man's game. He was getting too old for this.

He was glad that Audrey had shown up when she did. She truly was his angel. Claire had been right. Adding a baby to the mix was a lot more work and he'd *definitely* felt outnumbered. His plan had been to get through tonight and then wear them all out tomorrow by taking them to the park, down to the riverside, and maybe even to U Bounce, which was filled with inflatable castles and other structures that the girls could play on. He'd never been there, but he'd heard people that have kids swear by it as a life saver.

On the way back to the front room, he picked up two Barbie dolls, one of which had a very short haircut. He noticed there was a lot of hair in a pile next to a pair of scissors. He had no clue the girls had gotten scissors, and he knew Audrey hadn't seen it either. This must have happened when Audrey was feeding Braydon and he was cleaning up the soda that had spilled at dinner.

He walked out to the front room and saw that all of the girls were seated around the dining room table and were coloring. His heart was swelling and breaking at the same time. Every time he witnessed how amazing Audrey was with the kids it just solidified the fact that they couldn't be together. She was born to be a mom.

"Wow! That's such a pretty fish." Audrey said.

"It's not a fish it's a bird," Bridgette corrected her.

"Oh, right. Of course, it is. That is such a pretty *bird*."

"Princess Thor do you like my bird?" Bridgette lowered the paper down to where Thor was sleeping under the table. His only response was a soft snore.

He now understood why pits were called the nanny breed. Thor had worked harder than both he or Audrey had tonight, and he was out for the count.

"What are you coloring?" Bethany asked Audrey.

"I'm coloring flowers." Audrey showed his niece her picture. "What color do you think I should make this one?"

"Pink!" Both Bethany and Bridgette shouted.

"Pink it is." Audrey got a pink crayon and began to color in the daisy. He watched as she chatted with the girls about them starting kindergarten, which the twins referred to as their big girl class, and the things they were going to learn.

He had no idea how long he'd been leaning against the doorframe just taking in the scene when Audrey noticed he was there. She looked up and smiled at him sweetly. In a flash he saw what being with her, *really* being with her could be. He saw what his future could be if he wasn't so fucked up and circumstances were different.

An urgency unlike anything he'd ever felt before bubbled up inside of him. He wanted nothing more than to get down on one knee and ask Audrey to marry him. He had a ring. Nonna had given Josh her wedding ring after his father died. He'd told her he didn't want it and that he was never going to use it because he was never going to get married, but she insisted that he keep it. In his perfect world, he would put that ring on Audrey's finger tonight and be down at the courthouse in the morning to make it official.

He wasn't sure what his expression looked like as that epiphany hit him, but when Audrey glanced up at him again, a crease appeared between her eyebrows and she mouthed, "*Are you okay?*"

No. He wasn't.

But she didn't need to know that.

He smiled and clapped his hands. "Who wants to watch a movie?"

"Me!" Bethany yelled.

"I do!" Bridgette's arm flew up in the air.

He might not get to have his happily ever after with Audrey, but he did have tonight. And he was going to stop feeling sorry for himself and just feel grateful that he had her in his life.

THE CREDITS ROLLED and Audrey was surprised at how invested she'd gotten in the movie. They'd watched *Inside Out* and she'd even teared up. She hadn't seen any cartoons since she'd nannied when she was in college. She forgot just how amazing they could be.

She glanced beside her and saw that both the girls were sound asleep.

"I'm going to take them to the room," Josh whispered.

She started to get up and help, but he held out his arm and mouthed. "I've got it."

Audrey watched as Josh carried the girls one by one into his room. She honestly didn't think there was anything that man couldn't do. He could fix *anything* that broke, he was a good cook, a dog whisperer, could change a diaper with one hand, and he could say the alphabet backwards, which she supposed wasn't really that useful but it had always impressed her.

She stood and started cleaning up the movie snacks. She picked up the bowl, making sure to gather the popcorn that was scattered on the couch, and then grabbed the sippy cups. After taking the bowl to the trash she dumped out the unpopped popcorn and then rinsed it out, setting it in the drying rack and did the same thing with the sippy cups the girls had used after the soda spilling at dinner.

When she got back to the living room, she looked around and was amazed at how much of a mess two little people could make. It looked like a tornado had hit the place. She figured she'd start by cleaning up the dining room table and work her way out. She started straightening up the papers that she and the girls had been coloring on and gathering up the crayons. When she went to put them away in the cabinet a notebook fell out. It fell open to a page of handwritten words.

Firefly
Bright against the midnight sky

You shine light in the darkness
You luminate
You glow
The flutter of your wings
The whisper of your flight
The softness in your…

"THANKS FOR YOUR HELP TONI—" Josh's sentence dropped off mid word and she lifted her head and saw him staring at the notebook in her hands.

"Did you write this?" she asked.

All of the color drained from his face. "Yeah." Josh took the notebook from her hands, and she suddenly realized that it probably looked like she'd been snooping.

"I was just putting the coloring books away and it fell out."

"It's fine," his tone was clipped. She could tell that he was upset that she'd seen what she had.

"I didn't see that much. Just one poem and I thought it was beautiful."

"Thanks." He put the notebook into the cabinet and shut the door.

"Josh, I'm sorry." He'd never been mad at her before and seeing him like this made her feel sick to her stomach. She didn't know what to say, so she just repeated what she'd already said. "I was putting the coloring books away and it just fell out."

The corner of his lips turned up and she saw the light that she'd been missing in his eyes. "You were snooping. You got caught. Let's not make a big deal about it," he teased.

She knew if he was joking around about the situation

he wasn't upset, or if he was, he was going to get over it. A weight lifted off her shoulders and she chuckled and threw a crayon at him. He lifted his hand and easily caught it, because he had ninja-like reflexes, and the inner walls of her sex clenched. She must have it bad if just seeing him catch a crayon was making lady parts flutter.

"Before I caught you *snooping*, I was just saying, thanks for helping me tonight."

"Of course! I love those kids. They're great!" Audrey enthused.

He stared down at her and she could see that beneath his deep brown eyes there was a world of emotion swirling.

After several moments, she couldn't take the suspense anymore and she asked, "What?"

"You're gonna be a *great* mom someday," he spoke in an almost reverent tone.

She let out a forced laugh as she shook her head as she finished putting the crayons back into the box. "No. I won't."

There was a moment of silence before Josh insisted, "*Yes*, you will. Kids love you and you're great with them."

Audrey looked up at him, thinking that he must be kidding, but when she saw his "serious brows" she knew that he wasn't. "Oh, no, I wasn't... I didn't mean that I would be a bad mom. I mean I'm *not* going to be a mom."

Josh blinked at her several times. His expression was a mix of confusion and shock, which she didn't understand. Finally, he asked, "What? Why not?"

Audrey couldn't believe that Josh was asking her that. But then she realized that they may not have ever discussed whether or not they wanted kids before, just like they'd never discussed her dating life?

No, they'd *definitely* talked about kids because she remembered Josh saying that he wasn't going to be a dad.

He'd never given his reasons for not being a father, but she guessed she just assumed that his were the same as hers. Now that she thought about it, she might have been so happy to hear that he didn't want kids, that she never told him how she felt about the topic.

So, she did now. "I don't want kids."

"What? Why not?" he repeated, still looking at her in disbelief.

Audrey lifted her shoulder in a shrug, suddenly feeling judged. So many people assumed that every person who had ovaries wanted to reproduce. She tried to avoid the topic as much as possible, because people either dismissed her stance telling her that when "she met the right man she'd change her mind." Or she'd even had people go as far as to accuse her of being selfish for her choice.

"I just…never have. Not even when I was little. You know how the girls were playing with their baby dolls tonight? They were feeding them, changing their diapers, and treating them just like Braydon."

He nodded.

"Well, I inherited *all* my sisters' baby dolls and Viv says I never had any interest in playing with them like they were my babies. I used to read to them. I would pretend they were patients and I was a doctor. Sometimes they were clients at my beauty salon, or customers at my grocery store. But mostly, I just used markers and painted their faces like dogs and cats and pretended they were animals."

Josh was staring at Audrey like she was speaking a foreign language. "So, you don't want a family?"

"I mean, yes, I do want a family. I want to get married and adopt all the rescue animals in the world. I want to be an amazing aunt and sister, and wife, and friend. Family doesn't just mean having kids, Josh."

"No…" He shook his head. "I know that… I just

meant…I don't know, you're just so caring and nurturing and you started that program with preschoolers and kindergartners going to the senior center, and you read to kids at the library, and don't you work in the nursery at church?"

She nodded but wondered how he would know that she volunteered at the nursery at church. She'd never seen him there. But then again, this was Hope Falls.

"And tonight with the kids…" He motioned his arm toward the bedroom where all the kids were asleep, and she could see just how confused he was.

"I love kids. I do. But I also love my alone time. I love quiet. I love sleep. I love being able to make my own schedule. I love volunteering. And I just, honestly, I've never even *considered* becoming a parent. I *have* seriously considered becoming a nun, but never a mom."

He stared at her, and she felt like she had to defend herself. She never expected him, of all people, to be judgmental of her decision. Josh was the least judgmental person Audrey had ever met. He just accepted people, flaws and all. He'd told her that growing up, he'd felt like an outsider in town, because of his mom's mental health issues and his father's alcoholism. So she'd always attributed his open-mindedness to him not wanting other people to feel different.

But now, it was hard not to feel like he was looking at her differently than he had.

"What about *you*?" She turned the tables. "You're great with kids. I mean, they love you! Why don't you want to be a dad?"

His expression hardened. "I knew it was never in the cards for me."

"Why?" She crossed her arms in a defensive stance. "Because you don't *do* relationships?"

She'd never had a conversation with Josh that was this confrontational. She'd truly only had one confrontational conversation in her entire life. It had been with her sister Grace when she was going to let the love of her life walk away because she didn't think she was good enough for him. That conversation had to happen, and so did this one.

His shoulders dropped. "I got in a dirt bike accident when I was fifteen and there was...damage done." Josh lifted his arms and ran his fingers through his hair. As sexy as it was to see the inner side of his biceps when he did, she knew she was only getting the gun show because he was frustrated, and she felt bad that she had pushed him.

"Sorry, it's none of my business—"

"Yes, it is." He dropped his arms and stared at her. The intensity in his eyes sucked all of the oxygen out of the room. Or at least that's what it felt like. "Even if the accident hadn't happened, I don't think it would be responsible for me to have kids."

"Because the world is overpopulated?" she guessed. She'd heard people say that before, but she doubted that would be Josh's reason.

It turned out it wasn't.

"No." He grinned and seeing his face soften caused her entire body to relax. She hadn't even realized how tense she'd been, or that she had crossed her arms. She unfolded them and leaned on the couch that was behind her in a more relaxed position. "Not because the world is overpopulated. Because I wouldn't wish my genetics on my worst enemy."

Audrey felt her face scrunch up as she asked, "What are you talking about? You are ridiculously hot!" As soon as the words flew out of her mouth, she felt her cheeks flush.

He glanced down to the ground as a smile spread on

his face. She hadn't meant to blurt that statement out, and she was still embarrassed that she'd done it, but if it made him smile like that, then it was worth it.

"You think so, huh?"

"Yeah." She nodded.

"Well, I wasn't talking about those genes, but thanks."

He was standing so close to her. She wasn't even sure if he knew how close he was standing.

He reached up and brushed his thumb along her jawline. "I think you are ridiculously hot, too."

She felt herself holding her breath as his face lowered down. She had a feeling that if she didn't do anything, he would press his lips to her forehead and give her a hug. As much as she loved forehead kisses, she wanted more.

So she took it.

She lifted up on her toes and pressed her lips to his. At first, he didn't move. Neither of them did. She hadn't kissed anyone in a long time, so she was out of practice, but she was pretty sure that there was supposed to be some movement.

All she could hear in her head was the whooshing sound of her heartbeat and a high ringing noise. She felt lightheaded and dizzy. Was she going to pass out?

The next thing she knew one of Josh's hands wrapped around her neck, he tilted it back and his tongue swept inside her mouth. That's when she exhaled and realized that she'd been holding her breath that entire time.

Once she was receiving oxygen again, she allowed herself to melt into the kiss that Josh had thankfully taken over. His lips brushed against hers, and his tongue licked along her upper and lower lip. Then it would sweep into her mouth before he would back off again. He alternated sucking her top and bottom lip between his and he even lightly bit her as he did.

The kiss swept her away to another dimension. She felt like she was floating. Like the world around her was all fake and this was her only reality.

She heard a soft whimper and thought that it was coming from her. But when he broke the kiss, she realized it wasn't her that was making the noise. It was Braydon who was apparently awake.

Josh rested his forehead against hers as they both tried to catch their breath. After a few seconds he gritted out, "I have to go get him."

She nodded and he pressed one more kiss to her lips before turning and heading down the hall. As she watched him go her fingers lifted to her mouth. Her lips were tingling and it felt like every cell in her body was alive with sensation.

If he could make her feel that much from a kiss... what else could he do?

16

Audrey turned off the lights of Brewed Awakenings and sighed with contentment as she locked up the back door. She was proud of her business, and she knew that her late mom would be, too.

Cora Wells was a vibrant, full of life, force to be reckoned with. She'd done everything she could to instill in Audrey and her sisters that life was for living and each day was a gift. Before she got sick, no matter how bad things were, and as a single mom of four daughters whose husband left when the girls were five, four, three, and two, making her a single parent, things were not always good. But Audrey remembered her mom always said, "*If you're breathing, have a roof over your head, and food in your belly, you had it better than a lot of people and should be grateful.*"

Once she got sick, her mom didn't lose her positive outlook. Instead of giving up, she focused on preparing the girls for a future without her. She did everything she could to instill in them that there was no use feeling sorry for yourself under any circumstance. "*Life doesn't owe anyone anything, it's up to you to make your life what you want.*" She wanted her daughters to be fearless. To go after what they wanted. Not to take the future for granted.

Professionally, that's exactly what Audrey had done. She'd wanted to move to Hope Falls after graduation, and she had. She wanted to own her own business, and with the help of her sisters she'd opened a coffee shop without having any experience in food service or running a business. She'd gone after the life she wanted.

Personally, however, was a totally different story. She'd let eight years go by without telling Josh how she felt about him or what she wanted, and she knew that her mother would be so disappointed in her. She could join the club because Audrey was disappointed in herself.

But just like Carly's poem said she'd taken steps in the past week. She'd told Josh that she wanted him to be her first. She'd kissed him. Twice. Once had just been on the cheek, but the other had been smack dab on the mouth.

Sure, things hadn't exactly played out how she'd wanted them to. When Braydon woke up the mood was sort of shattered. She'd stayed and made a bottle for him, but then she'd gone home. She'd gone back the next day to help with the kiddos after she got off work, but she'd left when Josh had put them to bed.

Partly because he looked as exhausted as she felt, and partly because she'd been too chicken to be alone with him. She knew the next time they were alone together, she needed to lay *all* of her cards on the table. And that's exactly what she planned on doing…tomorrow.

She'd do it tonight, but she had to go see a man about a cabin. That wasn't a euphemism. Viv had asked her to go meet with the owner of a new spa retreat called Moonlight River Lodge. They wanted to offer several packages as part of a raffle during singles week and Viv had asked Audrey to go. Tonight, her sister had a very legitimate reason for not being able to go meet him herself. Viv was speaking in front of the city council to ask for more funds for singles week. She'd made a power point presentation and everything.

Audrey had gladly agreed to do the errand for her sister when she asked. Moonlight River was about an hour north of Hope Falls and Audrey was actually looking forward to getting out of town for the evening and clearing her head. She planned on listening to some podcasts on the drive and *not* thinking about Josh or the fact that they'd shared a kiss that would forever be branded on her soul.

Or at least that was the plan, whether or not she'd be able to keep her thoughts from drifting back to the hottest kiss she'd ever had in her life was anyone's guess.

When she walked out to the back parking lot, she intentionally did not look to her left. If she did, she'd be able to see if the bay door on the auto shop was open and if Josh was working. She knew that Claire had picked up the kids that morning, because Nonna had told Viv who told her. And she knew that Josh came in to work today because Tessa Maguire, who was married to the fire chief Jake Maguire, had stopped by and waited while he changed her oil.

Audrey kept her face intentionally staring straight ahead as she walked to her car. It was a small rebellion, but she just wanted *one* Josh-free night. She didn't want to catch a glimpse of his muscular arms as he bent over a car under the hood. She didn't want to gaze at his muscular frame beneath the thin cotton shirts he wore whether it was ten degrees or a hundred and ten degrees. She didn't want her eyes to linger on his perfectly rounded backside showcased in jeans that were worn in all the right places.

An overwhelming sense of undeserved pride flooded through her when she made it all the way to her car and got inside without sparing even a single glance in his direction. It wasn't something she should feel good about, but she had to admit, she did.

She was riding on that cloud of self-satisfaction when she put the car in reverse and started to back out. That's when her cloud evaporated. She felt and heard a loud clunking. She turned off the engine and got out to see that her passenger side back tire was completely flat.

She wished that her mom had taught her how to change a tire but unfortunately that wasn't one of the life lessons Cora Wells had given her. Audrey liked being independent and hated asking for help. The book that Carly had told her about sprang to mind. Audrey thought about the second parable where the horse said that sometimes asking for help isn't giving up, it's refusing to give up.

And thankfully, she knew a mechanic. It looked like it wasn't going to be a Josh-free night after all.

JOSH WAS IN THE ZONE. It didn't happen often. But today the parts that had been on backorder for his late father's '67 Chevy Nova had come in. It had taken him nearly a decade to finish this restoration. Mainly because he'd had to put so much money into the shop to get it back in the black that he hadn't had anything to put into the car. But after he installed the carpet kit and headliner he just had to put in the seats, radio, and gauges. After that he had the wheels and tires and then his baby was ready for the road.

When he thought back to the beginning of the project, he couldn't believe how far he'd come. He'd dismantled it, done all the body work, reinstalled the large components, then replaced the axles, and worked on the suspension, brakes, and fuel system. And he was finally at the finish line.

He was glad for the distraction. The last few days with the kids had been a lot of work and he hadn't slept that well thanks to the kiss that he and Audrey shared. He wasn't even sure how it happened. He was pretty sure she kissed him, but there was a chance his aim could have been off and he missed her forehead and hit her mouth. All he knew was one second he was leaning down and the next her lips were pressed against his.

It had taken him a full minute to get his bearings but once he had, he'd definitely been the one to take the kiss further. He'd never experienced a kiss quite like the one they'd shared. He'd forgotten where he was, who he was, and what he was doing.

If Braydon hadn't cried, he had no idea what would have happened. He could have easily gotten swept away and then what? What about the next day? Or the day after that? He couldn't lose Audrey, and that's what he feared would happen if things went too far.

His mind had just started falling down the what if rabbit hole as he reinstalled the scuff plate on the driver's side when he heard the faint sound of a quiet voice that washed over him like a cool breeze on a hot summer day.

"Hey."

He lifted his head and saw Audrey standing by the bay door. The sun was setting behind her giving her an ethereal glow. Just like the first time he'd seen her, she looked like an angel.

"Wow. This was your dad's, right?" she asked as she entered the garage and walked around the front of the car, her hand gliding over the sideboard.

"Yep."

"It's...beautiful," she breathed.

Pride swelled in Josh's chest. He knew that it was silly that the look on Audrey's face as she admired the Nova made him feel like he was Superman. But he couldn't help it. She had that effect on him. Other than Nonna, he'd never given two shits about what people thought of him. But with Audrey, he did. He wanted her to be awed by his work.

"Thanks again, for helping me with the kids this weekend." He stood and wiped off his hands with a rag.

"Sure, of course, it was fun." Audrey licked her lips nervously.

Now that he knew what her soft lips felt like brushing against his. Now that he'd tasted the sweetness of her mouth, now that his tongue had glided against hers all he could think about was wanting to kiss her again.

He wanted to make out with her like he had in middle school. He'd thought that maybe, just maybe kissing her was like an itch that needed to be scratched, and once he did it, he'd be able to move on with his life. But it was the opposite. Kissing her had been like taking a hit of the most addictive drug, and now he was feigning for his next fix.

"Um, I'm sorry to bug you but—"

"You could never bug me," his voice was raspy with desire.

She grinned and sucked in a shaky breath. "Um, right, well, um I have a flat tire and I was wondering if you could fix it. I need to head up to Moonlight River. I'm checking out a new resort up there because they want to offer a package for Viv's singles week. I would just ask if they could reschedule but—"

"I'll take you," he cut her off.

"What?"

"I'll take you up to Moonlight River," he repeated.

"Oh...no..." She shook her head and blinked the way

she did when she was flustered. "You don't have to do that. I just...all I need is my tire changed."

Seeing her reaction did not sit well with him. Did she *not* want to spend time with him? That was a first. Audrey always seemed happy to spend time with him. Had he damaged his friendship with her being a weirdo the past few weeks?

He grinned, hoping to disguise the sting of rejection he felt with charm. "Sooooo, you're saying you *don't* want me to take you up to Moonlight River?"

Her eyes widened and she shook her head. "No. I didn't mean that. I just don't want to take up your time. You're obviously busy and it's like an hour drive each way."

He wasn't sure if she meant what she was saying or if she really didn't want him to go, but to be honest he didn't care. He didn't want her driving up in the mountains when it was going to be dark in an hour meeting some guy about to show her around his resort.

Since offering wasn't working, he figured he'd try a different tactic. "A drive out of town actually sounds nice. Plus, I want to see how well Thor does on the mountain roads and make sure he doesn't get car sick." He motioned to Thor who was standing beside her.

As if on cue, Thor looked up at her giving her his biggest puppy dog eyes and whined.

She smiled down at him then looked up at Josh and her shoulders lifted in a shrug. "Then I guess, it's a road trip."

17

WAS THIS ACTUALLY HAPPENING?

One minute she was asking Josh to change her tire and the next they were climbing into his truck. They'd been on the road for about half an hour, and they'd barely said two words to each other. That wasn't unusual for them. He was a quiet person and so was she. Neither of them felt the need to fill the silence every minute they were in each other's company.

But usually, their silence was because they didn't have anything to say not because they were avoiding things that needed to be said. That's what she felt was happening now. At least on her part.

She needed to bring up the confession she'd made at dinner. The statement she'd made after the motorcycle ride. And the kiss that she'd planted on him at his house.

And she would. But not now. She would bring it up on the drive home. She'd had it all planned out. When they were headed back home and passed Coyote Junction, which was about twenty minutes outside of Hope Falls, she'd tell him that they needed to talk. She'd explain that

175

she had feelings for him and that she totally understood if they weren't reciprocated. She'd tell him that the most important thing to her was that they didn't ruin their friendship but that she had to be honest with him about her feelings and that she hoped he would be honest with her, too. Since she had zero experience with any sort of relationship "talks" she really hoped she didn't make a fool out of herself.

Audrey let out a silent exhale as she looked down at Thor's head, which was lying on her lap, and ran her hand over the top of it. He was curled up on the bench seat between them the same way he'd been when they left the shelter the night that Josh adopted him. She still couldn't believe what an instant connection Thor and Josh had had. Actually, she could. That's exactly how she'd felt about Josh the first time she'd seen him.

She was four years old at the time. It was the first time their mom had brought them to Hope Falls for their summer vacation. Their mom took her and her sisters down to the Riverside Recreation Area for the Fourth of July. Audrey remembered that the place was packed with crowds gathered to watch the fireworks. Somehow, someway, she became separated from her sisters and her mom and got lost in the crowd right before the fireworks started.

The whole thing was sort of blurry in her mind. But from what she remembered one second, she'd been holding Viv's hand and the next she was in a sea of people and there were bright lights and loud explosions going off.

She remembered standing frozen in fear as a stream of huge tears fell down her face. Then, a boy walked up to her and asked her if she was okay. She shook her head and he asked where her mom or dad was. That question made her cry even worse. She could still picture his face looking down at her as bright colorful bursts of light exploded behind his head. Even then she'd thought that he had kind eyes.

He bent down and said, "*My name's Josh. What's your name?*"

Audrey hesitated to answer because she wasn't supposed to talk to strangers. But then he smiled at her, and she just knew that she was safe. She told him her name right as another firework exploded. She must have flinched when it did because he took the sunglasses that were hanging off the collar of his T-shirt *Miami Vice* style and put them on her face. He explained to her that they were superhero glasses, and they'd make her brave. Then he asked her if she wanted to go find her mom. She sniffed back tears and nodded.

He held her hand and guided her through the crowd. She had no concept of how long it took to find her mom, but she did remember her mom crying and thanking Josh when they were finally reunited. He was her hero that night. Just like he'd been Thor's hero the night of the thunderstorm.

Out of her peripheral vision she noticed Josh glance over at her. "You're quiet tonight."

"Sorry." She looked down at Thor as she ran her hand over his head. "I was just thinking…"

"About what?"

Damn. Should she lie? Was it weird that she was thinking of the first time they met? Screw it. Before anything else, Josh was her friend. If she couldn't be honest with him, what was the point of any of this?

She turned her head toward him. "I was just thinking about the first time we met. On the Fourth of July."

A small grin lifted on Josh's face. "You were so *little*."

Crap. The last thing she wanted was for him to be

thinking about her as young. She wasn't little anymore. Was that why he wasn't interested in her? Did he think of her as that little girl? She was a thirty-two-year-old woman.

"But you were trying to be so *brave*," he continued.

"You gave me your sunglasses." She still had his glasses on her dresser. They were a pair knockoff Oakley's that had been popular at the time. "You said that they were superhero glasses and that they had special powers to make me brave."

"I was eight. It was the only thing I could think of to help you not be scared."

"It worked. And then you walked me through the crowd until we heard my mom calling for me and you took me to her."

"She wasn't that far away but it was so crowded down there." His eyes cut to hers and he smiled. "I can't believe you remember that. You were so little."

There was that word again. *Little.* She wasn't a little girl anymore and she would do whatever it took to prove that to him.

"I THINK THAT'S IT." Audrey pointed out the windshield.

Josh dipped his head so he could see what she was pointing at. When he did he saw that there was a cabin tucked away in the trees higher up on the mountainside. The only reason it was visible was because there was a light shining through the large windows that must have a spectacular view.

The Moonlight River Resort spanned a fairly large and very remote area. When they'd arrived at the front gate, a security guard had given them a map with a highlighted path on it. He told them that the owner Jeremy Mills would meet them up at the cabin when he finished with his current meeting, to give them a proper tour of the facilities.

Josh was thanking God or the universe, or fate or whatever had caused Audrey's tire to be flat. The thought of her coming out here, *alone*, scared the shit out of him. He followed the road they were on over a wooden bridge with a river running beneath it. They then continued climbing up the mountain for about another mile, the narrow road curved around large boulders and trees, before they finally entered a clearing and reached their destination.

Thor lifted his head as the truck came to a stop in front of a rustic cabin that Josh assumed had top of the line amenities from what Audrey had said the owner had boasted about to Viv.

They got out of the truck and made their way up the steps that led to the cabin. Thor stopped and relieved himself in the grass before clomping up the steps. The porch was oversized and had rocking chairs, heaters, and ceiling fans installed.

Josh opened the door and they walked inside and saw that the windows with lights they'd seen down on the road was an entire wall of floor to ceiling glass that overlooked the valley down below.

Both Audrey and Josh stood speechless by the door as Thor barreled inside between them.

"Wow. This is incredible." Audrey walked inside and he followed behind her.

There was a kitchen in the right-hand corner of the cabin. It had a large island that had a waterfall marble countertop. The cabinets were black and there was a marble subway tile backsplash. The large steel refrigerator was a smart fridge with screens on the doors.

They continued walking through the cabin and found a large bedroom complete with a spa bathroom and fireplace. And two more bedrooms with en suite bathrooms. There were rose petals strewn over each of the white bedspreads. All of the finishes were top of line and every appliance had all the bells and whistles. The toilet was an automatic open and had heated controls for the seat.

"It looks like a honeymoon suite or something," Audrey said as they made their way back to the front of the cabin where there was a large sitting area that faced the glass wall, a standalone fireplace, and farmhouse dining table with a wagon wheel chandelier hanging over it.

Her offhand comment had visions of him carrying her over the threshold in a white wedding dress. Nonna's ring on her left hand. He shook his head trying to erase the image like an Etch A Sketch, but it didn't work. It was seared into his memory bank.

Audrey's phone buzzed and she pulled it out of her purse. When she read the message that had been sent to her, her forehead creased.

"What's wrong?"

"It's Jeremy, the owner. He said that the bridge we went over washed out and he can't make it up here."

"It washed out?" They'd just crossed over it like ten minutes earlier.

Audrey turned her phone around and showed Josh a picture of water rushing over the bridge.

"What happened?" he asked.

"I don't know." Audrey turned her phone around and started typing.

If the bridge was washed out and the owner couldn't make it up here…that meant they couldn't make it back to the main road. Which meant they would be stuck here. In this cabin. Overnight.

Audrey was still typing when her phone rang and she answered it. "Hello."

"Yes, I got the photo."

Thor hopped up on the oversized couch, making himself at home. He circled three times and then plopped down.

"Okay." Audrey nodded. "Okay."

"Are you sure that…" She was silent again. "Oh, okay."

When she hung up the phone, he noticed that her chest was rising and falling in shallow breaths.

"What did he say?"

"He said that all the heavy rains we've been having overloaded the dam up the road and it broke causing the river to overflow. Road crews won't be able to get out until tomorrow morning. He apologized profusely but said that the fridge and bar are both stocked, and we should be fine until then, but we're basically stranded here overnight." Audrey stared at him for a minute and then looked down at her phone. "I need to text Viv to stop by and feed Frank and Lucy. And make sure that Frank's blanket is fluffed."

Josh was torn between being thrilled and terrified at that news. So many emotions were rushing through him that he felt his anxiety begin to build. They were stuck here. Together. All night.

His chest constricted at the thought of what the ramifications would be if anything happened tonight. For so long he'd been adamant that *nothing* could happen between them and one of the main reasons was because he couldn't have kids. Now that he knew that she didn't want kids, it changed things.

Just like finding out she was a virgin and her asking him to be her first had changed things.

But for some reason, he was still scared. Mainly because he didn't want to do something that couldn't be undone. Once you cross that line of intimacy with someone there is no going back, and also because he wasn't even sure he could do it if he wanted to.

So where did that leave them?

He didn't have any of those answers, but one thing he did know was that neither of them had had dinner. He might not have control of anything else tonight, but he could make sure they ate.

When Audrey finished texting her sister, she looked up at him and he noticed she was biting her lower lip. She only ever did that when she was nervous.

There was an electricity in the room that hadn't been there when they'd been expecting Jeremy Mills to walk through the door any second. Now that they knew it would be just the two of them until morning, the air was crackling with expectation.

Hoping to relieve some of the tension he clapped his hands together. "Okay, well there's really only one thing to do."

"What?" she breathed out.

"Eat."

A wide smile spread across her face.

He walked over to the kitchen area and saw that Mills hadn't been lying. There was enough food here to feed a family of four for a week. After a brief inspection he turned to Audrey and asked, "Do you feel like chicken or spaghetti?"

Her eyes twinkled with delight. "Spaghetti."

"Italian it is." Nonna would be furious at him for cooking Ragu, but desperate times.

"What can I do to help?" Audrey asked.

They worked together and prepared the food. He noticed that while they did she slipped out of her shoes and put her hair up in a bun. Audrey always loved to be comfy when she was at home. Not that she was home, but this was home for the night. He also realized that she was in her work jeans and T-shirt and they hadn't brought a change of clothes because this wasn't supposed to be a sleep over.

"Can you watch the sauce? I need to run out to the truck to grab something."

"Sure." She moved in front of him and took the spoon out of his hand. When she did her ass brushed across the front of his pants and he got hard. Not rock hard, but hard enough to make his jeans uncomfortable.

Even though it probably shouldn't, he had a little pep in his step as he went out to the truck. That was the first time in two years that he'd had any movement down below when he was with a female. He grabbed the Hope Falls Effect sweats that he'd washed and had planned on returning to Viv from behind his seat and brought them into the cabin.

"You can change into these if you want."

"Sweats?!" Audrey's face lit up adorably.

The girl *loved* to be comfortable.

Josh nodded and handed them to her then took the spoon from her hand. "I got this. You can go change."

He moved the sauce off the hot burner and was draining the noodles in the sink when Audrey returned. The pot almost slipped out of his hand when he saw that she wasn't wearing any pants. She was holding the sweats and they were folded up. His eyes were drawn to her bare legs which were peeking out beneath the oversized shirt that hit her mid-thigh.

"The sweats don't fit me, so I figured you could wear them."

He forced his eyes back up to hers and he nodded, not trusting himself to speak. They were stuck in a cabin together. Overnight. And she wasn't wearing any pants. He'd either died and gone to heaven or this was his personal hell.

18

AUDREY SAT ON THE COUCH, FIRE RAGING BESIDE THEM, her legs curled beneath her, sipping on a glass of wine. Josh was on the far side of the large sectional couch and Thor was sleeping in between them.

After dinner she'd cleaned up while Josh went and showered since he'd been working in the garage all day. When he came out of the bathroom, he was wearing the sweats, but he'd put back on his T-shirt, which she was very disappointed about.

They'd played a couple games of cards and now they were watching *This is 40*.

She knew that time was slipping away from her, and she was never going to get another opportunity like this. She needed to seize the day. Or the night, in this case.

She shifted her position so she was facing Josh, took a deep breath, and summoned all of the boldness that she knew had to be somewhere in her DNA since Viv was her sister. "Are we going to talk about the kiss? Or what I told you after the motorcycle ride?"

Josh's face was still staring straight ahead at the large

flat screen television, but even from his profile she could see his expression tense. He blinked and then turned the television off and readjusted his position so he was looking at her. "Yeah. We should."

The tone in his voice caused her stomach to drop like it did when Viv made her eat at a restaurant that was one-thousand feet above street level and had a glass bottom floor. It was *not* a happy tone. It was a let's-get-this-over-with tone.

He lifted his hands and ran them through his hair. Strike two on how well this talk was going to go. If he was running his hands through his hair that meant he was stressed or frustrated, neither of which were good signs.

"I've been wanting to talk to you about this…I was just trying to figure things out in my own head first. I just don't think…I don't see how we could…"

She felt tears begin to form in her eyes. She should have known he wasn't interested in her. She's seen *He's Just Not That Into You* fifty times. If a guy is interested, they tell you. They show you. They make it happen. They *don't* friend zone you.

Embarrassment washed over her, and she stood up. "It's fine. Don't worry about it. I'm just going to go to bed." She was trying to keep it together as she rushed past him but he reached out and grabbed her wrist. It was the same thing he'd done after they went to Dining in the Dark.

"It's not what you think. I'm not rejecting you…I just…even if we did decide that we wanted to be together, I don't know if I actually *could*. Physically."

"Oh," Audrey was confused and her self-preservation was screaming at her to drop this and just go to bed. She was pretty sure she'd met her embarrassment quota for… her life in this one conversation. But still she heard herself continuing, "I thought you said that you were attracted to—"

"I am attracted to you. You have no idea how *fucking* attracted to you I am. It's not that. It's just. The last few times I've tried to be with someone, intimately, I haven't been able to…perform. I don't know if it's mental or the medication I'm on."

Audrey could see how difficult it was for Josh to talk about this. His shoulders were tense, and his jaw was tight. She could even see the vein on the side of his neck popping out. She suddenly felt like an asshole for pressing him on the subject.

"I'm sorry I said anything. Just forget—"

His hand tightened around her wrist. "I can't forget it. Believe me, I've tried." His lips twitched in a grin but then it fell, and his expression turned more serious. "I want you…so badly…" His voice was strained, and tension was rolling off of him in waves. "I just…I don't want you to be disappointed or to ruin your first time."

"Being with you could *never* disappoint me." Audrey took a step toward him and lifted her free hand to his cheek. He tilted his head, so his face rested against her palm. "Besides, I don't have anything to compare it to soooo…"

A smile spread on his face. "That's true."

She loved that they could still joke around even in this situation. She could always be herself with Josh and she hoped that he knew he could always be himself with her. She also hoped that no matter what did or didn't happen tonight, that would never change.

His expression grew more serious as he asked, "How much experience do you have? Exactly?"

The raspiness in his deep voice spread through her like cream in hot coffee. She swallowed and felt her cheeks heat. Not from embarrassment, just from the subject matter they were discussing and the intensity in Josh's stare.

"Um, well, I had a boyfriend in high school. You know about him. I've told you about him. The one that's gay now. Or I guess he was gay then, too, but yeah him." She took a breath as her heart beat wildly. She didn't want to say or do anything that might change his mind. So she tried to calm down. "Anyway, I gave him a hand job once. At prom. He kept his eyes closed the entire time, which makes sense considering I wasn't exactly his type."

"That's all that happened?" Josh asked.

"Um, yes and no. After he finished, he tried to… pleasure me but it just wasn't working so I told him to stop."

"But he touched you?" Josh's voice was practically a growl.

Audrey nodded, loving the protective stare in his eyes. "It was over my underwear. He just sort of rubbed me, but it didn't feel good so I just told him not to worry about it. That I was fine."

"What about college?"

"I told you, I didn't date anyone in college. I just… I don't know…never wanted to."

"Have you had an orgasm before?" he asked.

She nodded. "But only by myself."

Josh's jaw tensed and his nostrils flared. He stared at her for a second and she started to get scared that he was going to change his mind about tonight. She didn't want to pressure him in any way, but she did really want this to happen.

"What?" she finally asked in a strangled whisper, not being able to take the suspense. If he changed his mind she just wanted to know.

"I'm just worried because…"

"Because why?"

"If I do anything you don't like, or if anything doesn't feel good and you want to stop, just promise me you'll say so."

That was never going to happen, but she nodded in agreement anyway.

"I'm serious, Audrey. I don't want you to keep doing something you don't like because you're being polite and you hate any sort of confrontation."

She smiled loving that he knew her so well. Because if it was anyone else, she probably would do that. But if it was anyone else, she wouldn't be in this position because she never would have been that bold. "I'll tell you if I don't like something. And if I do."

Josh must have liked her response because a soft moan fell from his lips as he lifted his hand and brushed her hair that had fallen across her face behind her ear. Then he leaned forward and pressed his lips to hers. The kiss was gentle at first. But once she opened her mouth and his tongue slid into her mouth everything changed. Her hands wrapped around his neck and she let herself fall into the heady sensation.

When she felt herself being picked up, her eyes opened, and she broke the kiss.

"Where are we going?" She'd thought that making love in front of the fireplace would have been really romantic.

"I don't want an audience."

"An audie—" Her words trailed off when looked to the side and saw Thor panting on the other end of the couch.

How had she forgotten Thor was there?

She tightened her arms around Josh and snuggled her head into the crook of his neck. When she did she saw his tattoo and she pressed her lips to it. She'd always thought his ink was extremely sexy, but she'd kept her appreciation to herself. Now she could show him how much she loved it.

From the groan that vibrated in his chest, it seemed he enjoyed the attention. She continued kissing him softly, even using her tongue to lick his skin which tasted a little bit salty, until he entered the room and she heard the door shut behind them.

He set her down and the moment her feet hit the floor she felt him tugging her oversized shirt up. She lifted her arms so that he could pull the material up and over her head, which he did. When she lowered her arms back down, she was standing in front of him wearing only her bra and underwear. And they weren't even matching, or that sexy. She had on a white lace bra and black cotton underwear. When she'd gotten dressed this morning, she'd had no idea that Josh would be seeing what she had on under her clothes.

She looked up at Josh and any self-consciousness she felt evaporated. The look in his eyes as they roamed up and down her body hungrily heated her from the inside out. The way he was looking at her made her want to show him even more.

Her hands were shaking as she lifted them behind her back and undid the hooks of her bra. Once it was undone, she lowered her arms and the bra slid down her arms. As the material fell to the floor, she slipped her fingers beneath the band on her underwear and pushed it down her hips and legs then stepped out of it.

When she stood back up Josh's chest was rising and falling in rapid breaths. "You are so fucking beautiful."

She swallowed hard over the lump that had formed in her throat. She wasn't sure if it was from nerves or lust or a combination of both. For years she'd fantasized about what Josh would look like naked. The closest she'd gotten was when they were down at the lake and he wore board shorts. But that wasn't enough. She wanted to see all of him.

"Your turn."

A little grin lifted on the corner of his mouth as he pulled his T-shirt up and over his head. Even though she'd seen his bare chest before, she still heard herself gasp quietly. His torso was just so incredibly sexy. He was like a Roman gladiator or something.

Her eyes were drinking him in when his hands moved to the waistband of his sweats. She watched as he pushed them down. When he stood back up, his erection was jutting out from a patch of dark hair. It was larger than she'd expected, which worried her a little, and was a lot thicker than the dick pics that Viv had shown her. She didn't ask her sister to see them, but for some reason Viv just felt the need to share.

He took a step toward her and his mouth claimed hers as his hands gripped her hips, just like they had in the yoga class. Except this time they were naked. She lifted her hands to his shoulders as his slid around to her backside. He cupped her cheeks with both of his hands and squeezed as his tongue slid between her lips.

She rocked into him and felt his erection pressing against her belly. He continued kneading her flesh and kissing her with a passion and fire that she'd only dreamt of.

Soon she felt herself taking steps backwards and realized that Josh was guiding them toward the bed.

This was actually going to happen. She was finally going to have sex and not just with anyone. With Josh. Her brain sort of felt like it was short circuiting with all the thoughts running through it and she did her best to shut it off. She didn't want tonight to be about thinking or analyzing. She just wanted tonight to be about feeling.

When the back of her legs hit the bed, Josh's hands moved up to her lower back and gently laid her down. He lowered down, hovering above her and didn't break their kiss. As his tongue met hers in a seductive rhythm his hands began to roam over her body. She wanted to feel his touch everywhere.

His hand dipped between her legs, and she spread them apart in invitation. The first brush of his fingers along her sex sent tingles spreading down her legs. As her legs widened, giving him better access, Josh began kissing down her neck. He continued traveling lower stopping at her breasts. With the hand that wasn't occupied between her legs, he cupped her mound as his lips covered her nipple. As he sucked her nipple his fingers continued teasing the sensitive flesh of her core.

"That feels…so good," she whispered breathless encouragements as he moved from one breast to another, taking his time to place open-mouth kisses on each of her nipples. Sometimes he'd suck her into the heat of his wet mouth, other times he'd trace around her nipple with his tongue before pulling it between his teeth and biting down with just enough pressure to send a shooting sensation straight to her sex.

His fingers continued their lazy exploration of her most intimate place. He ran his fingertips along the slit of her opening and then circled it around the sensitive nub that sat on the top.

With each pass of his fingers and each suckle of his mouth on her pebbled nipples her release built. Her hips began to rock needily into his touch, seeking more contact as soft mewing whimpers escaped from her lips.

"Please," she begged, not even sure of what she was begging for. Just needing more.

Josh answered her plea by moving down the bed and settling between her legs. His wide shoulders caused her legs to move even farther apart, exposing herself entirely. When he settled into place his face was a mere inch from her damp folds and she could feel the heat of his breath fanning over her.

She would have thought that being in this risqué of a position would make her feel self-conscious. That she might feel shy or uncomfortable. But it had the opposite effect. She felt bold. Brazen. And she loved it.

Her eyes lowered so she could watch him as he ran his fingers up and down her seam before parting her folds. When he did, she felt her inner walls clench and she wondered if he could see her body pulsing with need.

His eyes lifted and locked with hers and she watched as he licked her from the base of her opening to the tip of her clit. The moment his tongue touched her pleasure nub the orgasm that had been ebbing and flowing through her reached a critical mass.

One lick was all it took to get the center of her Tootsie Pop.

Her eyes closed when she felt one finger press past the barrier of her body as he continued licking her most sensitive button. The pressure of his finger combined with the sensation of his tongue flicking over her swollen tip sent her body up and over the top.

A dizzying explosion of cataclysmic proportions rocked her body. Simultaneous bursts of ecstasy ignited setting off an earth-shattering release. Her thighs shook as the delicious sensation of Josh's tongue and the pressure of his finger drew out her climax until she was completely and utterly satisfied. Her arms and legs felt heavy as she tried and failed to open her heavy lids.

She'd used vibrators and pleasured herself with her own hand, but it was such a different experience to come apart at the hands and mouth of someone else. She felt completely and utterly spent and more than anything she wanted to return the favor.

JOSH TASTED Audrey's climax on his tongue and he licked up every drop as her inner walls milked his finger. His erection was pulsing heavily with need, demanding to be inside of her tight, wet canal, but he ignored it. He didn't care about his own release, all he cared about was Audrey and her pleasure.

The entire time he was making love to her with his mouth, one word kept repeating in his head.

Mine.

Mine.

Mine.

He was getting high off of knowing that no other man had touched her bare skin. Or tasted the sweetness of her arousal. Or felt her body shake from an orgasm. Only him.

Mine.

Mine.

Mine.

As the word kept repeating in his head and he continued to softly lick her silken folds Audrey's eyes flitted open and looked down at him, her lips pulled up in a wide smile. "I liked that. A lot."

He smiled back at her as he moved up her body and began pressing soft kisses along her hip bone and waist. He continued kissing her across her stomach and up the side of her ribs to her full mounds. He pressed two kisses on each of her nipples before moving up her neck.

As he kissed her neck, he realized something that had him cursing beneath his breath.

"What? What's wrong?" she asked.

His forehead dropped to the pillow beside her. "This can't happen tonight."

"Oh," She moved her head to the side to look at him. "Are you not—"

"No. It's not that." He shifted his hips up and pressed his shaft against her still wet sex. When she felt the evidence of his arousal her eyes widened. "We can't because I don't have a condom."

"Oh." She stared at him blankly for a few beats before saying. "Um, I've been on the pill since I was fourteen, so…"

"You have?" Josh didn't mean to sound surprised.

She nodded. "My mom put me on it when I started dating Chris, and I knew I never wanted to have kids so I just stayed on it. You know, just in case."

Even though Josh couldn't get anyone pregnant, he'd still never had unprotected sex in his life just because he didn't want an STD. The thought of being inside Audrey without any barriers between them made his balls tingle and his dick pulse with anticipation. His hips began to move of their own accord, and he was sliding the girth of his shaft along her damp folds.

"Are you sure you want to do this without protection?" he asked, just to double check.

She nodded as she bit down on her bottom lip. He sensed some hesitation in her response. "What? What is it?"

"Before we…can I just…look at you? Touch you?"

Fuck. This girl was going to kill him. First, she stripped

down naked in front of him, then she said she wanted to have sex without a condom, and now she was asking to touch him.

He nodded, not trusting himself to speak and he rolled over onto his back. She spread her hands on his chest, the light touch of her fingertips. She roamed his body with what started as tentative grazes but soon turned bolder. His dick was throbbing painfully as her touch caressed him and his jaw tensed as he allowed her to explore him.

It was its own special brand of torture lying there and being a passive participant. But this is what she wanted. And Josh wanted to give her exactly what she wanted.

Her hands moved over his thighs and back up again to his stomach, chest, and arms. He watched her as she physically and visually explored him. There was something so sweet, so innocent about her tour of his anatomy. He'd never been with someone with so little experience and it was fucking endearing.

When she closed her fingers around his dick, he felt himself surge with arousal. When she started to move her hand, it was more than he could take. He was in the danger zone. One pump, and he would come all over himself. He grabbed her wrist and pulled it up as he shifted so that he was on top of her again.

Her eyes were wide. "Did that hurt?"

"No, it felt good. Too good."

"Oh," a small, satisfied smile pulled on her lips.

He moved his hand between their bodies and brushed his fingers along her seam to make sure that she was still ready. His fingers glided easily along her arousal and he lined his body up with hers.

"Are you sure?" he asked.

She nodded as she panted out her answer. "Yes. So sure."

He pushed past the resistance of her fleshy opening, and he felt her body stretch to its limit to accommodate him.

Her eyes widened slightly at the intrusion, and he stilled. "Do you want me to stop?"

"No," she breathed as she lifted her hips up. "Don't stop."

Josh closed his eyes and tried to think of anything other than how good Audrey's body felt clamping down around him as he sank fully into her. He'd been so scared that he wouldn't be able to perform at all and now he was scared that this was going to be over before it even started if he so much as breathed. That was how fucking good she felt.

So many factors were conspiring to bring his crescendo to a premature finish. Between how tight her body was, how long it had been since he'd had sex, the fact that he'd never been inside anyone without protection, the knowledge that he was her first, and the fact that this was Audrey, the woman he loved and he was fighting an uphill battle not to erupt.

Beads of sweat formed on the back of his neck as he tried to get his body under control.

"This feels so good. You feel so good."

He eased out of her slowly but as he entered her again, her body closed around him like a vice, and something took over him and he sank into her with more force than he had the first time.

She gasped at the intrusion and her back arched up as she clung to his back.

He froze, scared it had been too much.

"Are you okay? Do you want to stop?" he asked again.

"Yes. I mean no. I don't want to stop," she breathed out, her eyes wide. Her vulnerability and rawness shot straight to his heart. "Please don't stop."

He grinned, even in this intimate moment he just couldn't help but think how ridiculously adorable she was. Leaning down he pressed a soft kiss to her mouth, and she pulled his lower lip between hers and nipped at his tender flesh as she rolled her hips against his, drawing him even deeper inside of her. Her hands gripped his shoulders and her nails dug into his flesh. He loved that she wasn't holding back with him.

Lifting up on his elbows he rested his weight on his forearms which were framing Audrey's face. The position gave him the leverage to move in and out of her wet, tight heat. Each time he pulled out and then entered her again her breath fanned his face. He loved feeling the soft, shallow pants and the sting of her nails digging into his back.

He did his best to keep the pace steady and strong. He moved one hand down her body and tilted her hips giving him a better angle so he could drive into her and go even deeper. Her canal massaged his rock-hard shaft as her inner walls began to spasm. He knew that she was close, which was good because he was about to explode.

One more thrust and he closed his eyes as his entire body tensed as a powerful orgasm overtook him. Wave after wave of pulsating pleasure crashed over him and he rode each one out. The same word repeated over and over in his mind as he lost himself in his soul claiming release.

Mine.

Mine.

Mine.

When the last crest of passion faded away, he opened his eyes and started to shift to move off of her but she wrapped her arms and legs around him tighter. "Stay. Please."

"I don't want to hurt you." He whispered into her hair.

"You're not. I just…I love the way you feel on me. In me."

His dick twitched hearing her say that she loved how he felt inside of her. If it was up to him, he'd stay just like this forever. He knew this wasn't their reality. She deserved a man that could give her the world. He wasn't that man. As much as it broke his heart to face that truth, it was the truth. But he was her first. Nothing and no one could take that away from them.

And that was enough. It had to be.

19

AUDREY'S EYES OPENED AND IT TOOK HER A MOMENT FOR her senses to take in her surroundings. The room was dark. Pitch black. She blinked and as her eyes adjusted to the darkness she saw there was a ceiling fan above her head. Which was strange because she didn't have a ceiling fan...

Suddenly everything came back to her. She was in a cabin with Josh, and she was no longer a virgin.

A smile pulled at her lips, but it fell when she heard a muffled yell. Her head turned and beside her she saw Josh's arm jerk wildly up in the air. He was breathing heavily, and his face looked like he was in pain.

Oh no. He must be having a night terror. A few years ago, he'd mentioned that he suffered from them when she'd asked him why he'd been so tired. She thought it was because he was working too much but he'd told her that it was because he wasn't sleeping well.

Always one to try and fix a problem and help, she'd bought him melatonin. When that hadn't made a difference, she got him hot tea that had a sleep aid in it. After she still saw dark circles under his eyes, she'd showed up with a diffuser and essential oils. That's when he'd explained that he didn't have a hard time falling asleep, but he suffered from night terrors and once he had one, he was unable to fall back to sleep.

His admission had made her feel like an idiot and she immediately apologized for trying to put a Band-Aid on a gunshot wound. He'd laughed and told her that she was sweet and he appreciated the effort. Then he'd pulled her into a hug and kissed her on her forehead.

Beside her Josh let out another muffled shout and his body thrashed as he flipped over on his side. Her first instinct was to wake him up, but she had no idea if that was the right thing to do. After he'd told her what he suffered from, she'd googled it trying to find solutions. But that had been so long ago, she'd forgotten what she'd learned. She vaguely remembered reading that you shouldn't wake up someone having a nightmare, or night terror.

She needed to google it again.

Moving as gingerly as possible so that she didn't disturb him and accidentally wake him up, she slid off the bed and began looking for her phone when Josh shouted again. She spun around and saw that he was sitting straight up now. His eyes were open, but she had no idea if he was really awake or if he was still asleep.

Thor was now on the bed lying next to Josh. Thor didn't seem concerned by what Josh was going through which made her think this wasn't the first time the dog had seen him have an episode.

Audrey still wasn't sure what to do. Should she say something? Should she remain quiet? If she didn't say something and he noticed her, would it scare him? What if she did say something and it made him even more agitated?

So many questions were buzzing around her brain like race cars on a track.

Josh began looking around the room with a panicked, wild look in his eyes. But then, slowly, she could see the awareness of where he was dawn on him. He still hadn't looked in her direction and she figured she should make herself known and ask him what he needed.

"Josh," Audrey spoke barely above a whisper and squinted as she stepped toward him.

He turned his head and when he saw her, he closed his eyes and exhaled loudly as his shoulders dropped. She wasn't exactly sure how to interpret that reaction. Was he upset that she was there? Was he relieved that he wasn't alone?

There was just no way for her to know, so she just waited and didn't speak for fear she would make the situation worse.

After a few seconds, Josh shifted bringing his legs over the side of the bed, so he was sitting on the edge. His feet hit the wood floor with a thud. He was still breathing heavily as he hung his head down, leaned forward resting his elbows on his knees and ran his hands through his hair.

Audrey felt totally helpless standing in the middle of the room doing nothing. Thankfully, she'd pulled on the singles week T-shirt before they'd gone to sleep so at least she wasn't naked standing in the middle of the room doing nothing. That would be awkward.

Not that this was about her. It wasn't. This was about Josh, and she wanted to support him in any way that she could. What did someone need after a night terror? Water? A cold rag? A shot of whiskey? She had no idea.

"Do you need anything?" she asked tentatively.

His only response was to reach out one of his arms.

She stepped forward and placed her hand in his. The

second their palms touched he clasped her hand and pulled her toward him. She ended up standing between his legs. He wrapped his arms around her waist and pressed the side of his face to her belly. This wasn't a normal hug, he was holding her tighter than he'd ever held her before.

She stood perfectly still for a moment, unsure of what to do. She was standing and he was sitting so she couldn't exactly hug him back. Instead, she lifted her arms and ran her fingers through his hair. His body was vibrating. Literally she could feel his body shaking with what she assumed was unspent adrenaline.

As she stood there, she tried to remember anything she could about the research she'd done. She recalled that it was mainly something that children were affected by, but there were cases where adults were as well. Normally when it presented in adults it was due to a trauma, heavy or long-term stress, or mood-altering mental health issues.

Audrey didn't know much about his childhood or his time in the Army but she did know that he'd been blown up by an IED and that is why he was medically discharged. She assumed that would be considered a pretty serious trauma. As soon as he got back home his dad passed away while he was still recovering and he had to take over Pine Auto Shop, which she thought would be classified as long-term stress. And she knew that he'd suffered from depression and anxiety which were both considered mood-related mental health issues.

Knowing the cause of night terrors, it didn't surprise her at all that he had them. It seemed almost inevitable that he would.

His breathing was beginning to slow down, which she thought was a good sign. She wished that she could do something, anything to make things better for him.

She remembered when her mom was sick, at the end,

she and Grace were her main caregivers. Ava would get too emotional, and Viv couldn't even handle seeing their mom in such a weakened state. Grace, who was the oldest, did most of the heavy lifting. Audrey, who was barely fourteen at the time, tried to help as much as she could with their mom but there wasn't a lot either of them could do except to be there with her while she endured the pain.

That's exactly how she felt now. Like all she could do was just be there for Josh. If it was up to her, she'd be there for him forever.

As Josh held Audrey tightly, she raked her fingers through his hair which felt comforting and soothing. With her in his arms his heartrate slowly started to return to normal. He'd never had a night terror around anyone before because he never spent the night with women for fear that this would happen.

He'd always assumed that he would be embarrassed if anyone witnessed what he went through, but he wasn't. Maybe in the morning, when he was thinking clearer, he would be, but right now he just felt grateful that Audrey was there.

Although he wasn't embarrassed, he did feel bad that he'd woken her up. He knew how precious sleep was to her since four days out of the week she got up before the ass crack of dawn.

"I'm sorry," he apologized as he lifted his head and looked up at her.

Her brow furrowed as she stared down at him. "For what?"

"For waking you up."

"You don't have anything to apologize for. *I'm* sorry that you're still dealing with this."

He'd told Audrey about his night terrors a few years ago, but it's not like they talked about it on a regular basis. She'd always been there for him when he talked about his health issues, both mental and physical, but she didn't bring the subject up and pepper him with questions, which he'd always appreciated. It was probably why she was the only person he felt totally safe sharing personal things with.

Caleb was a great listener, but he would always follow-up on anything they discussed. His friend would check in for status updates, which academically Josh knew was his friend's way of showing he cared. But it always made Josh feel pressured and on the spot.

And Nonna was old school. She thought the best way for him to "feel better" was to drink water, go for a walk, and eat. That was her cure for anything that ailed you. It wasn't bad advice, but water, a walk, and food alone weren't going to cut it.

She didn't believe in psychologists, therapy, or taking pills to address mental health. Her generation didn't really discuss, acknowledge, or address any sort of problems in that area. They just ignored their feelings and pushed down whatever issues they were having.

Which, he'd tried to do. Unfortunately, he just hadn't been very good at it. So, after some encouragement and a few threats from Caleb, he'd gone and seen someone. Thankfully, over the years he'd learned tools to help with his issues and the medication Dr. Lowe had put him on definitely made a difference. He still battled with depression and dark thoughts, but there were a lot more good days than bad.

"Do you have these a lot?" Audrey asked as her fingers continued raking through his hair.

"No." He closed his eyes. "Not as many as I used to."

"Do you want to talk about it?"

He shook his head back and forth. Dr. Lowe had explained to him that most adults didn't wake up when they had night terrors and if they did, they didn't remember their dreams and were able to fall right back to sleep. Unfortunately, not only did Josh wake up, he remembered his dreams in vivid detail and was never able to fall back to sleep.

Typically, he just gave up sleep once he woke up from an episode and started his day. But that's when he was alone. Maybe with Audrey things would be different.

He could feel his muscles beginning to relax, and even if he couldn't sleep, just having her next to him sounded like exactly what he needed.

"Can you lay down with me?"

"Of course."

Audrey slid back into bed, and he wrapped his arms around her spooning her from behind. Thor snuggled up against his back and he felt something he wasn't sure he'd ever really felt in his life. He felt like he belonged. Like this was exactly where he was supposed to be. Like he was home.

20

The sun was shining, and the birds were chirping as Audrey walked along the river on the way to Belles Bridal. She was meeting her sisters and Blake for Ava's final dress fitting. The wedding was a little over a week away.

The past month had flown by so quickly, in the blink of an eye, yet she felt like so much had happened in that time. And she wasn't just talking about her losing her virginity, although that was a biggie. She'd also felt like she'd been dating Josh, even if it was by default.

Between the dinner, dancing, yoga, and the cabin getaway she felt like she'd had a real relationship. But the truth was…that's not what it was.

Yes, they'd shared all those experiences, but that didn't mean they were together, or even really dating.

Case in point: It had been four days since they returned from Moonlight River Lodge. She'd seen Josh several times. He'd come in to get his coffee, he was friendly, he joked around and they had the usual banter about him paying or not. Thankfully, since he'd just changed her tire and hadn't allowed her to pay for the tire or labor, he didn't really have a leg to stand on in the gratis category.

But that was it. Everything had just gone right back to normal. There had been no mention of the night they'd shared together or even a hint that anything had happened at all. Which was exactly what they'd agreed to. She'd promised him that nothing was going to change, and it hadn't. They'd had sex. It had been better than she ever could have possibly dreamed, and now they were back to being friends.

She was trying her best not to be disappointed and to try to take the glass half full approach to the situation. She was no longer the oldest virgin in the world. Not that she ever was, but that's how she'd felt. And she still had Josh in her life. He was still her friend.

But no matter how much she told herself that was enough, she still wanted more. She wanted a full glass.

Hopefully, this dress fitting would be a nice distraction. She'd barely seen her sisters over the past few weeks. It felt strange that she hadn't shared what was going on with anyone, including Viv. But why would she? It's not like it was real, no matter how badly she wished it was.

Across the street she saw Justin Barnes and his wife Amanda with their baby who was about six months old now. They'd had a daughter and named her Parker after Amanda's late father Parker Jacobs. The couple ran Mountain Ridge Adventure and Resort which was where Audrey and her sisters and mom had stayed when they had vacationed there. At that time, it was run by Amanda's father, who if memory served, had also been the mayor of Hope Falls.

Since her own father had left when she was two, Audrey didn't really have any memories of him. But she remembered when they'd stay at Mountain Ridge she used to watch Amanda with her dad and Audrey would pretend that her own father was like him. Audrey remembered that Mr. Jacobs had a booming voice, and he was kind and caring, especially with Amanda.

She remembered telling Viv that she wished she had a father like Mr. Jacobs and Viv told her, "*Yeah, and I bet Amanda wishes she had a mother.*" Amanda's mother had died when she was young.

Viv taught her a very valuable lesson that day. It was so easy to look at someone's life and envy it, but no one's life was perfect. Everyone deals with their own demons.

Most people would probably look at Josh and have no idea the things he suffered with. The back pain, the night terrors. He looked so strong and healthy, but inside he was dealing with so much.

When the couple noticed Audrey they smiled and lifted their hands in a wave. Audrey waved back and felt the same feeling she got nearly every day that she'd lived in Hope Falls, like she was home. She loved the tight knit community. Hope Falls really was her own personal version of Stars Hollow.

I just wish Josh was my personal version of Luke, she thought as she opened the door to the bridal salon and was met with a very dramatic greeting.

"Finally!" Viv lifted her arms in the air. "You're here!"

"We close at five." Audrey looked down at her watch. "It's five-o-eight."

"I *know*," Viv emphasized as if that was far too much time to walk four blocks.

In fairness, maybe it was. She had been in her head most of the way, and when she was like that she did tend to lollygag, as her mom used to say.

"Ava wouldn't come out until we were all here," Blake

who was seated beside Grace explained Viv's impatience to Audrey.

Audrey smiled at the teen and took a seat beside Viv.

"She's here," Grace called out.

"Are you guys ready?" Ava's voice sounded from behind the curtain.

"Yes!" Viv exclaimed.

Ava walked out and Audrey's jaw dropped. She'd never seen her sister *in* a wedding dress since she never made it to the actual wedding last time and she'd lived out of state so the sisters hadn't gone dress shopping with her. Seeing her sister in this dress made everything feel more real.

Ava was getting married. Grace was engaged. Viv was barely in the shop anymore doing who knows what. Yes, Audrey knew that the past month it was because her sister had been busy planning singles week, but even before then Viv had been taking more and more time off. The writing had been on the wall for a while that her sister was going to be moving on to bigger and better things. Which was totally fair. Viv's dream had never been to run a coffee shop. That was Audrey's dream that Viv had supported.

Audrey always knew that it was temporary, even if Viv said it wasn't.

All of the Wells sisters were starting new chapters in their lives, except Audrey. As the youngest she was used to being the last one to experience things, but to say that she was a late bloomer was an understatement.

Losing her virginity had woken something in her. Not just desire, although, she was definitely feeling a lot of that. If it had been up to her, she would have spent every night since they got back from Moonlight River in bed with Josh. But sadly, it wasn't up to her and he didn't seem like he was interested in a repeat performance.

What had been unearthed by her first sexual

experience was a new determination to live every day to its fullest. She didn't want to waste any time being scared or shy. She didn't want to spend the next eight years of her life not being honest about what she felt and what she wanted.

She didn't regret waiting as long as she had before having sex. It had been perfect. The perfect night. The perfect man. The perfect experience.

But just like the theme song to *Dawson's Creek* said, she didn't want to wait for her life to be over, she wanted to know right now what it would be. Would it be yes, or would it be sorry?

If Josh wasn't even interested in continuing to hook up, then maybe it was time to let go of the fantasy of the two of them ending up together. The one that she'd been dreaming of since she was four years old.

"What do you guys think?" Ava asked as she spun around.

"You look so beautiful," Grace smiled warmly.

"You look hot!" Viv exclaimed.

"Dad is going to freak when he sees you!" Blake smiled widely.

Ava couldn't imagine the stoic Asher Ford "freaking" when he saw his bride, but she guessed stranger things had happened.

Ava looked over at Audrey expectantly, waiting for her reaction.

"It's perfect." Audrey smiled, and she wasn't just talking about the dress. She was talking about the man she was marrying and the family that they would share together. Blake and Asher were a package deal, and Audrey couldn't think of a better person to be a stepmom than her sister Ava.

Grace, the perfectionist of the group, stood and walked

over to speak to Maria who was doing the alterations. Blake started filming a video of Ava in her dress who spun around and smiled. As soon as the other women were distracted, Viv hooked her arm through Audrey's and drug her into the corner of the shop and pretended to look at the tiaras on display.

"Okay, spill," her sister whispered as she picked up one of the jeweled headpieces.

"Spill what?" Audrey asked.

Viv smiled and spoke between her teeth without moving her lips. "The cabin."

Audrey wasn't sure why Viv was behaving like this was a covert mission and she was asking for state secrets. "I left you a message. It's amazing. You should definitely raffle off a package there."

Viv's eyes narrowed and she spoke at a regular volume. "Do you think I don't know that you were at the cabin with Josh?"

That was what she decided to say out loud?! Audrey's eyes widened as she silently shushed her sister. In her experience audibly shushing someone only drew more attention to the conversation.

"How do you know that I was there with Josh?" Audrey hadn't told *anyone* that the two of them had gone to the cabin together. She had texted Viv that she was stuck up at the cabin and asked her to go feed the kitties, but she'd made no mention of Josh.

"I know *everything*," Viv responded ominously.

Audrey wanted to argue with her sister, but she couldn't. Viv did have the inside scoop on a lot of the comings and goings around town.

Then her mind started flipping through a rolodex of who else might know something and also how her sister could have found out. Audrey mentally retraced her steps.

Besides Viv, the only other person that knew she'd even been up at the cabin was Manny. She'd texted him because he was opening with her the morning she got home, to let him know she wouldn't be in until later in the morning. When she got to the shop around nine, he'd asked her if everything was okay, and she'd explained that she'd gotten stranded up at the cabin. He'd gotten a funny look on his face and said that he'd thought he'd seen her car in the back, and she said that she'd gotten a flat tire the day before and that she'd gotten a ride from a friend.

Okay. That was it. That's how she knew. Because Manny had probably seen Josh drop her off so he'd put two and two together. And she guessed that he must have mentioned something about it to Viv. Audrey had never pegged Manny for a gossip, but he had been in Hope Falls for about three years now and it did tend to rub off on people.

"Soooo, what happened?" Viv prompted.

"Nothing," Audrey responded casually.

"Nothing," Viv repeated in a tone that conveyed she thought Audrey was lying. Which she was.

"Nothing," Audrey maintained.

Viv's brows lifted. "*Nothing* happened?"

Okay, this was getting them nowhere.

Audrey sighed. "I got flat tire, so I went to ask Josh to fix it. He offered to drive me up there because he'd been wanting to see how Thor did in the car to make sure he didn't get car sick. We drove there. Got stranded. Had dinner. Watched *This is 40*. Went to sleep. Came home. That's it."

"If *nothing* happened, why didn't you mention that Josh was with you when you called me to ask me to go feed Frank and Lucy? Why are you being so secretive?"

"Are you serious?" Indignation laced Audrey's tone.

"Look how you're acting right now. Look at what you *think* happened. Now multiply that by the entire town."

Viv stared at her, and she could see that her sister still wasn't convinced.

"Josh and I are friends. That's it." Unfortunately, that was the one thing she was telling her sister that was actually true.

21

Josh drove up to Nonna's house to the thump, thump, thumping of Thor's tail wagging wildly beside him. He'd only had the dog for a few weeks but Nonna's house for Sunday dinner was already Thor's favorite place to go.

The dog was whimpering and whining as Josh pulled the truck to a stop. He checked his phone and saw that he hadn't gotten a text from Audrey. Tonight was Sunday night which meant it might be a movie night. He'd been hoping that she would reach out and tell him that she'd just baked a pan of double fudge brownies or something equally delicious, but she hadn't.

He sighed and ran his hands through his hair. He hadn't wanted anything to change between them, but he'd been naïve in thinking that would actually be the case. He was sure that some people could manage to be friends with benefits but in those cases, he doubted that one party was madly in love with the other party, like he was with Audrey.

His relationship with her had already been complicated before he'd added sleeping with her. Now, it was…he didn't even know what it was. He was second guessing himself at every turn.

Since getting home from Moonlight River he'd gone into Brewed Awakenings, like normal, to get his coffee and chocolate croissants and, on the surface, everything was just as it usually was. But he sensed that beneath the surface, there was a lot going on. The dynamic between them had shifted. When she looked at him, he could see that there was something behind her hazel eyes, he just wasn't sure what it was.

Did she regret the night they'd spent together?

Did she just want to forget the entire thing ever happened?

Did she wish her first time had been with someone she was actually in a relationship with?

Those were the questions that had been whirling in his mind like sugar in a cotton candy machine.

She'd seemed fine on the drive back to Hope Falls the morning after. But almost *too fine*. She talked nonstop the entire hour drive, which wasn't like her at all. She spent twenty minutes listing the pros and cons of buying a new espresso machine. She barely took a breath as she spent half an hour discussing whether or not she should change the logo of Brewed Awakenings before the summer rush of tourists and whether or not it would hurt the brand recognition with return vacationers.

It wasn't that he hadn't enjoyed listening to Audrey talking. He could listen to the sound of her voice every minute of every day and never get tired of hearing it. It was just that she never just rambled on like that.

There was a voice in his head that told him she was acting strangely because of his episode. She'd witnessed something no one else had and it had made her uncomfortable. But he told himself that was ridiculous.

Audrey was the sweetest, kindest, most empathetic person he knew. There was no way that she would think badly of him because of something that was totally out of his control.

That same voice had also tried to say that she was probably disappointed after spending the night with him. Not because of the night terror, but the actual sex itself. She'd been a virgin for thirty-two years and maybe he hadn't lived up to what she'd hoped sex would be.

That voice was easier to silence. He'd read her body language and felt what had passed between them. He might have had some issues in that department in the past, but with Audrey everything had been firing on all cylinders. He didn't think he let her down in that regard.

But maybe after the fact he had.

Should he have bought her flowers?

Or maybe a card?

Did Hallmark make a card that said, *"Thank you for trusting me with your virginity. It was the best sex I've ever had."*

"Ruff!" Thor barked, demanding to get out of the truck so he could go see Nonna.

"Sorry, man." Josh shook his head. He'd gotten so caught up in his own thoughts he'd totally forgotten where he was or what he was doing.

He got out of the truck and Thor hopped down behind him. As the two walked up the back porch, Josh couldn't get over how strange it was that it felt like he'd had Thor forever. Like they'd always belonged together.

"There he is! Il mio bel ragazzo!" Nonna exclaimed calling Thor "my handsome boy" as he came bounding into the kitchen.

Josh never thought he'd be jealous of a dog, but he wasn't sure how he felt about being replaced as Nonna's favorite grandchild. Thor was clearly in the top spot now.

"Ahhh! Il mio tesoro!" Nonna patted Josh on his cheek as he bent down to give her a kiss on her cheek. When he did, he noticed that her skin looked pale and she had dark circles under her eyes.

He looked around and saw that she had made spaghetti with homemade sauce and meatballs, a fresh chopped salad, homemade garlic bread, and gnocchi. "You don't have to do this every week, you know. I could cook or we could order out."

She waved him away with her towel.

He loved Sunday dinners, but he was concerned it was getting to be too much for her. It was also one of the reasons that she wouldn't agree to move into Golden Years. The residents had mini kitchens, but there was no way that Nonna could cook the same way she did in her home. He'd offered, more than once, to pick her up every Sunday and bring her to his house to make it, but she refused to cook in anyone's kitchen but her own.

"Can I help with anything?"

"What is there to help?" she asked. "It's done."

Josh grabbed a plate and filled it from the stove. He loaded up on extra garlic bread because he'd forgotten to eat lunch.

When he got to the kitchen table, he saw that it was still covered in papers just like it had been for the past month that she'd been organizing singles week. She'd been working so hard on the project. He'd heard her when he was in the garage and she was in the office on the phone with vendors haggling over prices. She'd even learned how to email, and she'd been pouring over contracts and schedules. He was going to be happy when this week was over and she could go back to just her normal forty-hour work week at the shop, and he hoped he could convince her to cut back on that.

He moved some of the papers to the side and sat down. Nonna filled a plate with spaghetti noodles and sauce which he was happy to see. Normally, she didn't eat with him because she grazed when she was cooking meals and was never hungry by the time the food was ready. But his happiness was short-lived when he saw her set the plate down on the floor in front of Thor.

Josh knew he was wasting his breath, but still he said, "He shouldn't eat people food."

Nonna waved her hand dismissively. He knew it wasn't worth arguing with her. It was Nonna's world and he was just living in it.

He twisted his fork in the pasta and had just put it in his mouth when Nonna lowered down in the seat in front of him.

"So, you have something to tell me?!" she asked, crossing her arms.

Josh had no idea what she was talking about. He swallowed and got up to grab a Black Cherry Shasta from the fridge. It was the only 'soda' that Nonna had ever allowed in her house.

"I don't think so." He sat back down and popped the top.

"So, you don't think to tell me that you spend the night with Audrey in a cabin?"

He choked at her question and the soda went up his nose. He grabbed a napkin and wiped his face. How in the hell had Nonna found out about that?

Josh knew he couldn't deny it, but he could present it in a way that wouldn't give her false hope.

"Audrey had to go to the cabin because Viv needed her to go check it out because the owner wanted to raffle off a getaway there for singles week." Josh motioned to all the paperwork on her table. "When she was getting ready to leave she realized she had a flat tire, so I took her. Then when we got there the bridge up to the cabin washed out and we were stuck. We had to spend the night. That's it."

Nonna was quiet for a moment before asking, "Why?"

"Because of the heavy rains a damn burst and flooded the bridge."

Nonna grabbed a rolled-up newspaper that she somehow always had within her reach and swatted his arm. She might be in her nineties, but she still had an arm on her. It stung.

"What?" he asked, not sure why he was being disciplined.

"Not why the bridge flood? Why did you drive her up there?"

"She had a flat tire." Josh was sure that he'd said that already.

"So!" Nonna's hands flew in the air. "Why you didn't fix it? That's what you do! You fix tires!" She pointed her finger at him. "I tell you why? Because you love her! So why don't you tell her?! Why don't you make your girlfriend?!"

He did love her. And he wanted to make her his girlfriend more than he'd ever wanted anything else in the world. No, actually he wanted to make her his wife more than he'd ever wanted anything in the entire world. But it wasn't that simple.

"You need to, how do the kids say, put a ring on it!"

"Nonna, we're friends."

"If you make her your girlfriend, I'll move to the Golden Years."

Josh stared at his grandmother, sure that he'd heard her wrong. For over five years he'd been asking, no begging, Nonna to move in there. Now, all of a sudden, she was agreeing. Well, agreeing with conditions.

"Are you blackmailing me?"

Her hand balled in a fist, and she reached across the table and knocked it against the side of his head. "You are too thickheaded to do the right thing, so I help!"

"Nonna, you can't make me being with Audrey a condition to you moving to Golden Years."

"Who says?!" Her hands flew in the air. "You want me to move, you make Audrey your girlfriend."

"Nonna—"

Nonna made the tsking sound she always did when he was little and she wanted him to stop talking. She turned her show that was playing on the TV louder and he knew the conversation was over, at least on her end.

Josh wondered if she was serious. Would she really move into Golden Years if he and Audrey were together?

No. What was he doing? He couldn't drag Audrey into this. He loved her. And if he could be with her, he would. But he couldn't. And not even Nonna bribing him would change that.

22

Audrey smoothed the sheet mask over her forehead and on her chin. She hadn't heard from Josh so unfortunately tonight wasn't going to be a movie night. Instead of feeling sorry for herself, she'd decided to do some self-care. She'd taken a long bath, put on her most comfortable pjs and applied a collagen infused, vitamin C, coconut gel mask that purported to hydrate, tighten and reenergize her skin. Which she needed.

In her twenties, her four in the morning wake-up calls and six to seven days per week schedule hadn't shown on her face. But now that she was in her thirties, they were starting to take a toll.

Once the mask was in place she went to the kitchen and grabbed the cookies out of the oven. Lucy did a figure eight between her feet as she set them to cool on a rack on the butcher block island.

From the time Audrey was a teenager, she'd baked every Sunday. It was something she'd taken over from her mom once she got too sick.

Cora Wells was an advocate for healthy eating, but she

believed in balance. Every Sunday she would bake a treat as a reward for getting through the week. But before any of the girls could indulge in the baked goodness, their mom would put on the radio and they'd all have a dance party to preemptively burn off the calories. Once their mom got too ill to do the baking, Audrey had taken over. They still had dance parties, but their mom would lay in bed and Audrey and her sisters would dance around her.

That tradition was Audrey's way of keeping her mom's spirit alive. The baking, not the dance parties. She'd tried to do it by herself but dancing alone just wasn't the same. She wished that Josh was there and they could add slow dance Sunday to their movie tradition.

And actually, Sunday baking nights was how Audrey and Josh's movie nights had begun. After living in Hope Falls for about a year, she'd texted Josh that she'd made too many chocolate chip cookies and asked if he wanted her to bag them up and bring them to him the next day.

Had she been using it as an excuse to talk to him? *Abso-freaking-lutely*. And it worked even better than she'd planned. He messaged right back that he'd just left Sunday dinner and cookies sounded awesome and then he showed up with a movie.

It wasn't like they watched a movie every Sunday, but usually they did at least once a month. At least they had before all the singles week stuff had happened. Since then, there had been no movie nights. But, on the flip side, they had spent the night together and had sex. So, she guessed it was a tradeoff.

She'd just put the last cookie on the cooling rack when she heard the door. She figured it was Viv coming over to ask if Audrey could open tomorrow. Sometimes when her sister had a big ask, she would stop by since they only lived a block away from each other. Her reasoning was that it was harder for Audrey to say no if she saw her beg in person. The truth was, Audrey couldn't say no to her sister in person, in text, or probably in smoke signal. If Viv or any of her other sisters needed her, she was there.

When she opened the door, she was shocked to see Josh standing on the other side and he wasn't alone. Thor was beside him. He'd usually texted before he came over for movie night.

She smiled and the mask began to slip off her face. "Hi!"

"Am I interrupting something?" he asked.

"No. I was just…" *Depressed because I wasn't going to see you tonight so I was trying to distract myself by putting on a face mask.* "Trying a new facemask Viv recommended."

That wasn't a lie. Viv *had* been the one to tell Audrey about the mask.

She leaned over and petted Thor on his head. He sniffed her hand and started licking it, probably smelling the cookie dough. Butterflies were flitting around her stomach as she kept her attention focused on Thor.

Josh was here. At her house. And he'd shown up unannounced. That was the textbook definition of a booty call.

"Well, if you're not busy, I was thinking tonight would be a good Stepbrothers night."

Or not. Audrey lifted her head, glad that she had a face mask in place to conceal the disappointment she felt after thinking for a brief, glorious second, that he was here for an encore of their night at the cabin. Although looking at the context clues, she should have known better. Did people bring dogs to booty calls? Probably not.

"Sure, yeah. Um, do you think he'll be okay with the cats?"

The only reason Audrey hadn't brought Thor home

the day he showed up at the shelter was because she'd been worried about how Lucy and Frank would do with him.

"I think so. He's fine with Bullet and Batman."

"Oh, right, okay." Audrey opened the door and Thor walked right in.

Lucy showed zero fear and wobbled right over to meet him. Thor laid down in a submissive position and the cat proceeded to sniff all over his face. Once the sniffing was done, the bathing commenced. Lucy licked all over Thor's face and ears and neck. Thor seemed pleased as punch with the attention.

Frank was less welcoming. He sat perched on the top of the built-in bookshelf next to the television giving Thor a death stare.

"Something smells delicious." Josh inhaled. "Double chocolate chip?"

"Yep. But they aren't ready yet. They're cooling." After she double-checked that the animals were all getting along, or at least not having any issues, she said, "Um, let me go take this off."

She rushed down the hall into the bathroom and when she saw her reflection she gasped. Her Grateful Dead T-shirt, that had been her mother's, had a hole in the armpit. Her sweats were three sizes too big; they'd been hand me downs from Viv who had them because one of her many suitors left them at her house. Her hair was piled up in a messy bun on top of her head and the pièce de résistance, the white sheet mask that made her look like Michael Myers from *Halloween*.

After removing the mask, she considered changing, but worried that it would be too obvious. She didn't want to look like she was trying too hard. Usually, when she and Josh had movie nights together, she went for an effortlessly casual look. She wore cute, athleisure wear that matched.

This ensemble screamed depressed woman who had given up.

Oh well. She wasn't going to change. That just felt too weird.

When she walked out of the bedroom, she heard the click clack of nails in the kitchen. She came around the corner and found Josh with a mouthful of chocolate chip cookie. "Hey, those aren't cool yet."

He finished chewing and swallowed. "They're cool enough for me."

Audrey rolled her eyes. He was always so impatient when it came to her baked goods. That sounded like a euphemism but unfortunately it wasn't. She wished it was. He didn't seem at all as ravenous for her as he was for her cookies. Her literal cookies.

She went to the cupboard and pulled out a glass. Josh loved milk with chocolate chip cookies and brownies. When she made cupcakes, he drank water. And with oatmeal raisin cookies he preferred soda for some odd reason.

After filling the glass to the top, she handed it to him and he drank it halfway down. The two worked together to fill the plate with the baked treats and went back into the front room.

"How's Nonna?" she asked knowing that he'd had dinner with her since it was Sunday, as they walked to the front room and sank into the sofa.

"As ornery as ever." Josh picked up the remote and turned the TV on.

"Still no progress in getting her to move into Golden Years?" She'd thought that Josh would have been able to wear her down by now, but that woman was as stubborn as they came.

He opened his mouth to say something but then closed it.

"What?" she asked thinking maybe there had been some movement on that front.

"Nothing."

Audrey felt like it was something, but she dropped it. If he wanted to talk about it with her, he would have, if not, she didn't want to pressure him.

They easily fell into their routine. They watched the movie and chatted. When the talk turned to Ava's wedding, Audrey almost asked him to be her plus one, but she chickened out. They'd been each other's plus one on several occasions, but that was before they'd had sex.

At the bridal salon she'd been so amped up to take control of her life. To stop being quiet and say what she felt. To find out would it be yes or would it be sorry. But now that she and Josh were together her old fear started creeping up. She didn't want to do anything that would ruin their friendship or make things awkward between them.

She was internally battling with that conundrum as the movie credits began to roll. At the same time, they both looked down and saw that there was one cookie left. She glanced up at him and he said, "Quick draw?"

She nodded and assumed the position. They both sat on the edge of the couch with their hands on their knees and counted back from three.

They chorused, "Three, two, one."

Her hand flew down to the plate and she felt the cookie beneath her fingertips.

"Yes!" she whooped in victory when she felt his hand cover hers. He pulled his hand back, and she didn't let go of the cookie. He had much longer arms than she did, and when he lifted his hand above his head she ended up on his lap to keep a hold of it.

One minute they were both laughing as they wrestled for the cookie and the next they were face to face and she was straddling his lap. Their laughter died down and Josh lowered his arm. The hand that wasn't holding the cookie was on her hip.

The energy between them crackled with electricity. It was so thick she felt like she could cut it with a knife. She was scared to move, to breathe, to do anything that would ruin this moment, but…she was also scared to do nothing and allow the moment to pass.

23

"Audrey..." His tone held a warning, he just wasn't sure if he was warning himself or her.

"What?" she asked, her mouth barely an inch from his.

Josh had barely been able to resist Audrey before they'd shared a night together, now he had no chance. He'd tried to convince himself that if he could just come over here and be friends with her, everything would be back to normal. But now he knew, there was no normal now that they'd crossed that line.

Her innocent seduction was too potent. His feelings for her were too intense. Their chemistry was too explosive to deny.

How could he ever be alone with her and not want to tear her clothes off. He'd wanted to before, but now he'd tasted the forbidden fruit. He knew how soft her lips were and the soft sounds of pleasure she made when he was driving into her.

"We can't...I don't want to, I can't lose you." He voiced his greatest fear aloud.

In that moment he knew the deepest, darkest reason

that he'd never allowed himself to act on what he felt for Audrey. His psychologist had repeatedly told him that he had commitment and abandonment issues, but he'd basically written those comments off. He figured that was what every shrink said to their patients. Like a blanket statement to cover all sins.

But now he was thinking that Dr. Lowe might just have been right about it.

She lifted her hand to his face and cupped his cheek as she shook her head. "You won't. I promise. You won't lose me."

He didn't know if she was just saying that because she wanted to be with him tonight or if she really, truly meant it. He hoped it was the latter.

She began to move off his lap. "But we don't have to—"

His fingers tightened on her hips keeping her in place. He knew that he was sending her mixed signals, but his mind was all fucked up. He was fucked up.

She stilled and lifted her hands to his shoulders. She ran her fingers down his arm and back up again. She traced a tattoo on his neck with her fingertips. The gentle brush of her touch caused his arousal to spike. "Is this okay?"

"Anything you do is okay." His chest rose and fell in shallow breaths as his fingers clenched on her hips causing them to roll and press her core into his straining erection sending a surge of arousal to course through him. He closed his eyes as his head fell back against the couch.

As soon as his neck bent back, Audrey took the opportunity to lean forward and press a feather soft kiss to his neck. His jaw clenched as he inhaled sharply through his nose. For years, he'd had trouble feeling anything sexually. But when he was with Audrey, the slightest touch sent him plummeting toward the edge of completion.

She peppered kisses along his neck as her hands gripped his shoulders and her hips continued to roll seductively as she ground her sex against his rock-hard shaft. He hadn't dry humped since middle school, and he forgot how frustrating it was. He wanted more.

A deep growl rumbled from his chest as he flipped her over so that she was beneath him lying on the couch. He leaned down and covered her mouth with his taking what he wanted, what he needed. His tongue pushed past the barriers of her lips, sweeping into her mouth. Her tongue met his in a seductive dance.

Her arms snaked around his neck and her legs spread wider as she wrapped them around his waist. Even through the barriers of her sweats and his jeans, he could feel the heat of her sex. He broke their kiss and began trailing kisses down her neck as his hand slid beneath her T-shirt. His fingers grazed her ribs before he cupped her breast in his hand.

She arched her back as a soft moan vibrated through her. He teased her nipples, rolling them between his finger and thumb, pinching them lightly as he lavished kisses on her neck. Her body writhed beneath him restlessly, seeking more contact.

He shifted off of her and began to pull her shirt up when he noticed that she was looking at him like she wanted to say something. He stilled and she licked her lips nervously. "

What?" he asked. "What is it?"

"Do you remember when we were at the dinner and we had blindfolds on?"

He nodded as his dick pulsed painfully against the

barrier of its zippered confines at the mention of blindfolds

"Um…" She swallowed and then licked her lips again. "I was wondering if you've ever done that…you know… when you were having sex?"

"You want to blindfold me?" That had never been something he was interested in, but if that's what Audrey wanted, he'd do it. Happily.

"No, um, I want you to blindfold me."

"Fuck," he groaned as he rested his forehead against hers.

"You don't have to." She immediately backtracked, most likely misinterpreting his reaction. "I just thought—"

She didn't get her sentence out before he was standing and pulling her to her feet.

"Let's go."

He wanted to pick her up so badly, but his back had been giving him trouble so instead he drug her to her room. When they got inside, he shut the door to close out any four-legged friends that might want to come in and join the party.

"Do you have a tie? A handkerchief?" he asked.

Her lips pursed in the adorable way they always did when she was thinking. He waited as patiently as he could, but he was about to rip a sheet to create a makeshift blindfold because just the thought of her not being able to see what he was doing, anticipating what he was going to do to her next, had him about to come in his jeans.

"Um…" Her eyes widened suddenly. "I have the tie from when Viv and I were *Men in Black* for Halloween." She rushed into her walk-in closet and returned with a black necktie. "Will this work?" she asked hopefully.

He nodded and took it from her hands. He noticed her

breathing was growing more and more shallow as she watched him fold it in two.

"Do you want me to put it on you now?" he asked as the material slid through his fingers.

Her head began to nod up and down before she answered, "Yes."

He swallowed over the large lump of lust that had formed in his throat.

How is this my life? he wondered as he walked behind her. How had they gotten here? Things between them felt like they'd escalated at warp speed and also like it had taken them a lifetime to get to this point.

She stood perfectly still as he circled her and when he stopped directly behind her he saw that her eyes were locked on him in the reflection of the mirror that was attached to her dresser on the far wall.

He lifted his arms and gently covered her eyes with the material.

"Can you see?" he asked.

"No," she breathed out.

He fastened the binding in place, tying a knot at the back of her head. "Is that too tight?"

"No."

Once the blindfold was secured, he moved the hair that was falling over her shoulders to one side. Instinctively she tilted her head giving him better access to her bare neck. He leaned down and kissed the soft skin beneath her ear and she took in a shaky breath.

Reaching down he tugged her T-shirt up and over her head. She lifted her arms to accommodate him and then dropped them back down to her sides. Next, his fingers traced along the waistband of her baggy sweats. Her belly trembled beneath his touch as he slid his hands over her hips and pushed her panties and sweats down her legs. He supported her arm as she stepped out of her clothing.

He straightened and what he saw in the mirror took his breath away. He was standing behind her, still fully clothed, and she was in front of him completely nude wearing only a blindfold. It was the hottest thing he'd ever seen in his life.

His eyes roamed up and down her body, mentally memorizing every curve, every dip, every line. Perfect raspberry nipples sat in the center of quarter sized pink areolas that topped her full mounds. Her waist curved giving her a pinup-worthy hourglass shape. The flare of her full hips hinted at her rounded backside and led to long toned legs.

"Fuck, you are so sexy," he gritted out.

Her chest was rising and falling in short pants, and he sensed her heightened anticipation at what he was going to do next.

Needing to touch her, he snaked his hands around her waist, and his fingers spread out on her belly. He took a step closer to her, closing the distance between them as he pulled her against his body. She molded into his frame as her hand gripped his outer thigh.

"Spread your legs," he whispered against her ear.

She sucked in a sharp breath and moved her feet apart. Slowly, taking his time he moved one hand down her belly which quivered beneath his touch. His palm grazed the tiny bed of curly hair she had at the top of her sex. His fingers dipped between her folds, they slid easily along her wet seam.

With his other hand he massaged her breasts, moving from one to the other making sure to pay special attention to her pebbled tips. Some women he'd been with didn't have a lot of sensitivity in their nipples, but he'd noticed that Audrey did. Every time he pinched, sucked, licked, or bit them her sex would clench.

Using that knowledge to his advantage he began to softly rub his finger over her clit as he played with her nipples, stimulating two of her most sensitive erogenous zones simultaneously. He felt her arousal coating his fingertip as she gripped his leg tighter.

"Do you want me to make you come like this?"

She nodded her head up and down against his chest. "Yes."

He lifted his fingers to her lips and they parted in a gasp.

"Suck," he instructed and she parted her lips and did as he'd asked.

He moved them in and out simulating her giving him oral sex and his cock throbbed painfully wishing it was in her warm, wet mouth. After she'd coated his entire finger, he removed it and traced his finger around her nipples coating the delicate pink flesh of her areolas. He continued massaging her clit as he began rolling her now wet pebbled tips between his thumb and forefinger.

"Yes, yes, yes," she whimpered as he increased the speed of his finger working her sex button while pressing his finger and thumb together with more pressure.

He watched as her stomach contracted and her legs shook in an all-consuming climax. He watched as she convulsed in his arms as he continued teasing her to draw out her release. When her legs and arms went limp, he laid her down on the bed gently.

As he stood above her and began to undress the words he'd almost said to her a thousand times slipped from his lips in a whispered confession, "I love you."

AUDREY'S HEAD was still buzzing from her climax and the blindfold she was wearing was covering her ears, but she thought she heard Josh whisper something. She was going to ask what he'd said when she heard the very distinct sound of a zipper which meant that Josh was taking off his pants.

Her entire body vibrated with anticipation. She bit her lip wondering what was going to come next. Would he tease her or just get right to it? She had no idea and there were no visual clues to help her answer the question.

When the bed dipped beneath her legs, she felt Josh's fingers trailing along her calves. Her heartbeat sped as his touch reached her knee and he pushed her legs farther apart. Even though he'd been about as up close and personal as someone could get with her, she still felt very exposed.

She couldn't imagine doing this with anyone else, but she trusted Josh implicitly. Being laid bare in this way with her eyes covered only ramped up her arousal. Although she was at his mercy, she felt empowered because she'd spoken up. She'd said what she wanted. As much as she'd loved seeing everything that was going on, there was something so erotic about not being able to see.

His fingertips grazed her inner thighs and he let out a gruff moan. She might not be able to see him, but she could sense the intensity of his arousal radiating off of him. She loved that she affected him.

Her body quivered as his touch reached the apex of her legs, but then his fingers detoured up and over her hip bone. She felt him shift so that he was above her and she reached up and touched his shoulders. She loved the sensation of his body on top of her. The weight, the solidness, the pressure all worked together to make her feel like in that moment, she was his.

He shifted and she felt his arm move between their bodies. The next thing she knew she felt his mushroom tip pressing against her opening. She arched her back, wanting him to be inside of her. As much as she loved how he felt above her, the best feeling in the world was him inside of her.

Instead of entering her like she wanted, he teased her entrance with the head of his dick, running it up and down. She could feel her walls contracting with each pass, trying to pull him into her body.

"Are you ready for me?" he asked against her ear.

She nodded as she breathed, "Yes."

When he'd told her that he wasn't even sure he'd be able to perform the first time they were together, she'd felt honored that he'd shared it with her and had honestly tempered her expectations knowing that it might not happen.

Then once it had happened, she just assumed that if she was lucky enough to share intimate time with him again, there was a chance that things wouldn't go as smoothly. But that didn't seem to be a problem so far.

He sank into her slowly and her body stretched to accommodate him. Her mouth opened as she let out a tiny whimper at the sting of the intrusion.

Above her, Josh froze. "Are you okay? Do you want me to stop?"

"No. Don't stop."

Yes, it was a little painful, but it was also very pleasurable. She'd found out that there was actually a pretty thin line between the two. What might hurt one second felt like bliss the next. And that's exactly what happened when he continued pushing inside of her. Her body stretched and the pressure, the sting melted into a tingling intensity that spread through her entire body.

As much as she'd enjoyed being blindfolded, now that he was inside of her she wanted to see him. Since her arms were pinned under his, she moved her head trying to peek beneath it. Josh must have noticed.

"You feel so fucking good," He whispered against her ear as he slid the blindfold off of her head.

She blinked, her eyes adjusting to the dim lighting as she grasped his hips. He lifted his head and their eyes locked as he sank deeper into her body. Her lips parted on a silent gasp as he filled her completely.

He stilled for a moment, giving her body time to acclimate to him. She could feel her muscles pulsating around his hard, thick shaft. Every time her body contracted, Josh swelled inside of her causing a swirling pressure to build low in her belly.

Their eyes remained locked as he began to move. He pulled back gently and entered her again, and again each time with more force causing the pressure of her release to build.

His pace began to increase, and she arched her back as she tilted her hips up to meet his body. She was so close; she could feel herself about to come apart, but it was just out of reach. Each time he drove into her she would get right to the edge of bliss but then when he retracted it would pull her away from it.

As if sensing her frustration, Josh lowered his head and sucked her nipple into his mouth. She felt his teeth surround her pebbled nub and as he surged into her one final time he bit down. The sharp sensation shot straight between her legs and pushed her over the edge of oblivion. She gasped as her orgasm crashed over her in a glorious, wild eruption of pleasure. She rode the intensity until her body shuddered with completion.

Just as she was drifting back to reality, Josh shifted so

that he was lying on his back and pulled her with him so that she was draped over his body. Her head rested on his chest as his hand rubbed up and down her back.

"Is it always like this?" She didn't have anything to compare her experiences to, but he did. Josh had been with plenty of other women, and Audrey wanted to know if this was what it was like with them. If it was this incredible, this intense, this intimate.

"What do you mean?" he asked as his hand raked through her hair.

"Does it just keep getting better each time?" She lifted her head and looked up at him. "Is that normal?"

"No. This isn't normal. It's never been like this with anyone before." He leaned down and kissed her on her forehead and a warmth spread through her like hot cocoa on a winter day.

It wasn't what he said that made her feel so special, so cherished, so safe, it was the way he'd said it and the look in his eyes. She knew that wasn't a declaration of love, but she'd take it.

24

AUDREY TRIED TO PUT ON A BRAVE FACE AS SHE TOOK A deep breath while she sat in her car outside Tessa Maguire's house. The past week had been its own special form of torture. The only silver lining was that it had been singles week so Brewed had been slammed with the influx of tourists so she hadn't had time for the emotional breakdown she deserved.

After Josh had shown up at her house for a movie night and they'd ended up having sex, he'd stayed the night. Maybe she was naïve. Or maybe he really had been sending mixed signals, but when he'd told her he couldn't lose her, when he'd spent the night with his arms wrapped around her, when the next morning he'd woken her up by kissing her neck and telling her how beautiful she was, the very last thing that she expected for him to do was to say that he thought she needed to go to all the singles events and date other people.

As Viv would say, *what in the actual fuck?*

It had completely blindsided her. She'd just stood there,

totally speechless as he got dressed. She hadn't argued. Hadn't stood up for herself. She'd just said a faint, *"Okay."*

Because what was she supposed to do? Tell him that she was madly in love with him? Tell him that there never had been and never would be anyone else for her? Tell him that he was the only man she'd ever loved and would ever love?

They hadn't even used the L word.

Since none of those had been viable options, she'd spent the past few days going through the motions of life. She hadn't taken him up on his suggestion to date other people or do any of the events of the week. But she'd gone to work. She'd watched people flirt, and fingers crossed, fall in love.

The town was brimming with hopeful singles ready to find love. And she was heartbroken.

Her *phone buzzed and she looked down to see that it was a text from Viv.*

Viv: *Why are you sitting in your car?*

Audrey sniffed and replied.

Audrey: *Just finishing up a podcast. I'll be right in.*

The last thing she wanted was for her sister to come outside and grill her. This week Viv had been very distracted with all of the activities she was overseeing, so thankfully she hadn't seen her sister. She knew that if she had, she would have known something was wrong.

Audrey had only agreed to go to book club because tonight there was a special guest there who Viv had secured to speak at Read Between the Lines on Valentine's Day morning. It was sort of the culmination of everything her sister had put together. Dr. Vanessa Cupid who had written two New York Times bestselling books on relationships had been a huge get and Audrey wanted to support her sister. She also brought the leftover baked goods that she'd stocked up on over the week which would go to waste if she hadn't. It turned out heartbroken Audrey baked. A lot.

Her week had gone like this.

Monday night it had been double fudge brownies.

Tuesday was cookie night, she'd made peanut butter, oatmeal raisin cookies and M&M because they were the closest to chocolate chip without actually being chocolate chip. She figured it would be a while before she'd be able to make chocolate chip cookies again.

And last night she'd gotten really crazy and baked cinnamon rolls. From scratch. It was amazing how many hours were in the day when you couldn't sleep because the man you loved had slept in your bed and even though you'd washed the sheets twice you could still smell him.

She wondered if his scent had imprinted itself on her olfactory nerve. Was that possible? Could his DNA be inside of her? Well, that was a silly question. His DNA had definitely been inside of her.

Tonight, she was doing this, but as soon as she was done she was going to go home, have a glass or bottle of wine, and probably cry.

Tomorrow night, she was pretty sure she was going to go to the dance. She did love to dance, so she figured it would only be punishing herself if she didn't go.

Then, Friday was the rehearsal for the wedding.

Saturday was Valentine's Day and the wedding.

Sunday she was working a double and then she planned on taking Viv up on the offer to take a few days off. In the eight years they'd run the shop, she hadn't taken more than one day off at a time. But she needed it. And her sister had suggested it, since she'd been MIA because of her singles week project.

Audrey wasn't sure where she was going to go. Or what

she was going to do. But she needed to get away. For the first time in her life, Hope Falls wasn't her safe place. It wasn't the place where she felt happiest. Hope Falls wasn't her dream come true.

All week she'd seen people running around town with the sweats that Viv had designed with the Hope Falls Effect on it. Apparently, Audrey was immune. She wasn't going to get her happily ever after. She wasn't Lorelai and she wasn't going to end up with Luke.

Each day she thought that Josh would show up and tell her how much she meant to him. That he'd been an idiot for freaking out and leaving her house half-dressed, with his pants around his knees, carrying his shoes. She honestly thought that scene only played out in movies.

Audrey checked her reflection in the rearview mirror. Her eyes were a little red, but she could just say she was tired. Viv should buy that since she'd been the one holding things down at Brewed with the help of Manny and Carly, of course.

As much as she wanted to support her sister, she was hoping she could just do a stop by, show her face, drop off the goodies and be home within twenty minutes curled up on the couch with Lucy like she had every other night since she couldn't sleep in her bed. Last night even Frank had snuggled with her. As much as she appreciated him putting in the effort, it did make her realize just how pathetic she was that even her narcissistic cat felt bad for her.

She sniffed and grabbed the container that held the cinnamon rolls, cookies, and brownies. As she walked up to Tessa Maguire's house she saw Karina Black and Sam Holt-Reynolds seated at the kitchen table. The two women were her oldest sister Grace's age and had been friends since childhood. She remembered seeing them a lot at Mountain Ridge because they were also friends with

Amanda, and Lauren who was a realtor who her sister Grace now worked with. The four girls used to call themselves the Fabulous Four. Audrey remembered thinking that they were all so cool.

The Hope Falls Effect had worked on all four of the Fabulous Four. The women were happily married and madly in love. As was nearly everyone else that was at book club. Over the years that Audrey had lived in Hope Falls, she'd witnessed first-hand one love story after another play out. Heck, in the past six months she'd witnessed two of her own sisters.

But when it came to her own love life, it looked like Hope Falls had zero effect on it.

Karina's face lit up when Audrey entered the back door. "Ooh, are those goodies?"

"Yep." Audrey set the container down and Karina ripped into the aluminum foil like a kid at Christmas. Sam joined her and the two both went for the cinnamon rolls.

"There you are!" she heard her sister's voice behind her. "Finally."

Audrey turned around and smiled widely at her sister. "Sorry, I was listening to SmartLess. They had on Reese Witherspoon, so…"

Viv knew how much Audrey loved Reese, Sweet Home Alabama was her all-time favorite movie, so she was sure her sister wouldn't question her delay.

Viv's eyes narrowed. "You already listened to that podcast."

Damn. She never thought Viv listened to her, apparently she'd underestimated her sister.

"It's a good one." Audrey smiled with a slight shrug.

She started to head into the room where the rest of the book clubbers were gathered but she felt herself being yanked into the laundry room off of the kitchen.

"What are you doing?!" Audrey asked as Viv slid the pocket door shut behind them.

Her sister pointed her finger at her accusatorily. "You weren't listening to the podcast, and you've been crying. What's wrong?"

"Nothing." Audrey tried to step around her sister to get out of the small room but Viv put her hand on the door, blocking her exit.

"You are not leaving here until you tell me what is wrong."

Audrey didn't know if it was the lack of sleep, or the fact that she'd watched single people flirting all week, or if it had all just gotten to be too much for her to keep inside, but for whatever reason when she opened her mouth the Niagara Falls of confessions came spilling out. She told her sister everything from her intimate admission at Dining in the Dark, the motorcycle ride after dancing, her telling Josh that she wanted him to be her first, the cabin, the sex, him showing up at her house, the sex again, and finally him telling her that he thought she should see other people and her not hearing from his since he left her house half-dressed, carrying his shoes on Monday morning.

When she finished, she wasn't sure what she expected her sister to do, but staring at her blankly as she blinked her eyes several times definitely wasn't it.

Finally, Viv spoke. "You're a virgin?"

"What? No. Didn't you just hear what I said. Josh and I had sex."

"No." Viv shook her head. "Yes, I did. I mean before that. Before Josh, you were a *virgin*?"

"Yeah." Audrey wasn't sure why that was so shocking. It's not like she'd had Viv's dating life.

"But what about Chris? You two were together for like four years. Mom put you on the pill."

"Chris came out freshman year of college." Audrey knew that her sister knew that, but she figured she'd jog her memory.

"Yeah, I know but…I don't know… I just figured that you two had…you know that he was experimenting or something."

"We didn't."

Audrey could see that this news was mind-blowing to Viv. Like seeing the aurora borealis or the *Matrix* for the first time mind-blowing.

"Anyway, that's what's wrong. I'm going to be fine. I'm just hurt. I don't know why he would tell me to date other people this week." Audrey shook her head. That was the part that confused her the most. It had seemed like such a one-eighty. "I'm not going to do that, though. But I am going to the dance because, well, you know how much I love to dance—"

"Hold the fucking phone," Viv cut her sister off and Audrey saw fire starting to light in Viv's eyes. "So let me get this straight. You are telling me that Joshie boy knew you were a virgin, popped your cherry and then told you to go bang other people?"

"Viv, no," Audrey warned.

She knew that look. Whenever Viv got that look, bad things happened.

"No *what?*" her sister asked.

"Whatever you're planning on doing. No." Audrey knew that her sister was fiercely protective of her, but she was a big girl. She could take care of herself. She did not want Vivien making a scene or saying something to Josh that embarrassed her.

"I'm not planning on doing anything."

Audrey narrowed her eyes at her sister.

"I'm not!" Viv raised her voice for the first time.

"Shh," Audrey shushed her just as the door opened.

"Hey, is everything okay?" Tessa asked carrying what looked like a towel that had cleaned up wine, clearly surprised to see the two of them huddled in the corner.

"Yep. Everything is peachy-fucking-keen." Viv gave Tessa a thumbs up.

Audrey just wanted to sneak out the back door, go to her car, drive home, curl up on the couch and cry, but she knew if she did that people would talk. This was Hope Falls, by morning everyone would know that Audrey and Viv had been hiding in the laundry room and then Audrey left book club without even a glass of wine.

So instead of doing what she wanted to do, she put on a brave face and allowed Viv to thread her arm through hers and walk her into a room filled with women who had their happily-ever-afters. Instead of being jealous, Audrey decided to look around the room and take hope. If the Hope Falls effect had worked on all of them, maybe, just maybe it would work on her too.

25

"Don't look at me like that." Josh reached beside Thor to grab the spark plug gapper.

The dog whined as he looked up at him with the biggest puppy dog eyes known to mankind.

"I miss her, too," he sighed rubbing Thor's head.

It had been four days since he'd left Audrey's house in the early hours of the morning. He'd done the right thing. At least that's what he kept telling himself.

When they'd woken up the morning after spending the night together, he'd started kissing her neck and she told him she had to run to the bathroom real quick. When she did, he sat up and that's when he saw them.

His sunglasses. The ones he'd given her when he was eight years old down by the river. They were on her dresser next to some jewelry. He stood and walked over and when he picked them up, he saw pictures she had of Audrey and him. One was from three years ago when their bowling team won the championship. Another was from the time Tessa Maguire, who was a photographer, had asked them to pose for some promo thing she was doing. And the third was from Nonna's ninetieth birthday.

As he looked at the pictures and held the glasses in his hand, he realized something. Audrey hadn't had any other relationships. Not real ones. He'd always known that she had a crush on him. But seeing the evidence of her feelings was a totally different reality. That's when it hit him. She'd never been with anyone else. Never even dated anyone.

She'd obviously built Josh up in her mind for years, but she had nothing to compare him to. He knew that would never be sustainable. Even if, by some miracle, they actually did get together, how long would it last? Once the excitement and newness of their relationship wore off, once the reality of his physical limitations presented itself, then what?

It wasn't fair of him to expect her to accept him, flaws and all, if she didn't even know what else was out there. She needed to date. She needed to see if he was actually who she wanted.

An urgency washed over him that what was happening between them wasn't right. He couldn't trap her in a relationship. The thought of her getting bored and leaving him or worse staying with him because she didn't want to hurt his feelings triggered his fight or flight instinct.

He chose flight.

When she walked out of the bathroom and saw that he was getting dressed her face dropped and it took his heart and stomach with it. He hated disappointing her, but it was inevitable that he would. It was better to rip the Band-Aid off now than wait until they were in a committed relationship only to have it implode.

He'd told her that she needed to date other people and she'd agreed, which supported the fact that he'd done the right thing. If not, she would have said that she didn't want to date other people.

"What the *fuck* are you doing?" he heard Viv's voice and he lifted his head.

Viv was standing at the edge of the garage in a green dress that matched her eyes, which were staring at him like Frank had stared at Thor when they showed up at Audrey's house.

He was pretty sure Viv's question had been a rhetorical one, but he answered anyway. "Replacing spark plugs."

She ignored his response and asked, "So, what was the plan exactly?"

"The plan?" he repeated.

"You know, the plan where you pop Audrey's cherry and then tell her to go have sex with randos."

"What?" He shook his head. "No. That's not what—"

"That's *exactly* what you did," Viv took a step forward, pointing her finger toward his chest.

Josh continued shaking his head, knowing that nothing he could say would make it better, but still wanting her to understand. "I didn't tell her to go have sex with randos. I told her she should *date*. I just want what's best for her. She deserves better than me."

"Yeah." Her arms flew in the air. "No shit, Sherlock! That's fucking obvious. *No one* is good enough for *her*. But that's not the point. She wants *you*, so sack up, Sparky. Stop feeling sorry for yourself and go get the girl."

Josh could see that Viv wasn't getting his point. He tried to explain it in a way that she would understand. "Viv, she deserves someone who isn't broken. Someone who can give her everything she wants."

Viv crossed her arms. "Oh, okay. Well, then enlighten me. What does my sister want?"

Josh felt his anxiety building up and his mind blanked,

so he said the first thing that came to mind. "A family. I know she says she doesn't want kids but—"

"But *what?* You think she doesn't know who she is and what she wants?"

"No. I'm just saying that she would make such an amazing mom and—"

"Um...newsflash, Sparky, not every person with ovaries wants to reproduce."

That was the same thing that Audrey had said. "I know that."

"Do you?" Viv's eyebrows lifted so high they were basically kissing the sky. "Because it seems like you think you know what's better for her than she does."

Trying to fight the panic attack that was coming on he took a deep breath. He knew that Viv was just here because she loved Audrey, but he did too. They were on the same team, he just needed to show her that. "She's never even had a real boyfriend. And I'm...I'm *fucked up*, Viv. I just...I don't want her to settle. She needs to know what's out there."

"Does she?" Viv's voice went an octave higher, which was never a good sign. "Does she need to know what's out there?"

"Yes. That way she'll know what she wants."

"Do *you* know what's out there?"

"Yeah, I've dated peop—"

"No, Sparky, not out there for *you*. Do you know what's out there for *her?*"

Josh stared blankly at Viv, not exactly sure what she was getting at.

She waited and then said, "You don't? Okay, well, allow me to educate you. Let's talk about the guys that are *out there* for Audrey. I'll give you a few options from the winners I've dated over the past six months, and you tell me which one you think is good enough for my sister.

"Do you want her to date a guy for a month, start to really like him and then get a call from the dude's wife, who is pregnant with twins?

"Or how about a guy who asks her if he can suck her toes before the first drink even arrives at the table.

"Wait, you probably want her to date a dude who asks her out for drinks then sends her the address to a strip club because his ex *works there* and he wants to make her jealous."

"Okay, Viv, I get—"

"Oh no!" Viv lifted her hand. "I am not done. Should she date the guy who shows up half an hour late totally wasted and then proceeds to get in a fight with a statue, hit it and break his hand only to send her a text in the morning threatening to sue her for damages because she left his drunk ass crying in a fountain and didn't take him to the hospital?

"Or do you want her to go out with the guy who sends her a dick pic during dinner because he wants to be honest about how small he is?" She lifted her hands and put them about an inch apart to demonstrate the size. "Yeah, we're talking micro penis. That's something you can't *un*see."

He grinned, even when she was mad at him, she was entertaining.

"Or she could go out with the guy who takes her to a drive-in movie, she thinks everything is going great, she's eating popcorn, milk duds, and then halfway through the movie she looks over and sees that he has whipped it out and is jerking off beside her.

"Or she could always date the guy who tells her," Viv lifted her hand, her fingers spread wide, "within *five minutes*

257

of their date that he's into bestiality and asks her if she can moo like a cow."

Josh stared at Viv dumfounded. He'd always thought of Viv as this badass, take charge, woman, and she was all of those things. But he never considered that she had to deal with such losers. "He asked you to *moo* like a cow?"

"Yeah. And that is seriously just scratching the surface of what's *out there*."

The thought of Audrey being exposed to disgusting men like that made him want to put his fist through the wall. Actually, it made him want to go find her, get on one knee and put Nonna's ring on her finger. But he wasn't going to do either one of those things. Because the truth was, she didn't have experience and he wasn't going to take advantage of that just because he could.

Josh ran his hands through his hair. "I know that she has a crush on me but..."

"Eeeh," Viv made a buzzer sound. "Wrong answer. When she was *four*, she had a crush on you. Now, *currently*, she is in love with you. I would have thought the past eight years of blind devotion might have tipped you off but it turns out you're an *idiot* who has your head so far up your own ass that you missed that."

Josh was quiet, not sure what to say. "It's just...it's complicated."

"First of all, this is not a Facebook status. Second, no, it's not. It's *really* fucking simple. It comes down to three things. One, do you love my sister?"

"Yes."

"Two, are you *in love* with my sister?"

"Yes."

"And finally, three, if you were with her, would you do everything in your power to make sure she knew that?

Would you protect her? Would you care for her? Would you support her in her dreams?"

Viv was right. When she put it like that, he guessed it was really that simple. Not that he would give her the satisfaction and admit defeat. "I think that's more than three things."

"Now is not the time to be a smartass," she replied in a monotone.

Josh just stared at her.

"Okay, fine, there's no wrong time to be a smartass," she admitted. "And since you're being one then I know that you have finally seen the light and you know what you have to do."

"Do I?"

"Yep, it's time to go get your girl, Sparky."

"*Sparky?*" Josh parroted. Viv considered herself the queen of nicknames but that was definitely not her best work.

"You said spark plugs and it sounded condescending, so I went with it," she replied defensively. "Don't change the subject. This isn't about me. Audrey is headed to the dance at the community center and I think it's grand gesture time."

"No. It's not. Audrey is not a grand gesture girl."

"Ding, ding, ding. Give the man a prize." Viv smiled widely as she pointed at Josh. "That was a test. See, you do know my sister. Now take a shower, clean up, and go get her, Sparky."

If being called Sparky was the price he had to pay to be with Audrey, he'd take it. He'd do anything to be with her. Starting with telling her what an asshat he'd been.

26

"You look smokin' hot!" Viv whistled as she walked into the community center and looked Audrey up and down.

They were supposed to drive together, but Viv said that she had a quick errand to run so they'd met each other there.

Audrey still couldn't believe that she'd let her sister talk her into wearing this dress. Audrey never wore tight fitting garments, but Viv had talked her into wearing one of her dresses tonight.

Normally, Viv's clothes wouldn't fit Audrey since her sister was built like a real-life Jessica Rabbit, but this dress was a clingy material. It was a sexy take on a little black dress. It had a scoop neck, inch wide straps and was completely backless. The hem hit Audrey just above her knee which was the only reason she'd agreed to wear it, the one thing she'd never do is pull a dress down all night because it was riding up her thighs.

"You look amazing!" Audrey beamed at her sister. And she did.

Viv was wearing a halter neck forest green dress that highlighted her curves and made her red hair pop. She was a showstopper, truly.

The community center was packed, and the night had already begun with the instructors teaching the moves. Audrey had decided to skip that portion of the evening since she'd already learned them when she'd danced with Josh.

"It looks like a great turnout," Audrey commented.

"We sold out of eighty percent of our events. Next year, I'm going to try for a hundred."

"Next year?"

"Yeah, I loved doing this." Viv beamed. "I think I found my calling as an event planner."

Audrey had always known that her sister's dream was not to own and operate a coffee shop. She was so grateful that her sister had dedicated eight years of her life to help fulfill Audrey's dream, but now it was time for Viv to fly.

"Don't worry, I'm not bailing on Brewed, I just…I think I might want to start doing this on the side."

"I think that's a great idea!"

Viv's eyes widened. "Really? I thought you'd freak out."

Audrey just stared at her; she'd never freaked out in her life. Actually, that wasn't true. A couple months back she'd freaked out on her sister Grace but that was because she was going to make the biggest mistake of her life by letting a man who loved her and who she loved just walk away, but Viv didn't know that.

"Okay, not freak out," Viv corrected. "But be disappointed, which would be worse than freaking you out."

"I'm not disappointed. I'm so proud of you! This week has been a huge success. You're like the real-life Alexis."

In the show that had inspired the singles week Schitt's Creek, Alexis finds her calling in public relations.

"I am." Viv smiled widely.

"And I love this journey for you," Audrey referenced one of Alexis's famous lines from the show.

Viv pulled her into a bear hug and when she stepped back she said, "And I am still going to be at Brewed. Just maybe not as much."

"Brewed will be fine. I will be fine. I promise." Audrey knew that she would be, right after she mended her currently broken heart.

The door to the community room opened and both Viv and Audrey glanced over. When Audrey saw Mayor Walker come in, she smiled hoping to disguise her disappointment. She knew that Josh wasn't going to show up tonight. Just like she knew he wasn't going to come into Brewed Awakenings. But that didn't stop her from subconsciously hoping that every time a door opened, he'd walk through it. Or every time her phone rang or a text message came through, it would be from him.

This week had been one of the longest of her life. She used to think that pining after Josh was miserable, and it was. But this was worse. They say it's better to have loved and lost than to have never loved at all, but Audrey strongly disagreed.

In the back of her mind, she'd always thought that someday, somehow, just like Luke and Lorelai, they'd end up together.

Obviously, she'd romanticized the fictional relationship since even Luke and Lorelai's road to happily-ever-after was paved with a whole lotta drama, breakups, and heartbreak. But this wasn't a TV show. This was real life, and the reality was she and Josh had had their chance. For all intents and purposes, they'd spent the last month dating. They'd had sex, and spent two nights together, and he'd basically told her to go be with other men, which she knew wasn't going to happen. She'd been tempted to do just that, but she knew it wouldn't solve anything. Just like Lorelai sleeping with Christopher at the end of season six hadn't solved anything.

Audrey wasn't going to make that same mistake. If she dated someone else, she was going to be completely over Josh first. Which might never happen considering she'd been in love with him since she was four. So basically, for nearly thirty years.

"Okay, folks. Now that you've got the moves down, we want the ladies on one side of the dance floor and the fellas on the other."

"Are you going out there?" Audrey asked Viv.

She shook her head. "Nope. Have fun," Viv swatted Audrey's backside playfully as she walked away.

When she got out on the dance floor, she tried not to think about the last time she'd been there. Or how amazing it had felt to be in Josh's arms. Or about the motorcycle ride that had followed and the admission she'd made when he'd dropped her off.

The music started and she was paired with a guy named Jeremy. She'd seen him around town during the week and thought he was cute, but she didn't feel anything close to the way she'd felt when she'd danced with Josh.

The next song was with a guy named Locke, she was pretty sure that was his last name. He was a dentist from Palo Alto and told her she had good teeth, which was one she'd never heard before.

Then there was Steve. They were all nice guys, who were very complimentary, and Steve even had a good sense of humor. But by her third dance partner, she realized as much as she enjoyed dancing, she really didn't like strangers touching her.

So, when the song ended she tried to sneak off the dance floor. She was proud of herself for giving it the old college try and not just staying home and baking, but she knew when it was time to admit defeat.

"Okay, now it's time to switch partners," the MC announced.

She smiled up at Steve, thanked him for the dance, and started walking off the dance floor when she felt someone grab her wrist. She turned around to explain that she was leaving but then she saw who was holding her.

Josh, who was wearing a white long-sleeved shirt that highlighted his broad chest and sculpted arms. He'd shaven leaving only a five o'clock shadow covering his chiseled jaw. And he was wearing jeans that didn't have any grease stains on them and shoes that didn't have the word tennis in front of them. For Josh that was practically black tie.

Before she could ask him what he was doing there, the next song started and he pulled her into his arms.

Neither of them said a word as he gracefully led her around the room. There was so much to be said. He'd hurt her. Badly. And she wasn't going to let him off the hook just because he'd shown up looking sexier than anyone had a right to look.

But one dance couldn't hurt.

AUDREY HADN'T SLAPPED him in his face when she saw him and had allowed herself to be pulled into his arms which were all wins in his book. But she wasn't smiling. Her back was stiff as they moved together. This was nothing like the first night that they'd danced together. She didn't look happy at all. She looked upset. Confused. Angry.

And it was his fault.

"You look beautiful." She looked *fucking hot* but he didn't think she'd appreciate him pointing that out when people were in earshot. She was the epitome of a freak in the sheets and a lady in the streets and she wouldn't want him to draw any attention to her, even if it was positive.

"Thank you," her response sounded distant and formal which he deserved.

He knew that he owed her an apology, and as much as he didn't think this was the place to give it to her, he also didn't think he could let another second go by without telling her what an ass he was.

"I'm sorry, Audrey."

"For what exactly?" she asked in a clipped tone she'd never had with him before.

He kept his voice quiet enough that even the couples dancing within a foot of them wouldn't be able to hear. "For telling you to date other people. Which for the record, I do not want you to do."

"Then why did you say that you did?"

"Because, I saw the glasses, my glasses on your dresser. And there were pictures of us, and it just—"

"Freaked you out," she interjected as her eyes widened in horror.

"Yeah, but not in the way I think you think it did."

"Well, I think it freaked you out because you thought I had a creepy shrine to you."

"No, that wasn't it. It just made me realize that you had had feelings for me for a long time and that you really hadn't had any other relationships. I got scared because I thought that if by some miracle we were ever together, for real, then after the newness wore off, you would get bored. Or curious about what else was out there. I was just scared that you'd built me up into something that would never be sustainable and you would leave, or worse, you would stay and be miserable."

He stared down at her waiting for her to call him an idiot, just like Viv had so helpfully pointed out he was. But instead a crease appeared between her brows. "I'm sorry you thought that would happen, but it never would. It couldn't because I haven't built you up into something in my head. I *know* you. You're my best friend."

He should have known better than to expect her to react the same way Viv had. Just like she'd said that she knew him, he knew her. Audrey would never call him an idiot. Or if she did, it would be over something stupid. Not something real.

"I'm sorry, Audrey. I'm sorry that I've been an ass. I'm sorry that I didn't just talk to you. To find out what you thought. What you felt. The truth is you really do deserve a hell of a lot better than me."

"The truth, if we're talking about the truth, is that you are a good man. You're not perfect. No one is. But you are loyal. Honest. Hardworking. You would never hurt anyone intentionally. And you protect the people that you love. The truth is that you cheat when we play quick draw. And you sneak twenties into the tip jar when my back is turned. And, if we're talking truth then you sort of suck at bowling."

Josh chuckled. He'd only agreed to be on the damn league because he knew that she was on it. He'd never liked bowling and it actually hurt his back to play but he did it because it meant he got to spend more time with her. And she was worth the pain.

She lifted her hand and pressed it to his cheek. "And

the truth is that I love you Josh. I always have and I always will."

This was not a conversation he wanted to have with her in a crowd of people. Also, he was about three seconds from tearing her dress off of her which would probably be frowned upon considering there was roughly two hundred people there including the mayor.

"Come home with me." It came out as more of a statement than a question as he rubbed his hand up and down Audrey's back. "Stay the night."

Audrey's eyes widened. "Stay the night?"

"Yes. Stay the night."

"But what about your rule?"

"You break all my rules."

Her lips curled up at the edges. "Okay."

As much as he wanted to pick her up, throw her over his shoulder, and carry her out of the room caveman-style, he figured she wouldn't appreciate the scene. So instead, he grabbed her hand and tugged her off the dance floor. He saw Viv cheering them on as they passed by her but he didn't slow down.

He wanted Audrey. He needed Audrey. Now.

27

Audrey and Josh barely made it through the door before he slammed it, picked her up and pressed her back up against the wall. His mouth covered hers in a soul-claiming kiss that had tension curling low in her belly. There was a fire in their kiss that hadn't been there before, a passion that was just now unlocking.

She wasn't sure if it was because they'd missed each other so much or if it had to do with all of her pent-up frustration she had over being so upset this past week. But whatever it was, it was working. Maybe this is why people liked make-up sex so much.

She still couldn't quite believe that she'd told him she loved him, but she was glad she did. He hadn't said it back, but he had taken her home. It wasn't exactly a declaration of love, but she'd take it. Josh was a thinker. He did things in his own time. He had to process things, and she'd sort of sprung a lot on him lately. Her virginity. Him being the one that she wanted to take it. And now that she loved him.

In her heart, she believed that he loved her, too. He wouldn't have shown up tonight if he didn't.

Her hands roamed the strong planes of his back as he moved lower, kissing her neck. Then lower still, he pulled the strap of her dress down her arm and since she wasn't wearing a bra her breast was exposed. Within seconds his lips surrounded her nipple, and he bit down lightly on it as his tongue flicked across it.

She loved the feeling of his mouth on her, especially when it was there. Her hands moved to Josh's hair and she fisted them, keeping him in place.

Their breaths were both labored, but she heard a panting that she didn't think was coming from them. She opened her eyes and couldn't help but chuckle.

"Um…Josh…we have an audience."

He lifted his head and Audrey pointed at Thor walking in circles behind him in the entry way.

He turned back around to her and stepped back. "I'll go feed him. Don't move."

When he turned and walked into the kitchen Audrey was still trying to catch her breath as she began to slide the strap of her dress up her shoulder since one of her boobs was just hanging out.

"I said, don't move," Josh said from inside the kitchen.

She had no clue how he'd known what she was doing, but she immediately dropped her hand down to her side. She really, really liked his take charge side. But then again, she liked every side of Josh.

By the time he came back into the room there was a glint in his eye. A predatory glint that made her entire body tingle with anticipation. With each step that he took the tingle intensified. When he was within just two feet of her he reached behind his back and pulled off his shirt. Seeing his bare chest was always going to be one of her favorite views.

When he stopped in front of her his hand cupped her

breast without any preamble. He rolled her nipple between his finger and his thumb before pinching her just enough to sting which sent a shock of bliss exploding between her legs. Then he slid the other strap down her arm and removed her dress completely. As the material pooled at her feet, his hands were already back on her chest, kneading her full mounds.

The last time she'd been with him she'd voiced what she wanted asking him to blindfold her. This time instead of using words, she wanted to show him with actions.

Her hands slid between their bodies and she began to unbutton his pants. He continued massaging both of her breasts in his large hands as she slid his zipper down. Once she'd taken care of that she hooked her thumbs into the waistband of his boxer briefs and started tugging them down.

He reached between them and assisted her and within seconds he was stepping out of his pants. Her plan had been to lower down to her knees once he was naked, but before she got the chance to do that she felt her feet lifting off the floor. Instinctively she wrapped her legs around him and she felt the impression of his hard shaft against her wet panties.

In all the times that she'd hung out at Josh's house, she'd never been in his bedroom. A thrill rushed through her that she was finally going to see where Josh slept. And not only that, she was spending the night. The same feeling she'd gotten when he'd slid the helmet on her head and she'd known she was the first person to get on the back of his motorcycle washed over her, except this time it was even more exciting.

When they got to his room, he lowered her onto the king-sized bed, but before he could join her, she slid off the edge landing on her knees in front of him. She was eyelevel with his erection jutting out from a patch of dark hair.

Her mouth watered as she lifted her hand and wrapped her fingers around his thick, hard shaft. When she did she felt him pulse heavily against her palm. She tightened her grip and ran her fingers down lower as she pressed her lips to his tip and sucked him into her mouth.

She heard him inhale sharply as his hand moved to the top of her head. His palm and fingers gripped her gently as she took more of him in her mouth. She kept her lips suctioned tightly to him as her tongue slid along the underside of his shaft.

When she felt the tip of his dick hit the back of her throat she swallowed. She'd never given a blow job before but thankfully she had a sister in Viv, that spoke openly about technique and fan favorite moves. Audrey had paid attention and she felt as if she'd gotten a master class on the subject. Now all she had to do was put into practice what she'd gleaned.

So far, she thought it was going well.

When she swallowed, it apparently created a suction that felt good to him because Josh's fingers gripped her head tighter and she heard him take in a short breath. She kept her fingers tight and the suction of her lips firm. She moved her hand up and down in sync with her mouth, twisting her grip in a semi-circle as she went down and came back up and always giving it an extra squeeze when she got to the base.

Being in this position, on her knees in front of Josh as she sucked him in and out of her mouth while his hand gently guided her was so much more of a turn on than she'd expected. She'd heard women complain about giving blow jobs, it was amazing what people would talk about at a public place like a coffee house. But they did.

She'd overheard her fair share of women lament over the chore it was to perform oral sex, although they put it in much cruder words than that.

As MUCH AS Josh loved watching Audrey take him in her mouth, he knew that if she continued what she was doing he was going to come. And there was no way he'd take for granted that he'd be able to go for a round two if that happened. Hell, he was happy he was getting round one with her.

In one swift movement, he reached down, lifted her up and laid her on the bed.

When he did, she looked up at him and her nose scrunched as she asked, "Was that okay?"

"That was a hell of a lot better than okay."

The satisfied smile that tilted on her full ruby lips caused his chest to ache.

Most people didn't associate the words endearing or sweet when it came to blow jobs. But the fact that he had been her first was both of those things.

He opened his mouth to tell her that but instead said three words he'd been holding in for years. "I love you."

Her eyes widened and her jaw dropped open. He saw that her lower lids filled with unshed emotion but she sniffed it away. "Wow. I would have done that a long time ago if I knew it would make you say that," she teased.

"I'm serious, Aud. I love you. I think I've loved you from the first day I saw you when you were setting out the sign for Brewed Awakenings. I remember how much pain I was in that day and I was just...in a really dark place. And I looked up and there you were. You smiled and it was like the sun breaking through the storm in my head. You were so beautiful. So perfect. You were an angel. You were my angel and I love you."

"That's good because I've loved you from the first day I saw you when I was four years old and yes, I did keep your glasses, and I'm not ashamed of it. Because I love you, Josh. I always have and I always will."

He had so much more he could say to her, so much more he wanted to say to her, but first, he needed to be inside of her. She must have seen the switch in his eyes because she laid back on the bed and her legs parted in invitation.

Within a second, he was above her. Leaning on one elbow he started to reach between their bodies but Audrey beat him to it. Her fingers wrapped around his shaft and he sucked in a breath of air through clenched teeth as his balls tightened against his body. Her touch nearly put him up and over the edge but he managed to get himself under control.

Then she began to rub his engorged head along her damp entrance and once again the telltale signs of release began to build in his body. As much as he loved her taking control, if she kept teasing herself and him like this he was scared he'd explode before he was inside of her.

Her breaths were coming in pants now as the grip of her hand tightened. Through the cloud of lust that was fogging his brain he realized that she was concentrating her efforts to the top of her sex. His eyes opened and he watched as her cheeks began to flush. She was masturbating with his cock and it was the sexiest thing he'd ever seen in his life.

"Does that feel good?" he rasped against her ear.

"Yes," she breathed.

"Can you make yourself come like this?"

"Yes," she gasped as her thighs began to shake.

He started kissing her neck as her body began to shake and she moved his dick lower and guided him inside of her. Her walls clamped down on him, spasming as her orgasm claimed her. His own climax was a whisper away and he didn't try to hold himself back. Instead, he gripped her hip and tilted her body up so he could sink deeper into her warm, tight canal. When he was fully engulfed by her his world exploded in a jarring, pulsating release.

He let himself go, abandoning himself to the pleasure and a deep, primal groan ripped from his chest. As the climax subsided, he rolled over onto his back and collapsed in exhaustion, completely spent from utter and complete satisfaction.

Audrey laid her head on his chest and curled up against him. He pulled her tighter to him, pressed a kiss to the top of her head and said, "I love you. I love you. I love you." He repeated those three words over and over.

Now that he was finally able to express his true feelings, it was like a fire hydrant that had been popped and his emotions were spraying everywhere uncontrollably.

She lifted her head and smiled at him. "I loved you first."

"Is this a competition now?" he teased.

"Yep." Her smile widened. "And I won."

That was where she was wrong. She loved him, so he'd won.

28

———

AUDREY AWOKE TO THE MELODIC SOUNDS OF THOR snoring at the end of the bed. She wasn't sure when Josh had let him in the night before, but the canine was curled up at her feet sawing logs. It was still dark outside, and she checked the time to see that her alarm was going to go off in five minutes.

Normally, when she woke up a few minutes before her alarm she got frustrated deciding whether she should shut her eyes and try to get in every second of rest that she could, or if she should get up and start her day. Inevitably and without fail she chose door number two but would then feel robbed of the precious sleep that was stolen from her.

Today, however, she did not feel robbed and there was no decision to be made. She used her extra time wisely and basked in the glow of the night before. Not only had Josh shown up at the dance—which felt like her very own rom com movie moment—he had also told her that he loved her. That he was in love with her.

And she'd told him the same thing.

The talk that she and Carly had, came to mind, and she realized that she'd worked her way through all of the lessons. She'd taken the first step of admitting she was a virgin and telling him that she wanted him to be her first, even though she couldn't see how to get out of the forest. She'd asked for help when she'd gotten a flat tire. And she'd told Josh her feelings so that he knew he was loved.

That lesson wasn't one she'd needed to learn because she'd never doubted that she was loved. She'd grown up knowing her mother and sisters all loved her very much. But when Josh started talking about her building him up to something he wasn't and the possibility of her getting bored and leaving him she realized that he didn't know how loved he was, so she told him. That was it. It wasn't about him saying it back to her, but she was really happy that he had.

She turned her head and studied Josh's face as he slept.

He looked so peaceful with his eyes closed as he laid on his back with one hand above his head. She wished he could find the sort of peace he had when he was sleeping like this while he was awake. She hated that he had chronic pain and dealt with what he called demons.

She wished that she could save him like he'd saved her when she was four, but since she couldn't, she'd do the next best thing. She'd just be there for him. She knew that he had his doubts about her inexperience in other relationships, but if he gave her the chance, she would show him that she wasn't going anywhere.

Well, that wasn't strictly true. At the moment she did have to leave him to get to work.

As tempted as she was to lean over and give him a soft kiss before she left, she resisted on the chance that it would wake him up. He knew that she had to open the coffee shop early today, it was the reason that she'd insisted she drive herself to his house last night when they left the dance, so he wouldn't be confused when he woke up and she was gone.

Being as quiet as she could she slipped out of bed and grabbed her clothes. Her movements did nothing to stir Josh, but they did wake the other gentleman in the bed.

Thor lifted his head as she tiptoed out of the room. She gave him a kiss on the head and whispered for him to go back to sleep.

When she made it to the hallway, she used the guest bath to change back into her clothes. The entire time she was getting dressed she had a smile on her face. It hadn't dropped from the moment her eyes had opened.

It honestly felt like a weight had been lifted from her shoulders because Josh knew how she felt about him. She'd finally had the courage to tell him that it wasn't about her, it was about him and what he needed.

As she walked out to her car, she felt like she was floating on air. Like she was on cloud nine. She honestly didn't think anything could bring her down from this high she was on. She got into her car and as she was pulling away from the house she passed a taxi. It struck her as strange because normally, there was not a lot of people on the road at four a.m.

When she pulled up to the four way stop at the end of his street she glanced in her rearview mirror and saw that the cab had pulled up in Josh's driveway and a woman was getting out.

What in the hell was a woman doing showing up at his house at four a.m.?

Audrey watched as the woman walked up to the porch

and the motion sensor lights went off. She couldn't tell what the woman looked like from this distance, only that she had long blonde hair. She knew it wasn't Claire, who had short dark hair. She expected the mystery woman to knock on the door but instead she saw her reach for the doorknob.

Did she have a key to Josh's house? Why would this woman have a key to Josh's house? He didn't let people stay the night but he gave them keys? That didn't make any sense.

Those questions were running through her head when she heard a honk and realized that the cab was behind her waiting for her to go.

She pulled away and couldn't shake the uneasy feeling she had. She told herself she was being ridiculous and that there had to be a perfectly reasonable explanation for what was going on.

One that she would definitely be asking Josh for when he opened the garage today.

"Ruff, ruff."

Josh lifted his heavy eyelids at the sound of Thor's deep bark and the first thing he saw was the clock on his nightstand, it was barely four a.m. He rolled over to find an empty bed. Audrey had already slipped out. He knew that she had to open the shop this morning at five a.m. and figured she must have left to go shower before she had to be in.

He smiled to himself thinking of her face when he'd told her that he loved her. Her wide eyes and the flush that rose on her cheeks. Now that he'd said it to her, he felt a compulsion to keep saying it to her. He reached over to grab his phone to text her that he loved her but saw that it was dead.

Since he didn't have to be up for another two hours, he rolled over to go back to sleep. When he woke up, he'd go to the kitchen to charge it and text her then.

"Ruff, ruff," Thor barked again.

Josh lifted his head, realizing then that it had been Thor barking that had woken him in the first place. Thor had never woken him up before. He lifted his head and saw that his dog was standing close to the door and he wondered if it was because Audrey had left, and he was trying to tell him.

"She had to go to work, bud. But she'll be back." Josh loved that he could say that with complete confidence. With any luck, she would be moving in with him or vice versa. He didn't want to spend one more night away from her. He patted the side of the bed. "Come on. Let's go back to sleep."

Instead of hopping up on the bed, circling three times and plopping down, Thor barked again.

"Do you have to go out?" Josh asked.

When Thor barked again, he figured he better get up and let him out so he didn't have an accident to clean up. He was getting out of bed when he heard something that sounded like someone coming in the front door. Or someone trying to come in the front door. Audrey must have forgotten something. She'd probably called or texted but his phone was dead.

He grabbed a pair of sweats and headed down the darkened hallway. When he got to the front room he turned on a light as he opened the door. When he did, he saw a woman crouched over with a pocketknife in her hand who had obviously been trying to pick the lock. And not just any woman. His mother.

"Mom?" Josh asked. "What the hell are you doing?"

"I didn't want to wake you," she said as if that was a perfectly reasonable explanation as she stood and opened her arms to give him a hug.

He took a step back. "You thought breaking into my house would be better?"

Thor was beside him and when his mom noticed him, she knelt down. "You got a dog! Hi dog!"

"His name is Thor."

"Oh, what a handsome name for a handsome boy."

Josh ran his hands through his hair. He had no idea what his mom was doing here, but if he had to guess it had something to do with money. It was usually money. Sometimes she just wanted a place to stay for a few days, but even those times she'd ask for money, or just outright steal his money before she left.

As much as he wished he could turn her away, he knew that he couldn't. Even if that's what she deserved.

"Do you want to come in?" he asked as he stepped to the side.

It was strange how one minute ago, he'd felt like everything was right in the world and the next thing he knew, his entire world depended on whatever chaos his mother had brought to his front door, literally.

She stood and stared at him for a moment. "Look at you. So handsome." She reached up and patted his face but unlike Nonna the pat didn't make him feel loved and secure, it made him angry. "It's so unfair. Men just keep getting better looking the older they get, and women just wrinkle and get cellulite."

His mom was in her fifties but she looked like she was in her thirties. She was thinner than the last time he'd seen her and had a few new scars on her face and neck from scabs she'd picked. But even with those she was still stunningly beautiful. People had always told him that his mom reminded them of Angelina Jolie. She had large eyes and naturally full lips well before full lips were in style.

She walked inside and sat on the couch, making herself at home. "Your father, may he rest in peace, was more handsome the day he died than the day I met him."

Josh's entire body tensed at the mention of his dad. He'd always hated the way his mom talked about him, like he was a saint, which in fairness, to her he probably was. He'd always let her come home, no matter how long she'd been gone or what she'd been doing. She'd suddenly appear, out of the blue with no warning. She'd say that she wanted to be a family, apologize for all manner of sins, and he'd forgive her. She'd get cleaned up, and for however long she deemed to stay they'd be a family.

She'd cook, clean, and try to be a normal mom. But then one day, without any warning, Josh would wake up and she'd be gone. Or he'd come home from school, and she'd be gone. Or he'd come home from hanging out with Caleb, and she'd be gone. The running theme was she'd be gone. He never knew how long she'd be there or when or if she'd come back.

When he was young, he used to think it was something he did. So every time she'd show up he'd do everything he could to be on his best behavior. But once he got into his teens, he realized that her behavior had more to do with her mental illness and drug addiction than it did with him. And he'd been angry that his dad enabled her.

One time when Josh was fifteen and his mom showed up, stayed for a month, and then disappeared again, he'd confronted his dad about why he let her vacation in their lives. Why his father hadn't cut her out of his life. His dad just looked at him and said, "Because I love her."

His father's answer had infuriated him at the time, but

that was before he knew what unconditional love was. Yes, his dad had enabled his mom, but he'd done it from a pure place. A place of love.

"What are you doing here Mom?" he asked as he shut the door.

"I missed you."

"What do you want? Money, a place to stay, what?" Josh just wanted her to get to the point. His father might have had the patience of a saint with his mom, but he did not.

"Why do you always think I want something? Can't I just visit my only son?"

"Mom," his patience was running thin.

"Okay, fine. I need three thousand dollars and bus fair to Los Angeles."

She'd never actually just come out and asked for what she wanted this quickly before. And her answer was so specific that his curiosity was piqued. "What's in Los Angeles and why do you need three thousand dollars?"

"Rehab." She dug into her purse and pulled out a pamphlet. "Here. Look. It's legit. And they are holding a bed for me but I have to be there by noon. I know that you don't owe me anything. I know that you probably hate me. But I don't have anyone else to ask and I want to do this, this time. For real."

She'd agreed to go to rehab a few times when he was growing up but it had always been because his dad had pushed for it. To Josh's knowledge, she'd never been the one to initiate it. "Why? What's so different about this time?"

"I, um, I overdosed and it was…bad. The doctors said that when I got to the hospital, I was minutes, not hours, away from dying. I was in full cardiac arrest. If I don't do this, I'm going to die."

He'd never seen his mom take any responsibility before now, but there was no way he was going to put her on a bus with three grand. She was an addict and he knew that if he did that, she would use before she made it to rehab. So, it looked like he and Thor were going on a road trip.

29

THIRTY-SIX HOURS. IT HAD BEEN THIRTY-SIX HOURS SINCE she'd left Josh's house in the early morning and seen a woman letting herself in. And in those thirty-six hours Josh had gone MIA. She'd called and texted, but it went straight to voicemail, which wasn't alarming in and of itself. Josh's phone was often dead, or he forgot it at home.

That wasn't what worried her. What worried her was that he hadn't opened the shop on Friday or today. Nonna didn't know where he was and neither did Caleb. Audrey had been so worried the night before that after the rehearsal she'd gone over to make sure that the woman hadn't murdered him. When she got to the house she saw that his truck wasn't there and when she knocked on the door, there were no sounds of Thor barking.

There was no way that she was going to ruin her sister's wedding by making a scene, but she'd been on the verge of tears since she'd gone over to check on him last night.

"Sorry I'm late!" Viv rushed into the room like the hurricane that she was, wearing her bridesmaid dress. Her sister had been at the book event at Read Between the Lines with Dr. Vanessa Cupid. She'd worn the dress to the event because it ended right before the wedding was set to begin. Thankfully, Ava had gone with a simple, knee length, black cocktail dress for the bridesmaids so it's not like Viv was in bows and chiffon.

Ava, who was seated in a chair next to the window getting her hair and makeup final touches smiled. "No worries."

Her sister was whatever the opposite of a bridezilla was. All day she'd been the epitome of calm, cool, and collected. She didn't seem even the slightest bit nervous. Grace and Blake both seemed more on edge than Ava. Blake was just excited about her dad getting remarried, and Grace was a perfectionist so she was always sort of on edge.

After hugging everyone, and declaring Ava the most beautiful bride that ever existed, Viv migrated across the room to Audrey, who was sitting on a couch in the corner reading a book. So far, she'd been able to conceal her own anxiousness by just quietly reading, which was totally in character for her.

"Who died?" Viv asked as she plopped down.

Audrey put on her best casual look. "No one."

"Then why do you look like—" Her sister stopped mid-sentence and her expression changed. "What did he do?"

Audrey shook her head. "Nothing."

And that was the problem. He hadn't even had the decency to tell her that he was going out of town on a mini vacation with the blonde that had shown up at his door.

"Last time I saw you, you were being dragged out of the community center wearing the grin of a woman who knew she was about to have really good sex. Now you look like someone ran over your dog. There's only one reason that you'd look like that, so I am going to repeat my question. What did he do?"

Audrey looked past Viv and saw that Ava, Grace, and Blake were all distracted as they debated whether or not Ava should have a smokey eye.

"You can't say or do anything." Audrey lifted her hand and held out her pinky.

"Oh, hell no, if this is pinky swear bad, there's *no way* I'm promising not to say anything."

"This is Ava's day." Audrey kept a smile on her face as she talked to Viv so just in case either of her sisters or niece looked over, they wouldn't be concerned. "I just don't want you to say or do anything that makes today about me."

Viv sighed and lifted her hand, hooking her pinky around Audrey's. They both kissed their thumbs sealing the sacred pinky swear.

"So yesterday morning, when I was leaving Josh's—"

Viv clutched her hands to her chest and sighed as if she was having an 'aww' moment.

"What?" Audrey asked.

"Your first walk of shame. My little girl is finally growing up."

Audrey rolled her eyes. "When I was driving away, I noticed a woman walking up the steps and when she got to door it looked like she put a key in it."

Viv's eyebrows furrowed. "What woman?"

"I couldn't really see her that well, but from what I saw she was a pretty blonde." Audrey shook her head. "The point is, I haven't heard from him since. Neither has Nonna or Caleb. We've all called and texted and it goes straight to voicemail."

"Holy shit!" Viv whispered. "Did she Glenn Close him?"

"What?"

"Did she try and Fatal Attraction him?"

For once she and Viv were on the same page. "I was worried about that, too. So, I went over to his house last night to make sure that he was okay and his truck was gone and so was Thor."

"So what? He just took off with this mystery woman?"

Audrey could feel tears pooling in her eyes as she shrugged.

"Oh hell no. I'm going to kill him!"

"Shh!" Audrey silently shushed her sister but it was too late. Her outburst had drawn the attention of Ava, Grace and Blake.

"Kill who?" Ava and Blake both asked in unison.

Thankfully before Viv could reply the door opened and Monica, the day-of wedding coordinator, popped her head in. "It's time."

Audrey and Viv both stood up and followed Monica, Ava, Grace, and Blake out into the vestibule and took their places. Blake was walking first in the processional, followed by Audrey, then Viv, then Grace. Ava was waiting around the corner so no one would see her until it was her time to enter.

"This conversation is not over." Viv said beneath her breath as they waited for the doors to open.

From inside the sanctuary Ava heard the music change to the song that the wedding party was walking in to. She clutched her flowers in her hand and put on her best smile. Monica put her hand on door that led to the sanctuary when another door opened.

Everyone's heads turned around as Josh came through the double doors into the church. He was wearing jeans, a T-shirt, his hair was windblown, and he looked like he hadn't slept in days.

Audrey's first thought was relief that he was alive and

okay. Her second thought was that she wanted to kill him for putting her through the past thirty-six hours.

He rushed up to her and Monica dropped her hand from the door. "I'm so sorry. I'll explain everything after the ceremony."

Audrey nodded, not wanting to cause a scene.

Viv had no such impulses. "Where in the fuck were you?"

"My mom showed up. I had to drive her to a rehab in LA that was holding a spot for her until noon. But there was road construction over the Grapevine so we didn't make it in time. But then they found a spot for her in Arizona, but she had to be there by this morning." Josh was speaking so quickly and quietly it was hard to understand him.

"Why didn't you answer your phone?" Viv seethed.

"I forgot it at home. I'm so sorry. I would have figured out how to call you, but I was just trying to get back to you."

"Is everything okay?" Ava peeked her head around the corner.

"Yes. Sorry." Audrey apologized then looked at Monica and gave her the nod to open the doors.

"I love you. And I'm sorry."

Josh stepped to the side so he wouldn't be seen by any of the attendees. Audrey walked down the aisle and when she got up to the front, she felt all the emotions that she'd been keeping at bay come to a boiling point.

Thankfully, her emotional floodgates opened at exactly the same time the doors did and her sister appeared at the end of the aisle so anyone who saw her crying would just assume it was over how beautiful her sister looked.

She was doing her best to pull herself together when tissues appeared in front of her face. She had no idea where Pastor Harrison, er um Caleb had gotten them, but she was happy he had.

JOSH WATCHED as Audrey disappeared into the sanctuary. He stood there for a moment after the doors closed contemplating whether he should go home, shower, change and then head down to the Riverside Recreation Area where the reception was being held. Or if he should sneak in the side door and watch the ceremony.

He hoped to someday be a part of the Wells sisters' clan, so he figured it would be bad form not to witness the first of the sisters' wedding.

Ever so quietly he opened the door to the side of the sanctuary and saw that everyone was still looking at Ava who was walking down the aisle. He slid inside and shut the door without drawing any attention to himself. He saw that Nonna was sitting in her usual seat which was in the back pew on the side closest to the door he'd just entered.

She sat there so she could slip in and out if nature called during service. By the time Caleb told everyone they could be seated he was beside Nonna and lowered down in unison with the rest of the guests.

It took a few minutes for Nonna to notice him, but when she did, she smacked him on his leg and demanded in a barely-there rage-whisper, "Where have you been?"

He turned to her and tried to mouth that he'd tell her after the ceremony but the next thing he knew she had him by the ear and was dragging him out into the side hallway like she had numerous times when he was a child. Thankfully Karina Black and her husband Ryan were performing a duet that had reached number one on the billboard charts a few years ago, so no one heard the commotion.

When they were safely out of earshot, Nonna released his ear and wagged her wrinkled finger at him. "Where have you been?!"

"My mom showed up. I had to take her to rehab," he explained thinking she might understand.

"Why don't you call and tell anyone where you are? I call, I call, and it just go to your mail voice."

Josh knew that it was not the time to crack a smile, but he did think it was ridiculously endearing when his grandmother mixed up phrases like voicemail, or when she did things like call UPS ups, like ups and downs.

"I forgot my phone at home."

Somehow, like magic, she produced a rolled-up newspaper from her purse and the next thing he knew he was getting swatted upside the head with it.

"Stupid, stupid boy! You make us all worried sick. Caleb worried, I worried, and sweet, sweet Audrey worried."

He wasn't thrilled with being called a stupid boy, but he loved that Nonna had included Audrey in the group.

"I know. I'm going to make it up to her. I promise. I'm sorry. Can we please go in and watch the wedding of my hopefully future sister-in-law?"

Nonna's face brightened. "Sister-in-law?"

"If Audrey will have me." He hoped he hadn't fucked things up too bad. But he had faith in what he and Audrey had.

Nonna patted his cheek with a smile on her face. "Stupid, stupid boy, you finally smarten up."

He smiled. Nonna had no idea how right she was. Over the past thirty-six hours he'd had several revelations about himself, his childhood, and how much that had affected his adulthood.

"Come on, we're going to miss it." Nonna said as if he'd been the one to drag her out.

When they walked back inside, they slid into their seats undetected, and he looked up at the altar. Audrey had tissues in her hand as she looked lovingly at her sister as Caleb talked about the meaning of love and what it meant to love someone.

Josh didn't need to hear his friend's explanation, because Audrey had shown him the meaning of love and what it meant to love someone. Now, he just hoped she'd let him return the favor.

30

Audrey walked into the tent that was set up at the Riverside Rec Area and her breath was taken away. She was so happy that Ava had decided to have the reception at this venue. It was literally perfect.

The tent was somehow both grand and intimate at the same time. There were fairy lights strung from the outer wall to a center chandelier. A mixture of farm and round tables were scattered throughout the room, each with its own large bouquet of flowers in the center. There was a photo station in the corner with valentine themed props that guests could use.

It was the perfect balance of fun and classy. As she scanned the tent, she couldn't help but look for one person in particular. While she'd been taking pictures with the rest of the wedding party, she'd made herself promise that she would *not* seek him out when she got to the reception, but apparently her eyes hadn't gotten the memo.

"Hey." She turned and saw Pastor Harrison.

She smiled. "It was a beautiful ceremony, Pastor Harrison."

"Please, you can just call me Caleb."

She wasn't sure why he always tried to insist that people call him by his first name.

"It was a beautiful ceremony, Caleb." It felt weird not referring to him as his title.

"Thanks. Um, Josh wanted me to let you know that he went home to change and drop off Thor, but he'd be back."

Audrey did her best to keep her expression blank and passive. She knew that Caleb and Josh were close friends and she didn't want the good pastor to report back that she'd gotten excited when he'd relayed the message.

She shrugged. "Oh, okay."

She was going for casual cool, but feared she might have come off sounding a little bitchy. Damn, it was truly a fine line.

"I don't know if it's my place to say anything…"

Normally, she'd appreciate any advice from Pastor Harrison, er um, Caleb. He was a good man, a good leader both spiritually and in the community. He was all about service and relationships with people. He didn't stand at the pulpit and preach at people, he just shared with them his experiences and insights. Caleb wasn't religious, per se. He challenged his congregation to question things, not just blindly follow. He told them to seek out their own relationship with the big man above. Well, he didn't use those words. That's how Viv had described it after Audrey had drug her to church one Sunday.

"I don't know what is going on with you and Josh, but I do know that a couple weeks back, Nonna left a message on my phone asking me to meet you at the community center because you needed a dance partner for the evening."

"She did?"

"Yep. And then I got a text from Josh telling me not to worry about the message from Nonna because he was going."

Audrey remembered that he'd told her that he'd volunteered, but she hadn't known what that meant exactly.

"Like I said, I don't know what's going on with you guys. But I do know I've never seen him dance before. Not at prom, not at homecoming and not at every wedding reception he's ever been to. He never got out on the dance floor. But he did for you. Voluntarily. I know that might seem insignificant but, believe me, it's not. Josh might not be good at expressing himself, and he's probably going to mess things up from time to time, but he loves you, Audrey. He might be really bad at showing it, but he does."

Audrey nodded, suddenly feeling a little overwhelmed. She believed what Caleb was saying. She even believed that Josh loved her. It was the "he might not be very good at showing it" part, that was giving her pause.

"Pastor Harrison!" Sue Ann called out his name, waving at him. She was standing with Renata and a young woman who Audrey had met once or twice. She was new to town and had so far kept to herself. She had a son, who Viv had mentioned had some medical problems.

Caleb smiled at Audrey before heading over to his adoring public. The guy seriously was like a rock star in Hope Falls. Everyone clamored for his attention. She understood why. He had such a calming yet authoritative vibe. He made you feel like no matter what, everything was going to be okay. Well, usually he did.

In this particular situation, his talk had only made her feel more confused. As much as she knew that Josh loved her, and he'd had a good reason for taking off like he had, the past thirty-six hours had felt eerily familiar and Audrey couldn't explain why. But then, during the ceremony when Ava was walking down the aisle, alone, it hit her.

Their dad wasn't there. He'd taken off. And somehow the past thirty-six hours had tapped into a part of Audrey's subconscious memory and made her walls go up.

"We need to talk." Viv grabbed Audrey's arm and pulled her over to a table in the far corner of the tent next to the service entry, away from the dance floor and where most of the guests were congregated.

"Where did you go?" Audrey asked as she lowered down into the chair.

Viv had disappeared right after they'd finished pictures without any explanation.

"I had to get this." Viv plopped the folder that had the words Project Valentine on the table.

Audrey was confused. "I thought your last event was this morning."

"It was." Viv motioned to the binder. "Open it up."

Audrey was still confused, but she did as her sister asked.

"Turn to the Project Valentine tab."

Audrey looked at the tabs, they weren't color coordinated or in alphabetical order. Which instantly gave her anxiety, but she tried to ignore that. She finally found Project Valentine between vendors and balloons.

She pulled it open and saw a picture of herself and Josh. It had been taken at the Christmas Parade, the one where Easton had asked Grace to marry him. She and Josh were standing beside the carolers drinking hot cocoa. She didn't even know that Viv had taken this.

"Why do you have our picture?"

"Keep going."

Audrey flipped the page and saw the words The Plan,

centered at the top in bold lettering with a heart around them and below there were steps listed.

Step one: get Audrey and Josh both to Dining in the Dark.

Step two: fake back injury so that Audrey takes AcroYoga class with Josh.

Audrey looked up at her sister. "You faked your back injury?"

"Oh that's nothing. Keep reading." Viv waved her hand at Audrey.

Audrey turned her attention once again to The Plan.

Step three: Nonna asks Caleb to go to the community center to dance with Audrey in front of Josh to make him jealous.

Again her head lifted. "Did you really plan all this or did you just write this after the fact.

"I knew you would say that." Viv suddenly materialized her phone and turned the screen toward Audrey and she watched as a video began. When it played she saw that Viv was standing in front of the Christmas tree that the town put up each year downtown and she was with Nonna.

"Hi, Audrey. We are making this video as evidence that we have been planning Project Valentine for months."

"You two not know what's good for you, so we're going to help!" Nonna wagged her finger at the screen.

"We just had a meeting with Sue Ann and Renata and pitched the singles week. They agreed after looking at our proposal. But there is one piece of paper that Sue Ann and Renata didn't see. It is the real reason behind singles week."

"Project Valentine!" Both Nonna and Viv chorused together as Nonna held up the piece of paper that was in the binder with the words The Plan on the top.

Viv continued, "So get ready to fall in love, or fall even further in love because like Chris Lane, we've got 'Big, Big Plans.'"

Nonna turned her head to Viv. "Like whose plans?"

"Chris Lane. He has a song called 'Big, Big, Plans.'" When Nonna's confused expression didn't change Viv continued. "He's the country artist that is married to Lauren Bushnell, well now Lane. She was on the Ben Higgins season of The Bachelor and won."

"Oh yes, I like that girl. Very good girl." Nonna nodded in recognition.

They both turned their attention back to the camera. "So this is your friendly neighborhood cupids signing off. We love you both and we just want you to be happy."

"And get head out of butt." Nonna added.

Viv smiled in agreement. "Yes, and remove your heads from your asses please and thank you."

The video ended and Audrey looked at her sister who just motioned down to the binder. "Keep reading."

Audrey looked back down.

Step four: flatten Audrey's back tire so she can't drive up to Moonlight River Lodge so she has to go and ask Josh for a ride.

Viv was right, faking a back injury was nothing.

Step five: once Josh and Audrey get up to the cabin, have Jeremy text that the bridge is "flooded" stranding them at the cabin.

The quotations around the word flooded had Audrey lifting her head. "The bridge wasn't flooded?"

"It was. Back in November when I went up there to the grand opening of the lodge."

"But the night we were there, it wasn't flooded." Audrey clarified.

Viv shook her head back and forth, clearly proud of

her plots and schemes. Without her sister's prompting this time, Audrey looked back down at the paper.

Step six: Josh and Audrey finally declare their undying love for one another and live happily ever after.

Audrey looked back up at her sister in total disbelief.

"You planned all of this?"

"Yes. Well, I can't take full credit, Nonna was my partner in crime. But we did it for both of your own good. And it worked! Maybe not as smoothly as we'd hoped, but damn near. That boy loves you and you love him, so don't let some stupid mistakes get in the way of that or you'll ruin the plan that I slaved over for months."

Audrey continued staring at her sister.

"Or that Nonna and I came up with after two bottles of wine during a binge-watch of the Kardashians."

That made more sense.

Before she could answer she heard her name and looked up. Josh was standing there wearing a white button-down shirt and dark gray slacks. She'd never seen him in slacks before or a button-down shirt. He looked like he'd stepped right off the pages of GQ.

"Well, my work here is done." Viv stood and grabbed her notebook.

As she passed by Josh she leaned in close and said, "I'm rooting for you but if you hurt her, I will cut off your balls, grind them up, and feed them to you."

Josh, who was used to Viv's wild claims, just nodded his head. "Understood."

Viv continued on her way leaving Josh and Audrey alone. Well, as alone as they could be in a tent filled with two hundred plus guests.

"Can I sit?" Josh asked.

Audrey nodded. As he lowered down in the seat next to her, she said, "You look really nice."

"You look fucking hot," he replied, and she felt her cheeks warm.

He took a breath and said, "I'm really sorry, Audrey—"

"It's okay. I understand—"

"I'm not just apologizing for the past couple of days, although I am sorry for that, I'm apologizing for the past eight years that I've been too much of a pussy to tell you how I feel. I wasted so much time, and the shittiest part is, I convinced myself I was doing the honorable thing. I told myself you deserved better, that you should be with someone who you could have kids with—"

"I don't want kids." Audrey didn't know how many times she had to tell him that.

"I know," Josh grinned. "I'm just telling you what was going on in my head. I told myself you deserved someone who wasn't fucked up mentally, and physically. I told myself a lot of things, except for one thing, the truth.

"Spending the last couple of days with my mom was a very eye-opening experience. I saw her, really saw her, for the first time. She's just a person. She's a messed up, broken person. I think I had this idea of her as someone who didn't love me. Who didn't choose me. And deep down, I was scared to let you in because I thought if my mom doesn't love me, then how could Audrey? And I was terrified that you would leave, just like she had.

"I think that's why I reacted the way I did when I saw the glasses and pictures. I freaked out because my mind went down a path where you could logically leave me and deep down that was my worst fear.

"But I realized something after I dropped my mom off in Arizona, her not being there for me growing up wasn't about me. It was about her. Her not being there for me wasn't because she didn't love me, it was because she was sick.

"And you might leave me. And if you did, I would be heartbroken, crushed, but I'd rather take the chance at that than spend another day without you."

Audrey didn't know what to say. She'd never heard Josh speak this much in her life, especially about his feelings, much less his feelings for her. It was a lot to take in. "Josh, I…"

"Wait, I'm not done. I want you to see something." He reached behind him and pulled out three spiral notebooks like the one that had fallen on the floor when she was putting the coloring away.

What was it with people and showing her notebooks today?

"My doctor told me when I was feeling anxious to write down what was in my head. So, I did." He set them in front of Audrey.

"Do you want me to…?"

He nodded.

She opened it up to a random page.

Ladybug
You flit into my life
Landing on my heart
So beautiful
So delicate
Like a sunshine ray
I don't breathe
I don't speak
I don't move
For fear that you'll fly away

SHE TURNED ANOTHER PAGE.

Blink
My eyelids shut and I curse them
For those seconds they stole
The time they took from me
Not able to gaze upon your beauty
Your face
Your lips
Your smile
There is nothing more perfect
More sacred
More captivating
Just you

SHE FLIPPED through several more pages reading more entries. Gravity. Shadow. Angel. Mine. Each one heartbreakingly beautiful.

"They're all about you. Every single one."

She lifted her eyes to his and felt tears starting to well. "They are?"

"Yeah. I know that you say I saved you the day we met, but the truth is you saved me the day you came back. I was in a really dark place and you were like a breath of fresh air. You let me breathe again. You gave me hope. And I'm sorry it took me so long to realize it and, as Nonna likes to say, get my head out of my butt. I love you, Audrey. I always have and I always will."

"I love you, too." She leaned forward and pressed a kiss to his mouth.

He cupped her cheek with his hand and when their kiss broke, he rested his forehead on hers. "I know it's bad form to ask someone to marry them at another person's wedding. So I am not doing that. But, I am telling you that I have Nonna's ring in my back pocket and the second you'll let me put it on your finger, it's yours."

"Okay," she smiled from ear to ear.

"Is that a yes?" he asked with intensity in his deep brown stare.

"Yes."

The back of her chair was bumped, bursting the bubble of two that she had been floating in. She turned and saw one of the servers going out the makeshift door of the tent with one of the platters. Before the curtain fell back into place she noticed something and stood up.

She pushed the curtain out of her way and walked outside. Josh followed behind her.

"What? What's wrong?"

"This is it." She pointed to the large boulder in the center of the grass area beside the tent.

"What is it?"

"This is where I was standing when we met." Tears were in her eyes as she looked up at him.

Josh looked around and recognition dawned on his face. "You're right. This is it."

He took the ring out of his pocket and got down on one knee.

"I thought you said that this is bad form." She sniffed back tears she was holding in.

"It is. I don't care. Audrey Faith Wells, I love you. I want to marry you and have slow dance Sundays, and cheat during quick draw, and take AcroYoga classes with you, and adopt all the rescues in the world. Will you marry me?"

She nodded as tears fell down her face. "Yes."

He slid the simple, solitaire, oval diamond on her finger

and stood up pulling her into a hug. He kissed her forehead and she looked up at him at the exact time that fireworks exploded behind his head. She'd totally forgotten that the Valentine's Day Festival had fireworks.

A sense of déjà vu overcame her. He was looking down at her. She was crying. Fireworks were going off behind his head. But this time instead of sunglasses he put a ring on her finger.

She finally got her Hope Falls Effect. And it was perfect.

THE END

Flirting with Fate

Available for Preorder

Don't miss the final installment in the Hope Falls: Brewed Awakenings series featuring reader-favorite (and Jessica Rabbit look-alike) Vivien Wells who is the only Wells sister still standing from the Hope Falls Effect coming 3/10!

Author's Note: Flirting with Fate is a single dad, next-door neighbor, road trip, small-town romance.

A NOTE FROM MELANIE AND SHAWNA

Hello! *waves wildly* We hope you enjoyed this visit to Hope Falls! Audrey and Josh were a lot of fun (also frustrating, I'm looking at YOU Josh) to write. We tried to get back to basics with this one and give you (our readers) a character driven love story filled with quirky, well-meaning side characters in a town that we both wish was real. We hope you enjoyed the ride!

If you haven't picked up Ava Wells' story Falling in Fate, or Grace Wells' story Trusting Fate make sure you do! They both have very swoony heroes, if I do say so myself. ;) And next up is Viv's story Flirting with Fate. Fun fact: Viv is our most requested side character ever. She's shown up in many a previous Hope Falls story and we get A TON of requests for her to have her own book each time she's made a cameo. Well, the wait is almost over!

Her book will be the final Hope Falls: Brewed Awakenings book and will be completing this series, but do not fret, that does not mean we won't be visiting Hope Falls again. *she says being intentionally vague*

Now down to business, Melanie and I love connecting with our readers and there's a few ways that we do it.

Our Facebook page, our reader group: Club HEA with Melanie Shawn and our Instagram. (we're not cool enough for TikTok or Snapchat, lol)

Oh, and if you want to check out Audrey & Josh's playlist it is below.

Say You Won't Let Go — James Arthur
    Butterflies — Max (ft. Fletcher)
    Like I'm Gonna Lose You — Meghan Trainor
    If the World Was Ending — JP Saxe & Julia Michaels
    All of Me — John Legend
    Thinking Out Loud — Ed Sheeran
    Amazed — Lonestar
    A Thousand Years — Christina Perri
    Your Body is a Wonderland — John Mayor
    One Call Away — Charlie Puth
    Bleeding Love — Leona Lewis
    Just the Way You Are — Bruno Mars
    Perfect — Ed Sheeran

If you want to keep up with new releases, sales, and general book and life shenanigans make sure to sign up for our newsletter!

And as always we wish you love, laughter, and happily ever after! XO

Shawna & Melanie

OTHER TITLES BY MELANIE SHAWN

The Crossroads Body Guards

All He Wants

All He Needs

All He Feels

All He Desires

The Crossroads Bachelorettes

Just One Night

Just One Kiss

Just One Look

Just One Touch

The Wishing Well, Texas Series

Teasing Destiny

Convincing Cara

Discovering Harmony

Taming Travis

Claiming Colton

Trusting Bryson

Seducing Sawyer

Unwrapping Jade

Borrowing Bentley

Loving Jackson

Educating Holden

Kissing Beau

The Hope Falls Series

Sweet Reunion

Sweet Harmonies

Sweet Victory

Home Sweet Home

One Sweet Day

Snow Angel

Snow Days

Snowed In

Let It Snow

Perfect Kiss

Secret Kiss

Magic Kiss

Lucky Kiss

Christmas Wish

Fire and Love

Fire and Foreplay

Fire and Romance

Fire and Temptation

The Valentine Bay Series

Protecting My Heart

Rescuing His Heart

Rocking Her Heart

Playing By Heart

Unbreak My Heart

The Steamy Weekend Series

Charming Cupid

Seducing Cinderella

Resisting Romeo

The Someday Series

Someday Girl

One Day His

Forever Us

Chasing Perfect

Book Boyfriend

Embracing Reckless

Meet Cute

ABOUT THE AUTHOR

Melanie Shawn is the writing team of sister duo Melanie and Shawna. Originally from Northern California, they both migrated south and now call So Cal their home.

Growing up, Melanie constantly had her head in a book and was always working on short stories, manuscripts, plays and poetry. After graduating magna cum laude from Pepperdine University, she went on to teach grades 2nd through 8th for five years. She now spends her days writing and taking care of her furry baby, a Lhasa Apso named Hercules. In her free time, her favorite activity is to curl up on the couch with that stubborn, funny mutt and binge-watch cable TV shows on DVD (preferably of at least eight seasons in length - a girl's gotta have her standards!).

Shawna always loved romance in any form - movie, song or literary. If it was a love story with a happy ending, Shawna was all about it! She proudly acknowledges that she is a romanceaholic. Her days are jam-packed with writing, being a wife, mom aka referee of two teens, and indulging in her second passion (dance!) as a Zumba instructor. In the little free time she has, she joins Melanie in marathon-watching DVDs of their favorite TV programs.

They have joined forces to create a world where True Love and Happily Ever After always has a Sexy Twist!

You can keep up with all the latest Melanie Shawn news, including new releases and contests, at:

http://melanieshawn.com
and
http://facebook.com/melanieshawnbooks

Printed in Great Britain
by Amazon